I WANNA GET *Laid by* KADE

NIKKI ASHTON
&
VICTORIA JOHNS

Dedication

This book is dedicated to everyone who reads it, and to all those who helped make it possible.

A good friend knows all your best stories
A best friend has lived them with you
A great friend helps you to write them

MEREDITH HENNESEY

"So there it is, Meredith," the station boss of RTVN, Roddy Devenish smarmed. "You give us a hit or you're out, baby. We can't keep carrying you."

I fisted my hands by my thighs and took a deep breath. The bastard wouldn't know a hit if it lurched up and kicked the fucking half a million dollar veneers, from his stupid, plastic face. He had no idea what went on at this damn studio. How could he when he was never there? He was always, elsewhere with his scabby cock in some dirty bitch's pussy.

Roddy Devenish was the son of Milland Devenish, one of the richest movie moguls in Hollywood, and he had propensities for sex and coke, and not necessarily in that order. Milland had thought that buying his son a TV studio would distract him, keep him occupied, but everyone knew the SOB was still visiting Maison Noire - a local sex club - regularly, and did not have his eye on the game. That was why the fucker had me in his office, blaming me for poor ratings and the fact that the studio was losing money. I had the job title of Producer and

4

Head Scheduler for the station; in truth the damn buck stopped with me.

"Maybe we need to think about the genus of the programs we produce," I replied with a tight smile.

"Consider more serious programming?"

Roddy gave me a look as though he were trying to shit and couldn't.

"Genus means genre, Roddy," I explained.

Nope, the stupid fucker was still looking like a constipated aardvark.

"Type, Roddy. We need to think about changing the type of programs we produce."

"I'm not sure I get what you're trying to say, Meredith." He brushed at something on his slacks and let out a bored sigh.

"I think we need to consider what our competitors are producing, CSTV just won a Critic's Choice award for their serial drama about three generations of a military family. Maybe we should think about commissioning something more serious like that."

He gave me a smile that clearly said, 'you're a fucking woman who has no damn idea what she's talking about'.

"The clue is in our name, Meredith. RTVN: Reality TV Network."

He was right; I knew that, but fuck me, we'd done every possible reality TV program we could think of. Our lowest point had to have been, 'Celebrity Bathroom Drop', where a doctor examined the crap of celebrities and told us what they'd been eating and whether or not they were healthy. Not my finest fucking hour, I had to admit, especially when it had been dropped part-way through the first season. What Roddy had failed to tell the execs, though was that it had been his idea. An idea he and his friend, Charles Trent, MD, had come up with. The MD needed a quick dollar after being struck off for performing implant operations without the appropriate medical license, so Roddy had decided to help him out.

5

"Listen," he said impatiently. "The bottom line is you've not given me anything to argue your case with to the execs. Your last three programs have bombed, sweetheart, and you know it."

"I think that's unfair," I replied, managing to keep my tone level. "I was only responsible for 'Celebrity Dog Swap.' The others were your idea."

Roddy shook his head and smiled. "No, Meredith, you'll see it says Producer and Head Scheduler on your office door, not mine."

There was no point arguing with the stupid dickwad. There was no way he'd admit to being responsible for the shit that we produced.

"Okay," I sighed. "I'll get you your hit."

I pushed up from my chair and bent to retrieve my purse.

"I don't just want a hit, Meredith. I want a People's Reality Award."

I stared and felt the urge to throat punch him. We had no chance with the budget I had to work with, not when we were up against KBA. They were based in Kansas, and funded by one of America's richest men. The Financier Edgar Ormanstein, was worth billions and was number nine on the Forbes 100 list. Every damn show they made was slick, professional and super popular.

"Roddy..." I started.

He held up his hand and glowered at me. "I don't want your fucking excuses, Meredith. I want a fucking hit that gets me an award. I don't give a shit what or who you do to get it—you can rent your pussy out to congress for all care—but I want that award for this network. The awards are in eight months."

"That's impossible," I yelled. "The list of nominees has to be finalized in six months. We'll never be ready in time."

Roddy stood up and leaned across his desk, spittle forming at the corner of his sneering mouth.

"So move your fat ass out of my fucking office and get to work."

He strode around his desk and went to his drinks cabinet, and turning his back, pretty much dismissed me.

I walked down the hallway of the station offices, holding back the scream that was bubbling in my throat. I had five months at most, to broadcast something and get high enough viewing figures to even get past the first round of nominations. The brainstorming of ideas for programs usually took a month of the whole damn process. Shit, I was fucked.

At forty-nine, if I lost this job, no other network would touch me. Everyone was looking for young, pretty and tight assed these days. While my two hours in the gym four times a week, ensured the tight ass, I was not young and I was not pretty. I was attractive, with a decent body and some damn good hair that I'd paid a fortune to have stitched into my scalp, but I was almost fifty and there was no getting away from that fact. I couldn't even lie, seeing as my driver's license had been found and posted on social media by some generous member of the general public. Yeah, I was definitely fucked in every way.

"Daisy!" I bawled at my assistant. "Get your damn ass in my office now, and bring me a coffee and a drink."

It was the first thing I'd taught all my assistants- make sure there is always a bottle of *Dewar's* in the filing cabinet. That was how Bethany, my last assistant had lost her job. There had been no damn whiskey when I needed it.

"H-here you go, Meredith," Daisy stammered just three minutes later.

"Get the production team together," I snapped, snatching the tumbler from her fingers. "I want them in the meeting room in five minutes. We have to come up with a fucking award winning show that's ready to go in the next few weeks."

Daisy nodded and scribbled it down onto her pad.

"Can you not remember that?" I cried. "Do you have to write fucking everything down?"

She closed the pad, stuck the pen into the messy bun on her head and then pushed her black framed glasses up her nose.

"And get some contacts." I pointed at her glasses. "Those things make you look like damn *Waldo*."

"Y-yes, Meredith."

"Well, what are you waiting for?" I screeched, knocking back the last of my whiskey. "And where the fuck is my coffee?"

Daisy turned tail and ran out of the office, leaving me wondering how the hell I was going to save not only my job, but my damn reputation too.

Chapter 2

DAISY INGLES

As I let the door of the station offices slam behind me, I heaved a great sigh of relief. One more day down, only one hundred and ninety more to go until, I would have enough money to give to my pop to take him and Mom on their dream trip to Europe. Once I handed the money over, I'd be free to leave and go back to work at the animal shelter-a place I loved working-where I was loved by the animals and respected by my colleagues. Not at all like working here, or more specifically working for Meredith Hennesey. In fairness working for Meredith was like working for an animal anyway; an untrained dog that needed house training. I just had to keep telling myself it was a means to an end.

Mom had been ill for so many years, waiting for a kidney transplant, that she and Pop had never been able to go on vacation. It wasn't just that she was ill; it was also the cost. Her medical bills were huge, and the transplant had crippled them financially. So much so that they'd had to sell our old family home and move into my tiny two-bedroomed apartment with me. My older brother, Heath,

NIKKI ASHTON & VICTORIA JOHNS

had tried to help, but he was a State Trooper with only four years' service and a wife and a year old baby to support. Anyways, Mom and Pop would never take money from baby Allie's mouth. They loved their granddaughter and wanted her to have the best. Heath and his wife, Caitlin, had offered them a home with them, but that would have meant Mom and Pop sleeping in the living room. My apartment had, therefore, been the best option. Lucky for me, my love life was non-existent; no one wants their parents in earshot of any make out sessions.

Not long after Mom's transplant, I saw the vacancy for Meredith's assistant advertised, so I applied, not thinking for one minute I'd get the job. Apparently 'I was best of a bad load of shit.' Plus, word had got around the industry that she was a damn bitch, and no one wanted to work for her, so I got the job. A job that meant I could save money and send my parents on the trip of a lifetime. In a little over six months, I would have the money and I would be free.

As I walked a few steps down the sidewalk, my eyes searched until I spotted him-Kade. My face broke into a grin and I pulled the bag from my oversized purse, walking purposefully towards him. When I was only a couple of feet away, Brody let out a friendly bark and jumped up from his position next to Kade. As Brody's wagging tail hit him, he looked up and spotted me, returning my smile. His startling blue eyes sparkled beneath his scruffy beanie hat his dark hair poking out from underneath.

"Hey, Kade. Hey, Brody," I greeted them both, bending to give Brody a scratch behind his floppy ears.

"Hi, Daisy," Kade said, pulling his old, dirty, grey coat closer around him. "You're late today. Boss lady keep you in after school?"

I giggled, pulled the sandwiches and cookies from the bag, and passed them to Kade. "Yeah," I sighed. "She's been pretty crazy today. I think she's under pressure from her boss."

Kade watched me carefully as he snatched the wrapping from the food. I looked at Brody, not wanting Kade to see that I'd noticed how hungry he was. He may have been homeless but he had his pride. It had taken me almost a month, to get him to take fresh food that I'd bought specifically for him. The tins of food I'd brought for Brody were gratefully received, but unless it was my left-overs or day old food, he wouldn't take anything for himself. I didn't give up, though. I was like that '*Little Engine that could*'. I wouldn't give up, and eventually, he happily took a takeout coffee and some chicken noodles from me.

"So, you got plans tonight?" he asked around a mouthful of food.

"Hmm, let's see," I said, tilting my head as though I was considering it. "I was thinking of going to the ballet, or maybe dinner followed by a club, but..."

"Don't tell me, you're washing your hair." Kade smiled big and his whole face lit up.

Despite the dirt and grime, you could see he was real handsome. For a guy who was so dark haired, he had unusually light aquamarine blue eyes, which crinkled at the edges when he smiled. He had high cheek bones, a long aquiline nose and a square chin with a dimple in it, which I only got to see every three weeks or so, when a local barber went to the homeless shelter to give the guys a shave. The rest of the time, Kade sported a dark beard.

Kade had told me once that he was twenty-five years of age, and the only family he had, now his mom was dead, was Brody his beloved hound. I asked him how he'd ended up on the streets, but he simply shrugged, pulled Brody to his chest and said, "it's obviously the path I'm meant to take."

"Yes," I laughed. "Washing my hair seems a good plan. What about you? You have somewhere to sleep tonight?"

Kade nodded. "Yeah, I have a bed at the shelter tonight."

"You want me to take Brody?" I asked.

"Nope, it's fine. They've said it's okay to take him. It's the one on the east side of town."

"Okay," I breathed out. "If you're sure."

I reached into the bag again and took out a can of dog food for Brody.

"Almost forgot my favorite boy."

"Hey, Brody look what Daisy got you." Kade took the tin, pulled a pen-knife out of his coat pocket and dug it into the can, taking the top off and emptying the contents out into a tin bowl that sat in between him and Brody.

"Wow, he was hungry," I said as I watched Brody gobble down the food.

My heart ached as I thought about them both being hungry. I'd often thought about offering them a place to stay, but I didn't have the room. Plus, Heath had warned me not to get involved. In his words, "For fuck's sake, Dais, the dude could be a rapist or a murderer." I didn't think so, but thought it best not to upset my State Trooper brother.

"Anyway, I'd better go," I sighed. "I have hair to wash."

"Okay," Kade replied, holding his hand up for a high five. "Thanks for the food."

I slapped his palm with mine, took a step back, and walked straight into someone. I whirled around on my heels to apologize, only to come face to face with Meredith.

"Shit!" she yelled, a little louder than was necessary. "Watch where...Daisy?"

"So sorry, Meredith," I spluttered. "I didn't see you there."

"Well maybe you need to open your eyes a little more." She, brushed at some coffee that had spilled from her take out cup down her cashmere coat.

"Hey, she said she was sorry." Kade suddenly got to his feet and took a step forwards. "No need to be so rude."

"Who the hell do you think…?" As she looked up at all six feet plus of Kade, her voice trailed off and her eyes widened. Something akin to wonderment passed over her face. "Oh my. You. Are. Stunning."

Kade's heavy brow furrowed as he looked from Meredith to me, and then back again.

"Daisy," she said, slapping her hand against my arm without taking her gaze from Kade. "We just found our hook for 'Playboy Millionaire'."

My head whipped to Kade who was still watching Meredith somewhat warily. What was she talking about? Playboy Millionaire was the concept that she and the team had come up with this afternoon, but what the hell did Kade have to do with it?

"I don't understand," I stammered.

Meredith leaned back to peruse Kade before taking her cell from her pocket and snapping a photograph of him.

"Hey!" Kade cried, indignantly.

"Sorry, honey but you're just what I'm looking for," she said distractedly as she pushed buttons on the screen of her phone.

"Meredith?"

She looked up at me and grinned. "Your friend here-sorry, honey I didn't catch your name."

"I'm Kade, but-"

"Kade here is our hook, like I said. He's going to be our Playboy Millionaire," she responded proudly.

"But he's not a millionaire," I protested.

"I live on the streets," Kade said, grabbing a tight hold of the rope that he used for Brody's leash.

"Exactly!" Meredith stated. "That is going to win us our award. We're going to get all those sorority princesses and trust fund bunnies to fall in love with a homeless guy. It's pure fucking genius."

My mouth gaped open as Kade dragged his beanie from his head and gave me a WTF look.

"It's going to be brilliant," Meredith chuckled. "Absolutely brilliant."

Chapter 3

KADE SUTTON

"You did not just take a picture of me, lady," I shouted, and she kinda jumped a bit on the spot. Brody barked at her. She clearly thought he was backing me up, but I knew it was because the bitch was interrupting his meal. When you only eat once a day, you get seriously grouchy when the occasion is disturbed.

"Delete that picture," I said, stepping forward, pissed that she was sullying my daily visit from Daisy as well as the snack she'd brought for me.

When I raised my hand, she skulked backwards to some perceived safety, dragging Daisy with her. "I'll do it. I'll do it." She grimaced. It would have been funny if Daisy hadn't looked like she was being touched by some kind of contagion.

I was used to the masses of the world treating me as though I was some kind of scumbag. Daisy had never acted that way with me and the Brodester, but then I saw that the squeaky, uptight, fake assed bitch was clawing at Daisy's forearm in fear.

"Is she hurting you?" I asked.

Resting bitch face looked at me and dropped her safety link to Daisy. "Of course I'm not hurting her. What the hell do you take me for?"

"Someone with enough bad manners to take photos of a person less fortunate than themselves without bothering to ask." The grip she had on her fancy tech device was deathly. "Which reminds me, start deleting."

The huff that left her trout pout didn't pass me by, and it took some effort to hide the chuckle that was forming inside me. Truthfully, I couldn't have cared less about the picture, but now I knew it bugged her there was no way I was letting it go. I watched as she poked at the screen with a blood red talon and then went to pocket her cell. "Let me see," I requested and she spun the device around, waving it impatiently.

Brody was just reaching the end of his meal and I was debating whether to keep her there for a bit more entertainment. It wasn't unheard of for him to greet newcomers to our patch with his slobbery tongue and dog breath. I was looking forward to that fun and amusement when I noticed the look on Daisy's face. From their exchange, I'd garnered that this was Daisy's bitch of a boss, and I didn't want to cause her any trouble. Besides, Daisy had become a real highlight in my otherwise dull days, so the last thing I wanted to do was remove that beautiful smile.

I nodded in satisfaction and stepped back, ready to intercept Brody on his quest for desert in the lady's purse. "Daisy, I'll see you in the morning. My office, eight fifteen sharp—we'll be discussing this further," the woman snapped.

"Yes, Meredith," Daisy replied and we both watched as she strutted off up the sidewalk, trying her best to power walk in ridiculous shoes and a skirt so tight that she could have been endurance testing the thread holding it together.

When she was a safe distance away, Daisy sagged with relief. "Welcome to my world, Kade. She is one grumpy lady today."

"She needs to get laid," I said abruptly. "Although, I pity da'fool who takes up that challenge." I said it in my best *A-Team*, BA. Baracus impression and felt better when she burst out laughing. This girl was something else— nothing like the rest of the work demons I saw striding in and out of that building every day. Daisy was gentle and kind and didn't belong there, schlepping her ass off for the corporate monsters of the modern age. I watched as she carried on laughing with wild abandon.

"He's funny, isn't he, Brody?" she said, leaning down and scratching behind his ears with enthusiasm. Some of my homeless pals thought Brody was a bind, but the mutt was no trouble. I was a little bit more approachable when he was with me. People were okay turning a blind eye to a starving guy on the streets, but not to a dog. Their compassion came out in droves for him and money found its way out of wallets and pockets just that little bit easier when he was around. I couldn't get rid of him now. The donations meant for him had fed us both on more than one occasion and I owed him.

I watched as Daisy lapped up the dog's attention. She even stayed put whilst he smothered her cheeks with a tongue that had just licked clean a bowl of tuna dog meat.

"Oops," she said when he managed to butt her glasses off her face and onto the floor. Immediately reaching down for them, I began to panic that the lens glass might have broken when they hit the sidewalk. After a quick inspection, I was pleased that they were still in one piece, but feeling guilty that they'd been on the dirty sidewalk in the first place, I tried to clean them with my overcoat. The smear of grease that ended up on them was not pleasant, and the harder I rubbed, the more murky they were getting.

"Hey, don't worry about that." She smiled, taking them from me without cleaning them, not bothering that her clean, pretty fingers were touching my filthy ones.

As I watched her raise them to her face, I noticed things I'd never seen before. Her nose was small and petite, and covered in a smattering of freckles that the huge black rims seemed to hide. The eyes I'd always worked hard to avoid were almond shaped and the deepest chocolate brown. As soon as she placed them on her face, I watched as the glasses slid down her nose a touch and then settled to where I was used to seeing them.

"I'm really sorry about Meredith," she said on a breath.

"What're you apologizing for? People should take responsibility for their own actions."

"I know, but if I hadn't been here talking to you and Brody-boy then she'd have passed you by."

I nodded. Daisy couldn't have known that her words had an effect on me. People passing me by was what I'd been used to for most of my adult life, and the mundane visits from her at the end of her day, or the bitchy argument with that woman reminded me that I wasn't invisible. I was a person, the same as them, alive and breathing but a lot less fortunate.

But that was my choice.

The night was drawing in and I didn't have long left to get to the shelter. If I wasn't there before seven o'clock at night, they'd give my bed to another unlucky soul. There weren't many who were willing to take me in with Brody in tow, and I was always on my best behavior for that reason. "Time to move on for the night."

"Sleep safe, Kade." She smiled shyly, patted my boy on his head and then wandered down the sidewalk in the same direction as Miss. Prissy-Pants.

Chapter 4

KADE SUTTON

I made it in time to settle in for the night and have a quick shower before supper. The shower was something I was always desperate for and hated the minute I'd finished. I stood under the spray feeling my long, knotted hair growing heavy as the hot water saturated me. My hair was so knotted, in fact, that it was practically in dreadlocks now and a nightmare to get dry. The first time I stayed here, I was given the standard 'one towel per person' rule. The helpful old ladies in charge regretted it the morning after, though. The bed sheet, pillow and mattress were all damp, meaning they were down a bed for the night. I felt awful about depriving someone else of a bed, but the old girls were great. Apparently, it was a refreshing change for it to just be water from hair; they were used to seeing much worse. As a result, I now got two towels, one for me and one for my mass of dark hair.

My time in the shower lasted as long as I could drag it out. The feeling of washing away the grime from the streets was amazing but short lived, as I had to put the same clothes back on eventually. Where I was staying did a clothes swap once a month and sometimes it worked out great. I sometimes got lucky if someone donated their husband's old clothes, but at six foot three, it didn't happen often, so most of the time I left in the same clothes I came in.

The water and suds from the basic bar of soap floated down my body. My body's shape and my general state of health amazed me. I was in great condition considering how long I'd been living rough. Thankfully, survival had been the most important thing when I first ended up out there, and doing so high on drugs or boozed up on vodka wasn't going to increase my chances of making it through the nights unscathed. When I saw some of the regular faces and the lengths they went to just to forget why they were on the streets, I was thankful for the decision I made all those years ago to stay clean.

The tattoo I had before I hit adulthood still reminded me of the struggles of my life and my heartbeat always dipped when I saw the name 'Shelby' on my inner bicep. I could have been clichéd and had my mom's name on my heart, but having it there meant she was close to my heart. When I wrapped my arms around myself during the cold months, it was almost like she was hugging me and trying to protect me, like she would have done if she'd been there.

A bang on the bathroom door pulled me from my thoughts. "Time's up," grumbled a raspy voice on the other side. I dried off as quickly as I could and put my clothes back on, my nose crinkling in disgust at the smell. It turned my stomach, and I was surrounded by it constantly. That was how I knew Daisy was a saint—she never shied away from me, she got as close as I'd let her and acted like I was wearing expensive cologne. With my hair wrapped in a towel turban, I left the bathroom, ignoring the guy propped up against the wall opposite. I'd seen him before, and tonight, he was in bad shape. It was a wonder he'd managed to get there in one piece.

Back in the big dormitory, I moved to the bed they usually saved for me in the corner. Brody was on a blanket underneath, looking content. Daisy bringing him some food meant I could go and eat a hot meal in the dining room. When he hadn't eaten, I'd sneak him some food back, but that was more out of necessity. The last time I'd left him hungry and wandered off, he nearly got us both ejected. On his quest to track down both me and food, he wandered past the kitchen, and like the cheeky boy he was, managed to snaffle a pot roast. The cook had gone ballistic, demanding to know which one of us 'down and outs' had stolen from the kitchen. Her words nearly caused a riot, which meant she was the one who got ejected and quickly, but when I got back to the dormitory, I knew who the real culprit was. There was a trail of slobber and grease on the floor all the way to my bed. When you've been on the streets for any length of time, you become accustomed to following food scents. Usually, they lead to a trashcan or dumpster, but I knew what it was as soon as my nose picked it up at the door. That and the gnawing of bones I could hear were instant giveaways. I had to go and admit to Brody's crimes and was stunned when they didn't kick us out. I could only thank the bad-tempered cook whose harsh, truthful words had offended the other volunteers as much as the nightly inhabitants.

Tonight's meal was a steaming hot bowl of broiled meat and vegetables in a thick meaty sauce. It was served with a couple of chunks of crusty bread and a small slice of apple pie. I ate as slowly as I dared—after all, Brody was still a wily dog—and I savored the taste from the minute it passed my lips until it hit my growling belly. Looking around, I was reminded, again, of just how good a shape I was in. There were people eating so fast they were going to need another shower and others who were in danger of scraping the ceramic glaze off the bowls, such was their need to get every last drop of food up. Something else to thank Daisy for—the snacks of sandwiches took the edge off my hunger on the nights I was at the shelter. That meant I was able to act with a little decorum and show some table manners, unlike the rest of them.

I always washed my plate for the ladies; any little thing that kept Brody and me in favor wasn't a nicety so much as a necessity. Once back at my bed, I stripped down to my briefs and socks. One rule I abided by was that Brody wasn't allowed in the bed with me, so I always folded my clothes up to form a makeshift bed for him to lie on, covering him with the blanket. I used to tell myself that he kept them warm for the morning, but he was the best theft deterrent ever. No one ever attempted to steal my clothes.

Lights out came as soon as the beds were full, and it reminded me of some of the places I'd lived in as a kid before I went to my foster mom when I was eleven. The worst thing was that even though the beds around me were filled with drunks and druggies, I felt far safer now than I had back then and it was nothing to do with how I'd learned to defend myself.

Sleep came easier than it had when I first stayed there. You learned to leave an ear open in case of trouble, but most of the people around me were fighting their own demons, and as long as they didn't gang up on me and join my demons, I could ignore them.

The same faces rolled through my mind.

Daisy and her kindness—the sweet and pure nature of someone so untouched by the shitty existence I led—and my mom.

I worried that she'd fade from my mind the older I got. I'd learned to cope with the sadness her death caused me and remember the time she'd been in my life. It wasn't her fault; she'd done her very best for me until she took her last breath. Thinking of her and the way she loved me helped me to fight off my despair at my new situation.

We'd lived a simple life, just she and I in a little two bed rental, and I was her world. Everything she did was for me. I never wanted for anything, and the only friend she had was a neighbor next door who had a kid the same age as me. My mom and Paighton had an arrangement that meant they both had childcare. While one worked nights, the other worked days. I grew up thinking Cory was my brother, and when my mom fell ill, I relied on Paighton more and more. It's hard to understand when you're six why your own mother can't cook you mac and cheese anymore. As she got sicker, the days she got out of bed became fewer and fewer, and thinking back now, I wish I'd spent more time looking after her than racing round the yard with Cory. If only I'd known how precious those few years were.

I never knew who my dad was. It never seemed important enough to cross my mind because my mom gave me everything I needed. When Paighton finally called in the doctor, I remembered crying as they took my mom away in an ambulance, and that was the last I saw of her. She passed away a few days later, and that odd feeling of nothingness was still something I forced myself to feel now if I had days when I reminisced too much. I ended up in state care and learned when I was fifteen that the money my mom did have had been soaked up to pay for it. All of her savings were gone, just like that, to pay for substandard care.

I turned over and breathed deeply, forcing the happy memories back to the front of my mind. I was warm, I had a full belly, and my best friend was snoring beside me.

This was my choice, and whether I lived to see another day was down to me, not some state funded kids home run by a spiteful witch or foster family who took you in to treat you like a butler.

Chapter 5

DAISY INGLES

It was only just after eight when I turned on the Mac on my desk, but Meredith's office door swung open straight away. She stood in the doorway, tapping her foot, hands on hips with a face as red as the usual scarlet of her nails.

"You're late," she growled. "Get in here now."

I sighed, not bothering to tell her that I was actually fifteen minutes early. There was no point. She was a bitch and never listened.

"Tell me about the tramp," she said as soon as I closed her office door behind me. "What leverage do we have to get him to appear on the show?"

That was Meredith all over—talking at tangents, vocalizing the jumble of thoughts that bumped around in her head.

"I'm sorry, I'm not sure I understand," I replied, trying not to look her in the eye. I learned on my first day that you never met Meredith's eye; her stare could bring you to your knees. Either that or turn you to stone. She could have been Medusa in a past life.

"The homeless guy," she said, blatantly exasperated by

me. "I said last night, or weren't you listening? I want to use him on the show. He'll be our hook. He's going to be our millionaire, at least as far as the stupid bitches taking part think."

I tried not to gasp too loudly; it was best to never show Meredith that you were shocked by any of her ideas. Never let her think you believed her to be anything less than a genius, so shock was not a good emotion to display.

"What?" she snapped. "You're looking at me like I just shot your damn puppy. He'll be glad to be off the fucking streets, believe me."

I didn't doubt that, but from the little I knew of Kade, I knew he had pride and would hate being treated like some World Fair exhibit.

"I'm not sure it's really ethical, Meredith."

"Ethics, shmethics," she scoffed, with a wave of her hand. "He'll get paid, have a roof over his head, decent clothes on his back and food in his belly. You tell me what's unethical about that."

"You're exploiting him." I pushed my glasses up my nose and tried desperately not to end that sentence with the addendum – 'you selfish bitch'.

"I'm fucking not. I'd be exploiting him if I didn't pay him and didn't tell the viewers that he was some homeless schmuck, but that's the whole point. I'm not going to." She preened, running her long fingernails through her hair.

"Why don't you just get a real life millionaire? Having Kade won't win you an award if the audience don't know he's really homeless. The show will simply be another reality TV show about rich men and stupid women."

Meredith visibly winced; I'd obviously hit the mark with my description of her latest 'baby'. I had no doubt this was a great opportunity for Kade to get off the streets, but something about it didn't sit straight with me. I didn't like to think that Kade's life would become public property. He was a quiet and thoughtful man from what I'd seen, and I wasn't sure how he'd cope being under media scrutiny.

"How do you propose we keep it from the media?" I asked. "You know what they're like. They'll find out his real story and that will just spoil the whole concept for the show."

Meredith seemed to contemplate this for mere seconds, and then waved it away. "We can create him a back story that not even the FBI would be able to crack."

I doubted that, but Meredith was evidently more confident than I was.

Meredith stalked over to the plate glass window that overlooked the busy street below, and stared out at the city.

"Maybe we do tell the viewers," she said, tapping a long red nail against her teeth. "Hmm, I'm liking that idea. We all know, but the poor fucking bitches who want him don't. Shit, that would be good. It'll all be recorded. We'll keep them all on lock down in some rental mansion that they think is his, and none of them will know."

"But that makes the girls look stupid." I sighed.

Meredith turned to face me and shrugged her shoulders. "And?"

I shook my head. "I just think that it's unfair to put Kade in the spotlight just because he's homeless. If you want to help him, give him a job," I gushed, suddenly excited that maybe we could help Kade get into employment.

Meredith curled her lip and flopped down into the huge leather chair behind her desk.

"Okay, Daisy," she said with an air of weariness. "I'll put it as plainly as I can. Your homeless buddy is going to be my millionaire, and the show's concept will be 'Don't judge a book by its cover'. The audience will love it, the reality TV board will think it's genius to have a moral behind a reality show, and Kadey boy will finally be able to sleep safe at night without wondering whether he's going be robbed or pillaged in the biblical sense. You get me?"

"What if Kade won't do it?" I pouted, feeling braver than I ever had with Meredith before. I needed to ensure Kade wasn't manipulated just for Meredith's own ends. I hardly knew him, but I liked what I did know. He'd had a hard life—he'd told me he lost his mom when he was only a child, so, if I needed to stand my ground while shaking in my shoes just to help him, well, I would do it.

Meredith tilted her head back and looked down her nose at me. "Let's put it this way, Daisy Duke: if Kade and the Littlest Hobo aren't on board then you, sugar tits, will lose your job. Now, I don't doubt you would be grateful to be away from me, but for some reason you keep coming back every day, no matter how much shit I give you. That tells me you need this job, so get Kadey on board or get out of the door."

My stomach lurched and my heart hammered against my breastbone. It wouldn't be the end of the world. I had enough money to send Mom and Pop to Mexico or Belize; they'd love that just as much. She could shove her job as far as I was concerned.

"I tell you what," Meredith said, interrupting my thoughts. "You get Kade to agree, I'll not only let you keep your job but I'll give you a two thousand dollar bonus."

I opened my mouth to say that wasn't enough to make me manipulate the kind, handsome young man who had fallen on hard times, when Meredith continued.

"And if we win that award with Kade in the show, I'll give you another ten thousand dollars."

My mouth dropped open as a cold sweat formed on my brow. Ten thousand dollars, along with what I could save myself, would not only pay for my parents to go to Europe, but would help pay for Mom's medication for a while—a long while.

"Okay," I said quickly, hating myself as soon as the word came out.

Meredith smiled smugly and picked up the receiver of

the phone on her desk. "Well get out there and persuade him then."

"What if I can't?" I asked, knowing it was a possibility.

"Then you lose your job. Simple."

As Meredith waved me out of her office, I felt nausea rising in my throat. I hated the idea of manipulating Kade, but it was something I had to do. My mom and pop were depending on me.

Chapter 6

KADE SUTTON

Well that had been a total blast – not! The night in the hostel was one of the most uncomfortable I'd ever had. Not the bed—that had been good, comfy enough to send me to sleep pretty much straight away. The problem had been the guy next to me. The poor dude had night terrors most of the night, screaming about, of all people, Dolly Parton stabbing him with his damn underwear.

His screaming had set Brody off howling, which in turn made a guy a few beds down join in with him. Thankfully, the night officer had been pretty cool and didn't throw us out. He did have to move the Dolly Parton guy, though. He was hysterical and wouldn't believe Dolly wasn't gunning for him. My guess was he'd taken some pretty bad drugs—another reason I was glad I'd managed to stay clean.

Luckily, my usual spot next to Daisy's office building was free. It was funny how I always made for there these days. I tried to kid myself into believing it was because it was a busy sidewalk and I got a decent amount of food, but the way my heart stuttered whenever I saw her bouncing towards me told me that her pretty face and kooky dress sense were what pulled me there.

I'd been late this morning as I had breakfast at the hostel, so hadn't seen her going into the office as usual, so when I spotted her coming towards me, I grinned big. Today, her hair was in two braids, and she was wearing a huge sweater that fell off her shoulder, a pair of real tight jeans that stopped at her ankles and a pair of silver Chucks.

"Hey, Daisy," I greeted her, getting to my feet. "You going out for office coffees or somethin'?"

She gave me a tight smile and shook her head. "No, I'm here to see you."

"Me? How come?" I asked, giving Brody an absent-minded scratch. "Oh, let me guess… I won the lottery and you came to tell me."

I let out a laugh, but cut it short when I noticed that Daisy was chewing on her thumbnail and did not look happy.

"What's wrong?" My heart thudded. "You aren't leaving, are you?"

"No," she said, shaking her head. "Nothing like that."

"So what then? Don't tell me that bitch you work for has upset you again."

"Well," she sighed. "It is to do with her, but it's to do with you, too."

"She better have deleted that picture, because if she's done something stupid with it, I will not be happy."

Daisy looked up the street and then back to me.

"You fancy a coffee from Demetri?" She nodded towards the huge Greek guy who sold coffee and burritos from a cart just up the street. "My treat."

I laughed. "Well it would have to be. I kinda forgot my wallet."

Daisy cringed. "Oh God, I'm so sorry. I'm such an idiot."

"Hey," I said, laying a fairly clean hand on her

shoulder. "It's fine. I'm joking with ya."

She nodded and turned towards Demetri.

"Stay, Brody," I said to my best friend, but still tied him to the drainage pipe, just in case. He looked up at me with his big eyes, and if I hadn't known better, I have said he sighed before settling down onto the cardboard that I used to sit on. With a last scratch to his head, I followed Daisy.

"You have to be fucking kidding me," I hissed. "Sorry for cursing, but that is not happening."

"I did tell her," Daisy sighed. "But she wouldn't listen."

"I want to get off these streets more than anyone, believe me I do, but I'm not being paraded in front of millions of people like some circus freak."

Daisy grinned. "It won't be millions. I can promise you that. We're not exactly the most watched cable channel in the country. In fact, we're not even the fourth and when you consider there are only five reality channels, that's pretty bad, right?"

I sat back against the bench we were sitting on, and looked over towards Brody. It would be nice to sleep in a bed for more than one night a week, and to shower every day and put clean clothes on.

"Why do you look so unhappy about it?" I asked, taking a sip of the strong, black brew in my hand. "Don't you think I should do it?"

Daisy stared up at me, looking over the top of the black-rimmed glasses perched on the end of her nose. "Truth?"

I nodded.

"I think she's using you for her own ends. I don't think she cares that it will get you off the streets. All she cares about is winning that award."

"So she thinks that me being the 'playboy'," I said, making air quotes with my fingers, "will get her that award?"

NIKKI ASHTON & VICTORIA JOHNS

"That's about it. She thinks the reality TV board and the media will lap up the moral message the show gives."

"Which is what? Don't trust the rich guy? Because I have to be honest with you, I'm all in on that one."

I didn't expect anything from anyone, but those who tended to give me money and food were usually not those who could afford it the most. The haves were generally less generous than the have nots.

"No, the moral compass of the whole thing will be 'don't judge a book by its cover'."

"And I'll be the book?"

"I'm sorry, Kade," she breathed out. "I shouldn't have mentioned it. I should have told Meredith to stick her idea up her ass."

I watched as she rubbed at her temple. Something was worrying her. "So why didn't you? What's the old witch got on you, Daisy?"

She looked at me, startled, opening and closing her mouth like a real cute fish.

"I... Well, I..."

"Come on, Daisy, I thought we were friends—as much as a smelly homeless guy and a pretty girl can be."

Her cheeks pinked and I kinda wished I hadn't said she was pretty. She was, but I shouldn't have said it. The girl brought me and my dog food, for fuck's sake. I had no right to speak to her like that.

"She threatened to fire me," she suddenly announced.

"What?" I shifted on the bench to get a better look at her. "She did what?"

"She threatened to fire me if you didn't do the show, and I wouldn't care, Kade, I really wouldn't, but I need the money."

"What for? What's so important that you feel the need to work for her?"

She lowered her lashes and twisted her hands together between her knees.

"Daisy?"

"You'll think it's shallow, you know, with you being in the situation you're in. I think it's shallow to a certain point, but Mom and Pop, well they need it." Her eyes were pleading with me to understand, and she looked so sad I'd have needed a heart of cold steel to agree she was shallow. Whatever it was, it was a huge deal.

"Tell me," I urged.

"My mom had a kidney transplant and it took all their money, so they live in my apartment with me, and Pop always promised Mom that when he left the force he'd take her to Europe, but of course that wasn't possible, and she still has to have medicine, which is super expensive, and I just wanted them to have something nice, and if the show wins the award, Meredith said I'd get a bonus and that would not only get them a real nice trip but buy mom's medicine for ages…"

"Hey, Daisy?" I laughed, putting a hand on her forearm. "Take a breath."

"Sorry, I just feel so bad. Doing this for money when you have nothing." She let out a long breath and looked up at the sky. "Do you ever wonder what life would be like if you'd just taken a different route? You know, if you'd taken a different road to school one day would you have met someone who would change your life? Or maybe if you'd sat in a different doorway some really rich person might have come along and given you a job. I do, all the time." She turned her gaze back to me and shrugged. "All the damn time, Kade."

I had never wondered about my life. It was what it was. It was the fucking path a selfish bastard like me was meant to take, all because of Cory.

"I'll do it," I said, leaning forward to throw my empty cup into the trash. "I'll do the show as long as you promise me one thing."

"What's that?" she asked, holding a hand to her throat.

"That I can bring Brody."

The smile she gave me lit up not only her face, but the

damn grey day, too. It was bright enough to blind me.

"I can do that."

"Okay," I said with an air of resignation. "Where do I sign?"

Chapter 7

DAISY INGLES

I think Kade must have seen the shock his agreement caused me. When I left my desk to come and talk to him about it, I nearly packed up my belongings and brought them with me. Never did I think he'd say yes.

"You're sure about this, Kade?" I asked him, needing to hear him say it just once more.

"Well, I've consulted my busy schedule and I'm think I'm free for... just how long do we think this will last?"

This was the reason he didn't deserve to be the on streets. He'd thrown his hat into the ring of madness without even understanding what he was letting himself in for.

"I'm not sure of the details. We'll need to iron them out. The wicked witch of the west has said she'll give you a cast-iron, believable back story." Every extra detail I went into risked him realizing what he was letting himself in for and turning it down.

"So, this would be the time to think it through seriously before I sign my exciting life away?"

"How about I tell her that you've agreed in principle,

but you and Brody would like to hear some more in the morning?" Giving Meredith some good news would keep me employed for just another day, and giving Kade that extra time would help ease my conscience that he was only doing this because of my mom and pop. When I thought about it, he was really amazing. This guy had nothing and if he ever fell ill, he would be done for. At least my family could afford some level of medical care, but Kade had heard the desperation in my voice and was willing to help give those more fortunate than him a chance at life and happiness.

"I can do that," he told me. "Me and the Brodester can discuss our terms and conditions tomorrow."

I stayed with him while we finished our coffees. Sitting out there with him was definitely preferable to being in the office with that shark. In any case, the longer I was out there, the more she would think I was having a hard time persuading him, and if it helped Kade get better terms, I was all for it.

The minute my Chuck encased toes poked through the building door, Meredith was in my space.

"Well?" she demanded from the spot from which she'd been spying on us.

"Shall we discuss this upstairs?"

"No. I'm already here, and if you haven't convinced that hottie to get on board then there's no need for you to go back up there."

God, she really was a fudging bitch, and if I was going to make this work for Kade and still have some semblance of moral fiber left, I needed to play her game, too.

"I didn't say that. I just didn't think you'd want to discuss your award winning idea where others could hear it."

The spark in her eyes should have made me happy. Instead, it reminded me of when the T-800 Terminator robot kept refusing to die and the little piercing red eyes blinked signaling the evil death machine was coming back to kill someone.

"Yes, yes, you're right. Let's move."

Walking faster than I'd ever seen her move before, she hot footed it to the elevator and continued the annoying toe tapping she'd been doing first thing this morning while we waited.

"Right, tell me what he said. Is he on board?" she demanded as soon as we hit her office.

No small talk then. "He's agreed in principle, but would like the night to think it through. Kade will meet with us first thing in the morning to give you his final answer."

Meredith sneered back at me. "What is there to think through? I'm giving that vagrant the opportunity of a lifetime."

Yep. She was definitely a fudging bitch.

"It would be a big decision for anyone to make. Like I said, he's agreed in principle and has stipulated his first condition."

I watched as she halted her frenzied pacing behind the desk. Her actions were those of someone who was already working three steps ahead. Meredith was certain he was going to do this and she was plotting. A plotting Meredith was a dangerous Meredith, and she didn't appreciate that the main pawn in her path to award success was being cheeky enough to barter.

"And what would that be?"

"Brody. His dog. If Brody isn't allowed to come with him, it's a non-starter."

I noticed the tiniest exhalation of relief. She was desperate for this and that boded well for making sure Kade got more out of it than she planned.

"I suppose that's doable. After all, it's just another flea infested vagabond to help sell it to the public. It'll probably bring in the do-gooding animal viewers. You see, he's even helping us sell it." Meredith started to chuckle and there was a touch of craziness to it. "I may even be able to get a two-for-one discount at the vets. They can clean Kade up at the same time as his mangy mutt."

Thankfully, she was too busy scheming and celebrating her own brilliance to spot that I was one small step away from clawing her eyes out. My jeans were skintight and the pockets small, but in the interest of not getting arrested for assault, I'd managed to stuff my hands into them to keep them under control.

"Lydia," she screeched into her intercom. "In here now."

A younger version of the witch herself appeared in the room, smoothing down a skintight dress that was more fit for a nightclub than an office. Knowing Lydia, it might actually have been her outfit from the previous night. It was the norm for TV wannabes to roll in still half soaked in Martini and wearing fresh coats of makeup.

"What can I help you with?" she said superciliously, her shocking pink, coffin shaped acrylic nail poised over an iPad.

"The tramp has all but agreed. You need to start the search for an off the beat mansion we can hire. It needs to be secluded with no chance of outside paparazzi intrusion. Think 'Big Brother' private times ten."

"Yes, Meredith." The nail clicking on the screen of Lydia's iPad was grating on my nerves.

"I'll also need a plethora of females for audition. Shallow, vacuous Barbie creatures, a bit like you. I want them hungry for this, but believably interested in marrying into wealth."

At first, I thought Lydia hadn't noticed that she was being lumped into the same bucket as the Barbies we were going to need, but her smile increased just a smidge. The talentless tart was proud of her generation's 'this world owes me something' mindset.

Meredith was on a roll now. "Make sure a couple of them have a few skeletons in their closets. You never know when you might need to turn the heat up, and the possibility of last minute twists and turns will swing that award in my direction."

This was vulgar.

Lydia stopped typing and waited for further instruction, only to receive the bark we were all used to.

"Why are you still here? You have work to do. Get on with it!"

"Yes, Meredith." Lydia complied, but as she got to the door, she was stopped as Meredith continued.

"And remember, not one word of Kade's real status leaves this room. That knowledge is the key to the success of the show. We'll reveal it when the time is right. That means he can't come here for the discussion tomorrow morning. Daisy, find an alternative meeting place— preferably one where he won't have to sit too close to me."

That was it. I was done. With my fisted hands still in my pockets, I nodded at her and followed Lydia out of the door, praying I wasn't selling Kade down the river.

Chapter 8

KADE SUTTON

If I was going to get this much amusement out of working with Hennessey the Hag, perhaps it wouldn't be such a bad gig.

I'd taken the night to think things through like Daisy suggested, in the comfort of a bed, because the shelter had kindly offered me and the Brodester another night of warmth. Brody and I arrived and showered before pondering the possibility it could be my last night of sharing a room with twenty other guys, or on the streets for a while. Brody wasn't going to know what had hit him. Regular food and a roof over our heads—he was going to think he was in heaven.

When Daisy arrived at the office the next morning, she told me Meredith wanted to see me to firm up the deal. Because of my current status, being the real hook for the show, the meeting needed to happen away from the office. I agreed to meet them at Kirby's Cafe in hour and we'd negotiate from there.

She looked tired this morning, beautiful but tired. I didn't know her that well, but I imagined she'd had a sleepless night worrying about what she'd gotten me into.

Kirby's was one of the places I frequented if it was raining too hard to stay outside. I'd use some of the money that Brody had attracted and get a hot drink or two. It was pet friendly so the fact they had water bowls and blankets by a radiator for my best boy to relax on was just an added bonus. The owner of Kirby's seemed a good guy. He didn't kick me out in favor of customers who had washed. He just politely explained that if the place was busy I might need to sit away from others so he didn't lose customers. I could respect that. At least he was honest. Something about him hinted that he'd known hard times in his own life and was trying to pay it forward when he could.

"You'll need to sign this contract," Hennessy barked and threw the document across the table. She retracted her hand just as quick, in case there was any cross body contamination. It appeared she didn't want to be here with me, and being in a place like this was her idea of hell.

Decision made: I was going to drag it out as long as possible.

"I think I should read it first," I commented and flipped over the first page, putting my finger under the first word. "Th... Th... Th...isss. This," I began, rolling my tongue around the word and rubbing my dirty finger under the first paragraph, wondering how long it would take to break her.

"Jesus Christ," she finally muttered in frustration. "Give it here. I will read it to you. This is a binding contract," Meredith continued and proceeded to read the details of the first few sentences. When she hit the first line of the next paragraph, things got interesting.

"You will be paid the sum of $50,000 on completion of the filming."

"$100,000," I countered, causing her to look up and glare across the table at me. Meredith was perched on a chair, touching as little as possible as if she was worried she'd pick up a deadly strain of Ebola from the Formica table tops.

"That's double the amount stated in the contract."

"I think you'll find it's only $25,000 dollars more. The contract says $75,000 dollars. It seems you need to take notice of your own show's hook line."

"Excuse me?" she asked, confused, while Daisy struggled to hide a smile behind her hand.

"The 'don't judge a book by its cover' thing." I waited for the penny to drop.

"You can read!" she forced out through gritted teeth, clearly unhappy about being busted.

"I can. Pull that shit again and I walk. Now give me the damn contract."

Meredith handed it back to me, taking extra care not to risk making physical contact. The contract was simple enough. They wanted me to live in a big flash house and pretend to be someone of wealth and status. The production company would give me a legend and expect me to be available for filming twenty-four/seven. I'd be expected to evict a girl from the mansion daily for the first week to whittle them down before finally committing to dating the last girl standing. After our date, they would reveal my true status to her on a live show where they could televise the fall out. I would also be required to attend any talk shows and do PR for as long as the show remained current and aired on the TV network. Finally, the contract would be voided in the event of me revealing my true status before the show's finale.

"What do you think, Mr...?"

"Sutton," I barked, still looking over the paperwork. "I'll have my lawyer look over the contract at our next appointment." Hennessey the horror's jaw plopped open in surprise, whereas Daisy burst out laughing. "I'm fucking with ya."

"Of course, of course. Can we discuss some of the expected detail?"

"Knock yourself out. You may as well get them out

now. Just in case we need to renegotiate that big number you tried to con me out of." Reminding her of that again was funny. This woman had no clue about homeless people. The American movie stereotype had set her up to fail. Like many others, she assumed we were all bums, scurrying round the storm drains looking for our next fix. Not everyone was an uneducated miscreant. There were many people who could read and do math, and most of us had at least some basic schooling. It was only as we got older and life got difficult for us that we found ourselves sleeping rough. The amount of ex-servicemen living rough would have shocked the shit out of most normal people. Guys who had come close to making the ultimate sacrifice for their country were discarded, perhaps when they needed help the most. I'd made friends with some of them and the stories they had to tell were heart-wrenching. It was no wonder they struggled to integrate back into society. Seeing do-gooders whose only experience of real conflict came from *Saving Private Ryan* or some other Hollywood blockbuster stand proud for the national anthem didn't mean shit. It was an insult, and just looking across the table at this bitch reminded me of why they were forced to live the way they were.

"We'll need you to learn your back story. We're toying with the idea of telling the viewers your real status but for the ladies you are living with, you will need to be believed. I assume you have no objections to us sprucing you up a bit?"

"I don't want some fancy trendy hairstyle," I interrupted.

"To a point, I can agree to that. Maybe we could trim it, but you have to at least look as though you visit a barber regularly, and an expensive one at that. Make it more designer than disgusting."

I nodded. I wasn't against having my hair trimmed and tided up, but this bitch was not going to scrape away my individuality and make me some country club clone.

"You'll have a full wardrobe at your disposal and there will be a cook and staff at the Mansion to help maintain the façade of money, as well as the camera crew."

"Live in slaves. Agreed. Brody will need exercise so the place needs to have enough space for him to wander. If he isn't accommodated, I walk."

Meredith nodded in agreement.

Kirby came to the table with a fresh round of coffees and it smelt amazing. Both Daisy and I thanked him and reached for a cup, while Meredith peered over the plain white mug as if she were being asked to drink poison. For the first time it hit me that all the women they put in the place would be like her. I'd have to be friendly and courteous to a bunch of bimbos who probably couldn't read that contract for real. A glimpse of an idea hit me and I had the duration of Hennessey's prattling to give it some further thought.

"You understand that this show will be all access?"

"Consider me dumb and explain it to me," I poked back.

"Your waking hours will be spent in full view of the camera crew. Should you become very friendly with one of the women, we want it on camera. No full nudity or sexual activity will be filmed; that would get us kicked off the network. Bathroom activity won't be included in the filming either."

"Your camera lackeys will follow me round unless I want a shit, shower or shave, and should I get lucky you want it on camera, although fucking isn't acceptable?"

"Yes, that's it exactly."

Daisy was horrified that the discussion had gone into this level of detail.

"*Miss* Hennessey," I said, leaning in and emphasizing the 'Miss'. "You see my face, the strong cheekbones and brilliant blue eyes?"

"Oh, I do."

"You also see that, for a homeless guy, I'm in decent

shape, and you think that underneath these clothes I'm probably not bad to look at. If I wanted to fuck in a porn movie, I could have been doing it for years. I don't. So believe me when I say this: if there was any chance of me having sex in the house and I got even the slightest hint that it'd been filmed, you'd be looking for another damn stooge. And another thing, there will be no filming in my bedroom while I sleep. If these girls are as desperate as you hope, you'll get your 'movie action' in other ways."

I watched as she contemplated what my declaration would do to her show and then forced a nod as her face lifted. "Are you prepared to sign the contract?"

"Just one more condition."

"And that would be?" she expelled, unable to hide her irritation any longer.

"Daisy. She's a fake contestant in the mansion and you pay her as one, plus the amount you've already agreed to pay her."

Meredith's jaw hit the tabletop the same moment Daisy dropped her mug of coffee. Her boss was outraged but I wasn't sure whether it was at my condition or the fact that her tight ass, cream wool skirt was now completely ruined.

This job was going to be hard, but if I had a friend inside it might just be bearable.

Chapter 9

DAISY INGLES

"Kade," I gasped, absolutely floored by his idea. "I can't…"

"My damn skirt," Meredith bitched, snatching a napkin from the holder on the table. "Do you know how much this cost? You, Daisy Ingles, are so fucking stupid you can't even handle a damn cup of coffee and you think I'm going to trust you with my brain child? Deluded."

I looked down at the big wet, brown stain she was dabbing at, and tried to feel guilty, but couldn't muster up even an ounce of it. She deserved it, complaining about how much the too tight thing cost when poor Kade could barely afford a cup of coffee or a cream cheese bagel every day.

"Listen, lady," Kade said gruffly. "I'm sorry your skirt got some coffee on it, but I need to know your answer before I sign this contract."

Meredith stopped what she was doing and looked up at Kade, her top lip curling into a sneer. "You can't be serious?"

"As a heart attack. Now, what's your damn answer?"

Kade sat back in his chair and waited expectantly.

"Kade…" I started, but Meredith held up her hand to silence me.

"Why? Why do you want her on the show?"

Kade contemplated her question for a few seconds and then leaned forward, his arms resting on the Formica table.

"Short and truthful answer: I don't trust you and I know Daisy will make sure I'm not fucked over."

My chest constricted as I considered his words. He trusted me. This man who had no one but his beloved dog trusted me to take care of him. He wanted me to be the person who looked after his best interests, and while the responsibility was huge, it filled me with pride.

"She has no power," Meredith stated, throwing the sodden napkin onto the table. "She could be on the show and I could still fuck you over."

Kade nodded slowly. "I like your honesty, Ms. Hennesey, but rest assured, you fuck me over and the media will find out about it."

"So you don't need her on the show. Just sign the damn contract, Mr. Sutton."

"Nope," he said, pushing the papers towards her. "Not until it's altered to include all my stipulations. I'm doing this to help you win an award, which I'm guessing will save your ass, and believe me, spending weeks locked up with a bunch of walking, talking *Barbie dolls* is not my idea of fun. To combat that living hell, I want Daisy around. I want to be able to talk to my friend when the vacuum heads start jabbering about bikini lines and mani-peds, or whatever the fuck they're called. Oh, and don't forget the hair and room for my dog to run around in," he said, tapping a finger on the contract.

Meredith opened her mouth to argue, but Kade held up the same finger.

"Before you say anything, I suggest you consider your options. If I don't do this, who the hell will? Because, without wanting to come across as some egotistical idiot,

NIKKI ASHTON & VICTORIA JOHNS

the last time I looked, most of the people I share sleeping space with under the railway bridge are old and toothless. Added to which, they have pissed themselves so much it's ingrained into their skin. You'd never get rid of the smell; the Barbie girls would hate it."

"I don't know about this, Kade," I protested, glancing at Meredith.

"I know you need me to do this, Daisy," he said softly. "But I don't think I'll be able to stick it out without you. You understand?"

I nodded slowly, understanding every word. If he didn't finish the show, I didn't get my bonus and Mom and Pop didn't get their trip or Mom's medicine paid for.

Wanting to plead with him to let me off the hook, I looked into his startling blue eyes and saw a shimmer of insecurity and fear. He wasn't insisting on this to be cruel. He'd shown nothing but sympathy for my situation. He was doing it because he needed me. If he could give up his privacy for me then this was the least I could do to be a good person, a good friend.

"Okay," I said on an exhale. "I'll do it."

"Hey, boss lady here, people!" Meredith pointed a finger at her chest. "I make the decisions."

"So," Kade said. "Make them."

Meredith's nostrils flared as she grabbed the contract. "I'll get the changes made and Daisy will get it back to you."

She then stood up from her chair so forcefully that she almost pushed it over.

"When you've finished making puppy eyes at your boyfriend here, I want you in my office," she snapped.

"I'm not," I cried, totally embarrassed. I hadn't been, had I?

"Let's get one thing straight," Meredith hissed, leaning down to look into my eyes. "You will not, and I repeat *not*, be the one he chooses at the end. Do I make myself clear?"

"She'll need to be there until the end," Kade said matter-of-factly. "I want her there in the last week at least, so you'll have to have three girls in the final, not two."

"Who the hell do you think you are?" Meredith asked, shaking her head. "You do not make the rules. This is my show, and I decide what the format will be."

"Up to you, Ms. Hennesey," Kade said in a light tone. "She's in until the end or I'll walk with her."

"You little fucker!" Meredith poked a finger inches from Kade's face. "Do not mess with me, because I promise you it will only cause you heartache."

Kade raised his eyebrows until they disappeared into his beanie hat. "Okay, if you say so. Maybe I'd best walk away now before you cause me any harm."

My eyes widened at the balls of the guy. He was being offered a home, clothes, food and money, yet he would not be bought by the harpy shrew in the four inch red heels. He was bright and bold, and I had to wonder, again, how the hell he'd ended up on the streets.

"My office in an hour. I'll have the amended contract then," Meredith snapped at me then turned on her heels and fled.

As Kirby's door slammed shut, Kade chuckled while I stared at him open-mouthed.

"Well, that was fun," he said, picking up his mug of coffee.

"Seriously, Kade. I think you just made yourself an enemy. She hates being bested by anyone."

"Let alone a homeless guy," he replied flatly.

"I didn't say that," I protested.

"I know." He sighed. "I'm sorry, but she's pissed me off, thinking just because I have no home I mustn't have brains either. You know I had a GPA of 3.8 my last semester at college."

My eyes must have flashed amazement because Kade laughed.

"I know, go figure. The hobo actually has brains."

49

"Kade," I chided. "If I was amazed, it was not because you had a GPA of 3.8. It was because a GPA of 3.8 is damn near perfect."

"Now that's where you're wrong," he said, wagging his finger at me, any feelings of hurt gone from his demeanor. "A 4.0 would be perfect and a 3.9 would be damn near perfect."

I couldn't help but laugh at him, but still wondered how he'd gone from college to the streets.

"How did you end up homeless?" I asked, vocalizing my thoughts.

"Ah now, that is a story for those long nights in the mansion." He gave me a huge smile and stood up. "I'll see you later when she's amended the contract."

"Okay," I replied.

With that, he collected Brody from his spot by the radiator and left, leaving me worrying about the fact that I was kind of looking forward to those long nights.

KADE SUTTON

As I left the café, I had to wonder what the fuck I'd got myself in to. How the hell could this end on a positive? Okay, I'd be fed and clothed for a while, but I was under no illusion that once the show and all the furor around it died down, the network and, specifically, Meredith would cut me loose. I could end up back on the streets, and how would that feel after experiencing the wealth of something close to a normal life for a while?

Thinking about the wealth and the sheer crassness of it all, I worried that my mom would be disgusted with me. She'd hate that I agreed to living in luxury, for however short a time, while friends and people I knew were still living in poverty with a just pieces of cardboard and ripped, dirty blankets to their names. Maybe, though, she'd understand I was doing it for Daisy. Okay, a little bit of it was for me. I was getting tired of the constant battle to find food and a warm place to sleep, and the ongoing fight against joining the drinkers, just because the alcohol might help get me through the day, was becoming tiresome.

I hated to think that I'd let Mom down, but I needed to do this for me, as much as I needed to do it for Daisy. It may be the worst decision of my life; it may change me for the worse, but I had to do it, otherwise I wasn't sure how much longer I'd survive my current life, even if it was the one I deserved to have.

As I trailed back to my usual spot with Brody at my side, rain started to wet the sidewalk. It was only light, but it was enough to have those caught without jackets or umbrellas dashing into stores and coffee shops, while others pushed up their umbrellas and jostled with each other as they rushed along.

I pulled my coat collar up and urged Brody to go faster, heading for our spot under the overhang of Daisy's office building. She needed to be able to find me with the new and revised contract, so it was the best place to go. Yeah, okay, so Daisy herself might have had something to do with the reason I headed there every day, too.

The thought of her made me smile just as it always did, but her face when I told her about my GPA had been a picture. She'd looked as shocked as if I'd just got my dick out and flopped it on the table. Then, when she asked how I'd ended up on the streets, part of me wanted to tell her, let it all out, set myself free. Maybe talking about it would ease the pain, lessen the guilt, but how would saying the words do that when it was so deep within me it was part of me, part of my soul?

Paighton forgave me. She said it was an accident, it wasn't my fault, but Cory was dead because of me. Her only son died because I drank too much tequila one night.

I'd been back in touch with both Paighton and Cory for about a year. Social media did have its benefits, and reconnecting with the guy I'd considered my brother had been one of them. Cory had been so excited when I messaged him, and immediately insisted I go with him to see his mom and have a meal with them. Walking into their apartment had been like coming home. Paighton's familiar perfume hit me as soon as she pulled me into her arms. The memories of her caring for me when Mom was ill came flooding back. Some were good and some not so much, but they were memories of a time when I'd felt loved. Since leaving the kids home at eighteen, I'd had no one. I had college buddies, and a few girls were pretty happy to keep me company from time to time, but none of them were part of my history; they weren't family.

After that night, Cory and I spent a lot of time together either at his mom's apartment or at his shared house or mine. We partied a lot, we hooked up with *lots* of girls and we tooted the occasional line, but nothing too serious. One night, I went to a frat house party and lost real bad at beer pong, only there'd been a slight alteration and it was actually tequila pong. Only two hours in and I was wasted, and I mean really wasted. I was puking up so badly that I burst a blood vessel in my eye. Some of my hockey team put me to bed and left me to sleep it off while the party carried on downstairs. When I woke the next morning, I reeked of tequila and vomit and could barely stand. I considered just staying at the frat house and sleeping the day away, but I had to get an English paper in the next day, and I hadn't even started it.

My own house, which I shared with three other guys, was about a half hour walk away, and I could only just walk to the bathroom without thinking I might pass out, so I needed a ride. Everyone I knew had been at the party, so the few numbers I tried either went to voicemail or I was told to 'fuck off'. The only other person who could help was Cory.

When he answered his cell, I could tell by his voice that he'd been partying himself, so I tried to brush him off and say it didn't matter. Cory was one of the good guys, though, and said he'd come get me. He said he'd be there in an hour after he'd washed up and grabbed breakfast.

Two hours later, there was no sign of him, so I dialed his number again. He didn't answer but I got a text that said he was ten minutes away. An hour later, there was still no Cory, and I knew something was wrong. It took me almost another two hours to pluck up the courage to call Paighton, and a guy answered. He said he was a police officer and I couldn't speak to Mrs. Mulrooney. I yelled and screamed down that phone until, eventually, Paighton came on the line. Cory had been using his phone to text and had crashed his car into a truck when he missed a stop light. He'd been texting me. He'd been okay, or so they thought, when the cops had breathalyzed him. He was three times over the limit, and was just about to be pushed into the police cruiser when he collapsed. He was twenty-one years of age, and died from a massive brain bleed from banging his head on the side window of his car when he smashed into the truck.

When Daisy asked me whether I'd ever wondered where I'd be if I'd changed the route of my life in some way, I said I had never wondered about it, that I was on path I was meant to be on. Mom had always told me that we'd always end up on whatever path we were meant to be on. I truly believed her, and never thought about where I could be. I believed that this was my destiny because of my selfishness in calling Cory. I did, however, think about him. If I hadn't drunk so much that night, where would he be now? He was meant to join the NFL as a linebacker. He didn't care who for as long as he played professional football. He was not meant to be six feet down in the ground.

After that, I bombed out of pretty much everything. College, my part-time job teaching English to immigrant kids and hockey all went down the toilet. I got kicked out of college for missing too many classes and turning up late to those I did attend. That meant I lost my home, and seeing as the community college I taught at had fired my ass for missing my sessions there, too, I had no money to rent anywhere. A few nights sofa surfing with an old college buddy turned into a month, until in the end, his girlfriend kicked me out. I couldn't find another job so couldn't help pay for anything, and for his girlfriend, Tiffany, the final straw came when I finished off her favorite breakfast cereal and left them without milk.

So, that was the story I had to tell Daisy. That was how I ended up homeless at the age of twenty-two. My best buddy died because of me and I was so fucked up by it, I ended up on the streets. It was not *Disney*, it was not pretty, but it was my life, the path that I was meant to be on.

As we neared our spot, Brody gave a little grunt, as if to say 'we're home', and I felt a sense of peace as I saw my blanket roll and pile of cardboard still there. I didn't take it everywhere with me like most people on the street. I always thought if I were meant to keep it, it'd still be there when I got back. I'd been lucky so far, and in three years, this was only my second bundle.

"Home sweet home, Brody." I sighed, giving him a pat on the head. "Make the most of it, buddy, 'cause soon you'll be living in the lap of luxury."

Brody grunted again and I wondered whether he was telling me I'd made a huge mistake. If this was my path and I was meant to be on it—my penance for Cory— should I really fuck with that, just for the smile of a pretty girl? Then that pretty smile flashed through my brain and I knew this was what I had to do.

Chapter 11

DAISY INGLES

I had about an hour and a half of peace while Meredith went to change out of her ruined skirt. I could feel the cold breeze of her mood when she walked back past my desk, though. I was in for some serious shit. To say that things were bordering on arctic would have been an understatement.

I kept myself busy wandering through some of the emails that had built up over the last few hours and nearly jumped out of my skin when she slammed a bunch of paperwork on my desk.

"Here," she pointed, "is the damn revised contract for that fucking hustler in hand-me-downs outside. This," she said, sneering and separating one pile from the other, "is your paperwork. I think you get that I'm extremely unhappy about this. No one fucks with my plans. Ever."

"Meredith, it-"

"Save it. Whether you cooked it up together or not, you've just cost me a lot of money. The rise in his fee and now yours means I'm going to need more drama on the show."

I didn't want to point out that the rise in Kade's fee was purely a result of her attempt to swindle him. Reminding her of that would probably send her over the edge. "Not to mention the fact that I'm going to need to find a replacement dogsbody in the office." Her head was shaking so much that I was beginning to think her weave might come undone. "Go and get that excuse for a human to put his grubby, disgusting paw print on that contract and then come back here."

As I went to shove back my office chair to leave, she continued, "I've reserved a room for him and that mutt from tonight at the Diamond Days Motel. Tomorrow morning, you'll need to escort them to the various places for defleaing."

Meredith stormed off into her office, the door almost bending with the force she used to slam it.

Kade was sat outside, his head bobbing up and down and his fingers tapping a rhythm on his leg. He was completely content in his place and I felt bad again for dragging him into this. Meredith would pull out all the stops to get him back for what had gone down, and now I didn't just have to protect him, I had to look out for myself.

"Hey, here you go. I have to take it back with your signature."

He reached up for the paperwork and pen and looked confused when I held a pile of papers back. "What's that? More shit she's trying to shaft me with?"

"No. This would be my contract." I sighed.

"Daisy," he said, concerned. "Pull up a pew for a few." He indicated the paving slab next to him. "Can I read yours?"

It was a legal contract so I guessed someone should. I handed him the papers and he discarded his own in favor of mine. While he paid attention to the words from the witch, I gave Brody a good old pat down.

"Yours is identical to mine. The fees look the same and there are no hidden clauses as such. We're good to sign."

Kade signed his and handed it back to me along with the pen. I slowly flipped open the pages, the feeling of dread mounting the closer I got to the page where I'd see dotted lines awaiting my scrawl.

"It's not the hidden clauses in this document that worry me. She'll be lining up twists and turns for both of us now and I won't know about them in advance. I won't be able to warn you or protect you from that. The depths of exposure she's prepared to go to will be pretty low."

"I'm sorry, but I'm going to need a friend in there and I couldn't think of a better one." Kade took my hand and squeezed it in his own.

"Ignore me, I'm just grumpy. I know the money will help, but I don't know how I'm going to tell my parents, and what about the animal shelter? They'll be down a volunteer."

Kade was still holding my hand. "Only for a little while, and afterwards, they'll have a famous volunteer who could use her newly acquired fame to get publicity and donations."

He was right.

"I better go." I stood up to leave.

"Sign the papers, Daisy. Let me see you jump in this crazy boat with me and the Brodester."

I did as he requested and decided to get over myself. I wasn't the one about to live a lie. Kade could come out of this looking really bad. Duping a bunch of women would make him a target for some serious public hatred. I could just blend into the background if I chose to, and collect the money at the end of it.

"The witch has booked you a room at the Double Days. I believe your transformation starts tomorrow."

I walked back into the office and sucked in a lungful of confidence. Meredith's office door was open and I could hear her bitching down the phone at someone.

"You're back. Did the fraudulent motherfucker sign it?"

"He did, and mine is here, too."

I watched as she punched her intercom button and, in a repeat of yesterday, barked for Lydia to appear before her. When Lydia materialized with her *iPad* and sickly sweet smile, I decided to look on the bright side. Maybe I could treat the madness in the mansion as a vacation from the office, but I knew that I'd be swapping one madhouse for another.

"Lydia, there's been a change of plans. Daisy is taking your slot in the house and you're taking hers behind that desk." Lydia was going to be a contestant and I knew nothing about it. The confusion must have been clear for them both to see.

"But I thought we had an agreement, Meredith," she whined.

"We did, but this little madam and the tramp cooked up a new deal and the agreement is no longer viable."

Lydia shoved a hand on her hip so fast the *iPad* was forgotten and crashed to the floor. The look on her face was pure evil, and if she'd been capable of snarling like a rabid dog, she would have been.

"I didn't... We didn't," I began.

"You bitch!" she shrieked. "You've ruined my chance at breaking the big time. Look at you! Look at her!" she wailed, flinging her arms in my direction, not caring how deranged she looked. "No one will believe that you belong in that house, you frumpy, ugly, boring nobody."

"Enough!" Meredith barked. "We have to make it work, but we're going to need a couple of... 'normals' in the mansion to help her blend in or no one will believe Daisy belongs there. That's your job now, Lydia."

"I don't know people like her," she bleated.

Meredith completely ignored her and turned to me, "You can be in charge of getting that mangy fucking con artist and his animal into shape. Go and get a company

Amex from the finance team. He will need a few outfits and as much of that shitty hair lopping off as he will agree to. I want him ready for meetings and photos in a couple of days."

Both Lydia and I were gobsmacked at our change in roles. She was not a PA and Meredith was going to learn that really quickly. No doubt that would be something else she'd take out on me. Even more worrying was the fact that I was expected to find a salon on short notice that would take Kade and turn him around. I didn't do beauty parlors. They were inhabited by creatures I had no understanding of. Getting Brody through his transformation would be more my area of expertise.

Then the thought really hit me. They were inhabited by the same creatures I was going to be living with under the microscope of a TV camera, and if Meredith got her wish, millions of viewers.

Chapter 12

KADE SUTTON

Brody and I had an odd night. The bed was twice the size I was used to from the shelter. There was no rush to get through the shower, and because I was feeling such a king of luxury, I even dragged my boy into the tub with me and gave him a little spruce up. I don't think he appreciated my attempts to give him a soapy Mohawk, though.

Checking in at the front desk was hilarious. Before I even walked through the door the old cow behind the desk was screaming, "Out! We don't take your kind here." It took some convincing for her to check the register and see that I did actually have a reservation and it had been paid in full for a whole week.

A whole week!

Brody and me were going to lap up this little bit of luxurious privacy while we still had it.

I slept in the nude and loved the feel of the soft cotton on my body. I spent at least thirty minutes grasping the fabric between my toes until I spotted my toenails. They were not pretty and whoever ended up with the task of hacking them into shape was going to have their work cut out for them.

There was a locked mini bar in the room, and a quick call to Gloria at the front desk had housekeeping coming over with a key. It was full to the brim with liquor, beer and snacks. During my early days on the street, I broke into an empty motel room once. It had been raining for days and I could feel swamp rot setting in. I knew that if I didn't get some respite from the cold and wet, I'd end up with infected feet and be in bad shape. I stayed long enough to take a shower and dry my clothes. I whacked up the thermostat in the room in an attempt to dry them and my boots that I swear the room was hotter than a Caribbean island.

That entire law-breaking night I sat behind the window drapes wrapped in a towel, praying I didn't have to make a quick getaway, and as the hunger settled in, I spotted the mini bar in the corner. I jimmied it open with a knife and it was like finding the crown jewels when I looked inside. I made a decision that what I didn't manage to eat that night, I would steal for future supplies. I gorged on peanuts, pretzels, candy bars and beef jerky. My stomach had been so empty that I didn't even stop to breathe and digest in between each one, and by the time I was finished, I had a little pouch in my belly that I hadn't had in years.

As I fell asleep in my guarded position by the window, I could feel my belly beginning to tumble and turn, and I knew what was coming. I spent about three hours puking my guts up and the next three days shitting through the eye of a needle. When your stomach has been so deprived of processed foods and fats, overloading it with them in a short space of time is a bad idea, and I needed to remember that lesson for the mansion.

I watched a little bit of TV, flicking through the channels like some mad man. Living in a mansion wasn't going to be the only strange thing. I wasn't a functioning member of society. My manners were sketchy at the best of times, and I had no idea about current affairs or topics of interest to talk about. The legend that Meredith was creating was only a small part of the deception. I needed to learn about culture and the privileged lifestyle so I could be convincing as a millionaire.

The next morning, there was a banging on my motel door and Brody was instantly up at the window checking out who had dragged me from the depths of another night down memory lane. Whoever it was on the other side of the door, he was pleased about it. His tail was wagging back and to so quickly I began to fear he might start to hover. When I pulled open the door, Daisy stood there holding a large duffle bag, whereas I was only holding a towel around my middle.

"I thought you might be the grumpy old bag from the front desk. She is not keen on having my sort under her roof."

"Sorry, did I wake you? It's just that we have things to do. Can I come in?"

Interestingly, Daisy seemed nervous about my state of undress. I could tell she was trying to avert her eyes and the bobbing around like a cat on a hot tin roof was new. She'd always seemed so certain around me. My first conclusion was that she was shocked by my appearance but it didn't take a genius to figure out that what really shocked her was finding herself attracted to me. Her quick intake of breath and constant fidgeting gave her away and I loved it. I fucking loved that there was still some part of me this pretty girl actually found appealing.

We were both silent over the awkwardness of what we'd learned about each other in those few seconds, before I remembered that she was there.

"Can you give me a minute to put my clothes back on?" I asked, taking pleasure in reminding her I was as close to naked as I'd been for any female in a long time but trying not to embarrass her further. If we both stood like this for much longer, my excitement would be obvious to her, something else that hadn't happened in a while.

"Sure, you'll need this." Daisy swung the holdall at me through the door. "A few clean outfits to tide you over until we can get you... you know... sorted."

It was already starting to happen. The TV network were keen to get the show on the road. "Give me half an hour. I'll meet you at the *Wendy's* on the corner."

Daisy nodded and wandered off. As the door was shutting, I hurled the duffle at the bed. Whatever was inside was going to set the tone for what they expected of me. Brody came and stood next to me, regarding the bag with just as much fear, as if he knew that opening the zipper was some big event for both of us. I couldn't put it off any longer and carefully tugged it back. Inside were black and white chucks, a few pairs of cargo pants, some three quarter sleeved Henley's and a bomber jacket. No underwear, but still, not too disastrous and as soon as I spotted the Chucks, I knew that the selection was more Daisy's doing than Meredith's. Shuffling round further inside the bag, I found some popular masculine body wash, a can of deodorant, a toothbrush and toothpaste. The last item my fingers fell upon was a beanie. It felt like it was made of the softest wool and stylishly, it was me all over.

"She did good, buddy," I muttered to my pal, who had his nose in the bag, searching for any goodies that he could lay claim to.

Daisy was tucking into a plate of pancakes when I walked through the door. I'd had to tie Brody up outside, so I wasn't planning on staying long.

"Breakfast?" she asked. The look on her face was different. It didn't take long to figure out what had her attention.

It was me. I was different. I was wearing clean clothes and I looked like a regular patron. Her attention made me blush a little bit. I was so used to being ignored that to finally be under someone's gaze was embarrassing.

"Nah, left the big guy outside and I don't like leaving

him too long." She didn't need to know that I was still full from my mini bar feast last night.

"About Brody, the places we need to visit won't take too kindly to him tagging along. One of the volunteers from the animal shelter works at the vets on the corner of Seventh Street. They can keep an eye on him. Joel said he'll take us to the shelter so we can leave Brody there. They'll give him some doggy pampering."

I knew from the look on her face that she wasn't sure whether I would agree to being separated from my pal. If Meredith had made the arrangements, it would have been a no for sure.

"Guess we're going to meet some new friends." I smiled and watched as relief swamped her face.

When Joel pulled up at the dog shelter, Brody went nuts. He could hear all the barking and the commotion, and in his own head, translated it to, 'gonna get spoiled.' We left Joel, and Daisy introduced me to her supervisor, Pat, who promised to give my pal the works until we returned to collect him.

An hour later, we got an *Uber* back into the city and stood outside some godforsaken place called 'The beauty Zone'. The outside was nearly as drab as the insipid colored walls of the inside, and the desire to run had never been stronger.

"Let's be clear." I stopped her as she put a hand on the door. "I'm not gonna walk out of here looking like some dancer from a Broadway show."

"No, I promise," Daisy said. "But you are going to walk out looking like the son of a rich billionaire who's been living large on a Caribbean island and enjoying the high life. You're going to retain your individuality because millionaires who wear boating shoes and have neatly coiffed hairstyles exist in every gated, security guarded mansion, on every street corner in Beverley Hills. You, Mr. Sutton, are going to be the exception to the rule. The intrigue will kill the mansion bitches and the public."

Before I could argue with her or summon up a front to hide my fear about the person she was describing, Daisy was already inside confirming my arrival.

First up was a full body polish. I was wrapped from head to toe in some stinking mud and left to dry until I had a thick crust covering my body. If I closed my eyes for long enough, I could believe I was back on the streets I smelled that bad. Then some blonde in a therapist's dress appeared and brushed it off with a dry brush. I nearly asked her whether she'd mistaken me for a horse in the Kentucky Derby. The same girl then ushered me into a shower where I was blasted with jets of water, both hot and cold, until the shower tray beneath me looked like some kind of mud slide had happened, all while wearing damn paper underwear!

I was then wrapped in the fluffiest towels ever and plonked in a mani-pedi chair. One girl ground away at the skin on the bottoms of my feet and then proceeded to clip my toe nails. I did my best to ignore the way she was gritting her teeth and trying to ignore the state of me in general. At one point, she was hacking so hard at my toes that I nearly suggested she call in an industrial ground worker with an angle grinder.

When she was done, another girl in black pants and a tunic appeared and started to rub some sort of cream into my hands. At one point, it smelled so bad it reminded me of a night where I'd been so cold I pissed myself. Seriously, if I knew they were going to use materials that I'd been living in for years, I'd have been giving these treatments to myself on street corners. When she'd finally finished clipping, rounding and filing my finger nails with an emery board, I was about to get up when she approached me with a pot of clear nail polish.

"Uh, no. I don't think so. I do not need that shit," I protested.

This was getting ridiculous. These women, who all

looked exactly like each other with their high ponytails, rose pink lips and extra-long eyelashes, were determined to make me into some sort of pretty boy. A pretty boy suitable for the women I'd be on the show with; shit, they'd probably be primping and pampering them, too.

The hand girl looked in Daisy's direction for confirmation, and as I was gearing up for a showdown with her, too, she lowered her magazine and nodded in agreement with me, effectively dismissing the girl who was insistent that it would do wonders for my natural nail growth.

Next, I lay back in a chair and recieved a facial. Bony fingers felt like they were trying to poke holes in my cheeks, and probably the only part I enjoyed was the hot, wet shave that made my skin feel so tight I could have rivaled Meredith in a face lift competition. As I relaxed and breathed in through the hot towel wrapped around my nose and mouth, I felt a warm liquid being applied to my eye brows. It felt like just another piss useless cream being applied to my skin until she rubbed a small square of cloth over the top of the cream and pulled. Hard.

"Motherfucker!" I shouted and felt the instant need to slap my own eye sockets to quell the pain. "What the hell are you doing to me?" I shouted through the towel, causing the Barbie inflicting the agony to step back sharply in fear. Daisy was by her side in an instant, getting ready to talk me down from my angry outburst.

"I believe she has just shaped one of your eyebrows," she confirmed.

"Shaped? With what? A blow torch?" I cried, watery tears forming beneath my eyelids.

"No. Hot wax," torture girl replied.

"Well, no more of that shit. I'm not a chick or gay. There is nothing fucking wrong with my eyebrows."

Daisy was struggling to hold in a laugh. "You have to do the other one, Kade."

"I do not," I protested, spinning around and sitting

upright to look in a mirror. "Jesus Christ, what have you done? Make it quick," I conceded, seeing that my face would look ridiculous with only one done. "How you women do this is beyond me?"

The therapist began to whisper to Daisy who replied with, "I think we should give that a miss."

"What? What are we missing?" I enquired.

Once again, Daisy giggled. "You were down to have a back, sack and crack wax, too." As soon as she saw the look of horror on my face, her giggling turned extreme and I wasn't the only one with tears rolling down my face.

I'd been here forever and no one had approached the subject of my hair yet. "Daisy, are we going to be here much longer? I'm beginning to feel like some kind of beauty experiment."

"You're nearly done and then we move on to the dentist and barbers."

When I was finally allowed to put my clothes back on, I felt weird. I could smell my own natural body odor and it wasn't unpleasant. My hands seemed to glisten when I moved my fingers, reminding me of those girly vampire films all the girls in college were obsessed with. As for my face, that felt as tight as drum skin when I grimaced or smiled. I was starting to feel like someone else. It had been a long, long time since I'd felt this clean or smelled this good.

At the dentist, I was given a serious scale and polish. The hygienist who did the work was dressed up in some kind of hazmat suit, she was that worried about what she would be excavating, and I don't use the word excavation lightly. It felt like someone had been between my poor ivories with a pneumatic drill. For the first time ever I could feel air flowing between my teeth and around my gums after she'd finished. Quickly, I was ushered into a second room, and a different woman covered my lips and gums in some kind of rubber shield and began to paint them with a brush and some solution. I was left to bake in that room for God knows how long before being dispatched with some kind of mouth contraption and the words, "You can use this solution yourself to stay on top of your own whitening program." One look at the woman handing it over convinced me I was never doing it again. Her own smile was so bright they should have issued *Ray Bans* to protect anyone who was forced to have a conversation with her.

By this time I was beginning to doubt whether Brody would recognize me when we went to pick him up. Hell, I wasn't even sure I'd recognize myself when this was all finished. Daisy's interest in my transformation was getting more and more as the process continued. We'd never spent so long in each other's company before, and while I was trying to get a closer look at her, I could tell she was doing the same. Although, to say she wasn't very covert was an understatement. Every time I caught her glancing my way, she'd jump a little bit and raise the magazine she was pretending to read. At one point in the afternoon, I noticed she hadn't actually turned a page for nearly two hours. I had to be honest—I liked her gaze on me, and for the second time that day, it was perking up parts of me that hadn't been 'perked' in a while.

Then came the words I didn't want to hear: "Kade, one more stop and then we can go and get Brody. Time to visit the hair salon."

Chapter 13

DAISY INGLES

I had to admit Kade was looking pretty hot since he'd been polished and shined. His skin, without the grime, was remarkably clear for someone who'd lived on the streets for three years, and the way he filled out the cargo pants I got for him... Well, he did *Ralph Lauren* proud. I know, I shouldn't have spent that much, but I figured Meredith would want him to have the best, and his long legs were perfect for the straight cut, designer pants that cost what I would spend on two weeks' worth of groceries.

"I'm keeping some of the length," Kade muttered as he lifted his palms to smell his hands. "I did say that, right?"

"Yes, Kade." I grinned. "You did say, and yes you can keep it longer in length. We just need to tidy it up." I looked up at his hair. It was so unkempt I wondered if something could be living in it. "So tell me, is the long hair a product of living on the streets, or have you always worn it that way?"

Kade shook his head. "Not totally. In the homes we had our hair pretty much hacked off—to keep away the lice apparently. It wasn't until I moved in with my foster mom that I was allowed to grow it."

"That sounds awful," I replied, guiding him across the car park towards my ancient *Smart* car.

"Yeah, I know." He sighed. "When I left the home and started my new school, the kids used to make fun of me and shout baldy at me during every recess."

"What?" I gasped. "They shaved you bald?"

"No, it was just real short, but kids of eleven don't think about those deets when it means they can get a laugh."

"God, kids sure are cruel," I whispered, a lump forming in my throat at the thought of Kade being bullied. I really felt his pain.

"Ah, don't worry about it," Kade said, waving a dismissive hand at me. "I kicked their butts, and once my hair started to grow, the girls were putty in my hands. The other guys in the class didn't get a look in. Not wishing to sound like an egotistical idiot, but with wavy brown hair and bright blue eyes, I was kinda pretty."

Irrationally, I felt a small stab of jealousy at the thought of a group of eleven-year-old girls fawning all over him. They were probably the cool girls—the mean girls—who made it quite clear that the nerdy, quiet girls were not allowed to even look Kade's way. Holy fudge! What was going on with me? I couldn't peel my eyes away this morning, and now I was getting jealous over a bunch of girls I never even knew.

"Okay," I said, letting out a long breath. "This is me."

Kade looked at my car and smiled. "Loving the flowers."

I shrugged. "I love daisies."

I'd bought the car from an English lady who'd had it imported when she came to live here, and I loved it. The problem was, it was a little bit boring being all black, so I'd pimped it with huge daisy stickers on the sides.

"Not sure I'll get in it, though." Kade groaned. "It's a pretty small car."

As I got into my seat, I giggled as I watched him fold his long legs into the passenger seat. His knees were practically under his chin.

"You can put the seat back," I said. "My mom was the last person I had in here, and she's pretty small and likes to be right upfront where the action is."

"How small is she?" Kade muttered as he slid the seat back. "Is she a munchkin or an Oompa-Loompa?"

"She's very small." I laughed, thinking about my tiny little mom. "So, you okay?"

Kade nodded. "Yep, let's do this."

As I thrust the stick shift into gear, Kade blew out a long breath and I knew he was not looking forward to the next part one little bit.

When we pulled up outside Dominique's, I thought Kade was going to have some sort of fit and pass out. He was practically jumping in his seat with a huge Cheshire cat grin on his face.

"Seriously?" he asked.

I couldn't help but reciprocate his smile as I nodded. Dominique's was the most exclusive hair salon in the city, probably in the whole of the state, and appointments were at a premium. It was amazing, though, what Meredith's offer of some network TV advertising could get you: an appointment with Dominique, their top stylist and owner.

"Okay, let's…" I started to say, but Kade was already out of the car.

I got out and stood next to him on the sidewalk where he was gazing up at the signage. It was black with scrolling gold letters and its logo—a gold silhouette of a crown on the head of a woman with extremely long, flowing hair.

"Wow," he gasped. "My foster mom used to rave about this place when I was a kid?"

"Really?"

"Yeah. She'd never shut up about the place, talked about it a lot."

I looked up at his handsome face as he stared up at the sign with a wistful smile, and my heart did a little flutter. Okay, so the reason we were here wasn't ideal, but the fact that I, well the studio, could bring back a happy memory for him made me feel as though I'd done a really good thing. He was obviously thrilled and that made me beyond happy.

"Yep," he said, taking a deep breath. "A real lot. Bernadette, my foster mom, she didn't have much, so her dream was to come here one day. I used to tell her I'd pay for her one day, when I was older and got a job, but of course that never happened. Then, when I was thirteen, she had a heart attack and her husband, Larry, couldn't cope with looking after us kids and Bernadette, so the three of us had to leave her and go back into a state home, so…"

He trailed off and looked down at the ground, hanging his hands off the back of his neck.

"Hey," I said, laying my palm on his back. "You okay?"

Kade looked up at me, his eyes full of emotion, and gave me a small smile.

"I'm okay. Bernie would've loved this, you know? I wish she was here to see it."

"Do you still have her number or know where she lives? We could call her," I said excitedly.

"She died," Kade said, turning back to look at the signage. "We all visited for a couple of years, but then she had another heart attack and went."

"Oh, Kade, I'm so sorry. I didn't mean to upset you." I wrapped my arms around my waist and worried my bottom lip with my teeth, concerned that all of this coupled with reliving old memories was too much for him.

"I'm not upset," he replied. "Just a little disappointed she didn't get to fulfill her dream."

I had no idea what to say to him. It was hard hearing about more misery he'd had to live through. He'd obviously loved her, and for her to have died must have been heartbreaking for him. Two special women in his life and they were both dead. I knew how I would have felt if my mom had died. I mean, she very nearly had. Only the dialysis was keeping her alive until the transplant, but she was lucky. I was lucky because she survived.

"I think," I said with a long exhale, "that Bernadette probably knows you're here, and she's real happy for you."

Kade looked at me and grinned, nodding his head. "Yeah, I think so, too."

"Come on then, let's see what Dominique can do for you."

"Shit, you're kidding me," Kade cried, lacing his fingers at the back of his head. "*The* Dominique is doing my hair? Shit, Bernie will be sooo jealous."

"Yes." I giggled. "So, come on or we'll be late and that would never do."

Kade almost ran to the doorway, and seeing his joy made me feel happier than I had in a long, long time.

KADE SUTTON

"Woah," I gasped as Ginny, one of Dominque's girls, placed a bottle of beer in front of me. "This is so cool, Daisy."

Despite the fact I was sat under a big ass hairdryer that looked like some sort of brain reading machine with a plastic cap on while oil soaked into my damaged hair, this really was cool. I looked a real idiot, but shit, it was *Dominique's*, and *the* Dominque Jeffers had touched my hair. Admittedly, I'd been a little scared at first when she sheared my hair to shoulder length, but she assured me it'd look great once it was styled properly. I had to admit it looked better even before all the conditioning treatment. She knew exactly what she was doing.

Daisy grinned and pushed her glasses back up her cute nose. "I know, right?" She lifted a plate with a selection of pastries and cakes on it. "Want one?"

I thought about saying no after my binge in the hotel room, but that had been hours ago now and there'd been no adverse effects so far.

"Okay, something small," I said, peering at the plate

and picking a cookie shaped thing with a few nuts on one side and covered in chocolate on the other.

"Florentines are my favorite thing in the whole world," Daisy chirruped with a little stamp of her silver chucks.

"You want it?" I asked, offering it back to her.

Her cheeks pinked and she lowered her lashes. "I had two already," she said with a little grimace.

"Wow, greedy girl. All mine then." I took a bite of the cookie and had to stop myself from letting out some sort of sexual gratification groan.

It was amazing. The crunchy nuts combined with the chocolate and caramel was like nothing I'd ever tasted before; well, nothing I'd tasted since I'd been homeless anyway. Cookies, candy and cakes were things you avoided when you had no idea when your next meal would be. That swift pleasure the sugar brought didn't last long, and before you knew it you were hungry again. To be able to eat this and not worry about it brought a lump to my throat. I hadn't realized how hard life had been, and yet just these few hours of being normal, of wearing clean clothes and simply being clean myself had been like a sledgehammer to the head. My life had been shit for almost four years, and not just because I'd been on the streets for three of them, so I was grateful for the calm and peace. I was grateful for Daisy.

"You know, Daisy," I said, finishing off the Florentine, "I know I shouldn't, but I'm kinda looking forward to the show."

She looked at me wide eyed, a little cake thing halfway to her mouth. "You are?"

"Yeah. I know I'll probably live to regret saying that, but it'll be nice to talk to other people, dress up a little and eat good food. I wouldn't have that if Meredith hadn't railroaded me into it."

"Oh God." Daisy gasped. "You're not starting to like her, are you?"

The look of horror on her face made me laugh. Her

glasses had dropped right to the end of her nose, and her mouth was wide open.

"Shit, no!" I exclaimed. "She's a damn bitch, but that doesn't mean you and I can't have some fun while we're in the house."

"Mansion," Daisy corrected.

"Okay, mansion. Whatever it is, we can still have fun."

Daisy's eyes glistened like the sun on a pool of water, but her brows were furrowed and I knew instantly that she was feeling torn.

"I'm not suggesting anything really bad," I said, trying to placate her. "Just let's make the most of it. We'll treat it like a vacation."

"Funny thing, that's exactly what I thought earlier. It'll be a vacation away from Meredith if nothing else."

I watched as she rubbed her temple and narrowed her eyes.

"Why are you so worried about it, then? I know you are. I can see it in your face."

She shrugged and placed the plate of goodies onto the side table beside her. "I have to tell my mom and pop that I'll be gone all summer, and I'm not sure they'll like why. They hate that I work for Meredith as it is, so if I tell them she's pushed me into this, they'll be real mad."

"It was kinda me really, though, who pushed you into it," I said, feeling bad. "I understand if you want to change your mind."

Daisy shook her head. "No, no way. Apart from the fact I signed a contract and the money will help my folks an awful lot, I also promised you and I don't go back on a promise."

"Yeah, I know, but I'd understand and I'm sure Meredith would prefer you *not* to be on the show."

"Hmm, probably," she said, bobbing her head. "Which is why I'm definitely doing it."

We both laughed and I felt a little better.

"Do your parents know why you're working for

Meredith—to send them to Europe, I mean?"

"Nope. They just think the animal shelter couldn't afford to pay me any longer." She looked thoughtful as she stared ahead.

"You think you'll go back there, once you have the money you need?"

She grinned real wide and nodded. "Oh yes, Pat and Sonia already said I could. They didn't want me to leave in the first place, but the pay isn't great so they understood."

"And the pay is great at the studio?" I scratched at my head under the cap, wondering what the hell Dominique had put on it.

"It's good enough. Much better than the shelter, but nothing like Meredith earns," she replied with a laugh.

We fell into silence for a while, and I nodded off for a few minutes, but Dominique removing the cap from my head startled me.

"Oh hey," I said, wiping a little drool from the corner of my mouth.

"You're nice and cooked now," she said in her rich, Jamaican brogue. "Come, I make you even more handsome."

Dominique moved me to the other side of the salon, away from Daisy, and pushed me down into a chair.

"So, is she your woman?" she asked, nodding his head towards Daisy as she placed a pot of creamy stuff on a cart next to her. "She's beautiful."

"Daisy, oh no," I replied, shaking my head. "She's just a...friend."

Dominique chuckled, flashing her beautiful, pure white teeth. "Okay, whatever you say."

"No really, she is." I looked across the salon through the mirror, and watched as Daisy messed with her cell phone.

"She's still beautiful," Dominique said and started working the cream into my hair, combing it through with her fingers.

I looked in the mirror again and saw Daisy was watching. Catching my eye, she smiled shyly and pushed her glasses up her nose before reaching for a magazine. Dominique was right; she was beautiful, but she was also out of reach, off limits and too good for me. That meant I should stop looking at her, because being around a pretty woman for the first time in years meant that my dick was twitching against the zip of my pants. Yep, if I looked away and concentrated on Dominique, who while beautiful herself was also probably twenty years older than me, Kade junior would go back to sleep. The problem was, Kade junior wasn't on board with that train of thought, and almost two hours later when Dominique had finished with me, he was as hard as hell. That was kind of a surprise, because when I'd been that shallow jock in college, I probably would never have looked twice at a sweet little thing like Daisy, no matter how beautiful she was. Life on the street had shown me many things, one of those being that true beauty was *so* much more than big tits and pouty lips.

Chapter 15

DAISY INGLES

Kade played it cool with his hair at first. He tried to shrug off how totally amazing it looked, but when I asked him what he really thought, the beam on his face told me that it had been one of the best things to ever happen to him. It was a real stroke of luck that Dominique's was a happy memory for him, but I was so happy that it was.

"Every time I turn my head, there's this insane scent of cedar wood and lime. And my head feels so much lighter since she cut it," he yapped on in the car. "If we weren't in the car, I'd need to turn around to see who the fantastic smelling dude was behind me."

Dominique had indeed done a brilliant job, cutting Kade's dark hair just below his ears and teasing it into soft waves that fell into his eyes in a disheveled, just got out of bed look. He looked amazing and I couldn't stop myself from stealing glances at him. He took my breath away. I was starting to imagine him with a couple of days of stubble and what that would feel like against my skin. My thoughts were making me a little hot and breathless, and Kade was the star of those visions.

Kade's own enthusiasm lasted right up until we were back at the animal shelter. "What if my main guy doesn't recognize me?"

"Of course he will. Your scent is just a small part of who you are. Dogs have this instinct, kind of like magic, where they can see through to your core. At the shelter, we call it the 'The Good People Radar'. A dog's initial reaction helps us judge whether the person will connect with the animal they are trying to adopt.

Before he was reunited with Brody, I took him on a bit of a tour of the facility, and I was proud to show him what we did with people's generous donations. It was truly amazing. There were so many dogs who had been dumped by so-called animal lovers it wasn't true. The city pound was overrun and we liked to work with them. After all, if we didn't do something, most of the dogs the warden picked up would be destroyed. Subconsciously, people were shallow and they viewed dogs in the city pound as feral, dirty animals, whereas ours were seen as rescue pets. In essence, they were one and the same. When the pound's capacity was at bursting level, we'd take some dogs in as our success rate for re-homing was better, simply because people had huge misconceptions about the types of dogs that came from the pound as opposed to a shelter.

When I stopped at our 'wall of wonder', I watched as he stood and gazed at the hundreds of photos. Each was of a dog with a name we'd given them and the team member who had been involved with the dog's primary care. It was like I was seeing it for the first time, too. Not only were there so many photos, but there were dozens and dozens with me in them.

"You love what you do here, don't ya?" he said very simply.

"I do."

"It's obvious. This place is lucky to have you, Daisy. Although I'd question the person who let that thing in."

He laughed, pointing at a picture. "Is that a horse? It looks like you're trying to hug a damn horse."

"That was Tiny. The dog warden found him on the beach. Apparently he was holding an ice cream truck hostage. Kids were screaming and parents were wailing like the National Guard needed to come in and deal with some monster on the beach. He gave the warden no trouble, although he was lured into the back of his vehicle with a tub of rocky road *Ben and Jerry's*. There was no room for him at the pound, so they swung by here and we took him." I laughed at the memory. That was a good day—the kind when you know you're doing something good and worthwhile.

"Anyway, as soon as the truck door opened, he launched out the back and bowled me over. He was licking my face with a tongue so big it was like a facecloth. One of the last things I saw, before my glasses became so fogged with slobber and bits of marshmallow, was a nametag on his collar. It said 'Tiny'. That's what happens—people buy them as pets, not understanding that the dogs are going to grow and, in some cases, grow really, really big, so they just dump them."

"Well that dog had the 'good people radar'," Kade said, and when I turned to respond to him, he wasn't looking at the wall any more, he was transfixed, looking at me.

Feeling a little flustered, I nearly forgot why we were there. "Let's go and get Brody!"

As he wasn't a resident at the shelter, he was being treated to some TLC in the office, and when I pushed through the door, I saw his head pop up from under a desk and bark in recognition.

"Hey, boy, look who's here." I stepped aside and revealed Kade who was definitely nervous behind me.

Brody paused for a few seconds, titled his head to one side and then barked again.

"Well, look at you," Kade crooned.

Brody had been treated to a good scrub and coat trim,

and he looked great. As soon as he heard Kade's voice, he was up and moving. The crazy dog didn't scoot round at floor level, though. He jumped up and launched from desk to desk like he was a contestant on *Ninja Warrior*. Paperwork, pen pots and pamphlets rained down around us.

"Aw, shit! Brody, settle down," Kade told him, but it was only half-hearted.

Kade was relieved that his best friend still knew him after they'd both been through the beauty ringer, and their reunion hit me in the same spot it always did when we managed to reunite a dog with their owner.

I drove Kade and Brody back to the motel—Brody had to sit on Kade's knee, so that was fun—and watched as they both strutted their stuff across the parking lot. They both had a spring in their step that was good to see. If only all the homeless people out there could have been shown some compassion and made to feel clean and human. Wasn't that what those more fortunate should have been doing?

As much as I hated how Kade had been pulled into Meredith's master plan, at the moment, he was benefiting from it.

I agreed to pick him up again the following day at the same sort of time, and before he left the car, there was an awkward silence that neither of us could fill. I couldn't get it out of my head as I drove home. Even though it was awkward, it felt good, and I was happy to do anything to take my mind of what I was about to do.

Mom and Pop were sat in front of the TV watching the Dollar Dilemma. It wasn't a show I was a fan of, but then again I'd seen what went on behind the cameras. The main host and the girl who operated the big game board despised each other one day and then screwed like animals the next. The poor girl who had to try to keep them on an even keel just for filming had one hell of a job. Then there were the contestants—the network went out of their way to find the dumbest people possible, mainly because the questions the production team came up with were beyond stupid. It was just irritating all round. Mom was screaming the answers at the TV and Pop was screaming at her because she was getting too excited over some stupid game show.

My mom was looking tired today. Her next check-up and meds review was due and you could tell by the worry lines on her face. It was really sad that I could run a monthly calendar based on her wrinkles. My pop was a great guy; we both had the same heart and soul, but I knew he suffered with not being able to ease my mom's suffering and the dent his pride had taken by having to move in with me. It didn't matter how many times I told him I was okay with it and that I wouldn't have it any other way, I could still see that he felt like he'd failed.

"Here she is." My mom smiled as soon as she saw me. It was a genuine smile. She was always pleased to see me, and she loved to hear tales from the TV network office.

I only hoped she liked the one she was about to hear. There was no easy way to approach it, so I decided to just blurt it out.

"I'm going to be working on one of the TV shows. I'll be away for a few months on location."

"Oh my! Did you hear that? Our Daisy is going to be on location." I knew my mom would get a kick out of it.

"I'm right next to her, Heather. Of course I heard it." Pop was more reserved. He hated that I was working there at all. He knew my heart lay at the animal shelter.

"Tell me all about it." Mom's enthusiasm was something else. She didn't have much excitement in her life and was happy to live vicariously through me.

"It's a new show. A sort of matchmaking, reality documentary thing set in an exclusive luxury mansion."

Pop wasn't asking any questions and that worried me.

"When do you start?" she asked, her pupils fighting to shine brightly through her tiredness. Mom's body had been through a lot, and although she grabbed forty winks when her body needed it, she much preferred to be up and talking to me when I was home.

"Some time over the next week or two. It's going to be like a vacation for us all," I told them. "You get some space and I get to do something other than sitting behind my desk."

"You hear that, Robert? No more desk sitting for our girl. She's going on location!"

My dad wasn't impressed, but I suspected it was more to do with his failure complex than what I was going to do. As he got up and wandered to my kitchen, I followed. Whatever he had to say could be said without my mom hearing.

"What's wrong?" I asked him.

"I hate that you're taking a job elsewhere to get a break from me and your mom."

I knew he genuinely believed that. "I'm not. It's an opportunity and I couldn't turn it down."

I watched as he regarded my face for the briefest hint that I was lying to him. When he'd scrutinized me enough, he pulled me in for a hug. "I hate that we've taken over your life," he whispered, kissing my head.

"I wouldn't have it any other way. You guys are my world," I mumbled back, tightening my grip around his middle in an effort to ward off the emotion he always managed to bring out in me.

"Can I hear the jug?" we both heard mom shout, breaking our moment. Her intuition into how we were all dealing with the final stages of her post-op rehabilitation and living arrangements was uncanny.

Pop dropped the hug and reached for the kettle, sniffing. "Pot of earl gray coming up, Hev."

I went back into the living room to sit and watch the rest of *Dollar Dilemma*, doing my best to tune out the visuals of the hosts humping like rabbits in their shared dressing room. I refused to acknowledge the fact I'd been more than a little bit economical with the truth about my new job. At some point, I was going to have man up and tell them I was going to be in front of the camera instead of behind the scenes.

For now, though, that could wait. Mom's next check up was only days away. I'd do it after that, when she was stronger.

Who was I kidding? She wasn't the one who needed to be strong. It was me. I was dragging it out as long as possible until I could face the predicament I'd gotten myself into.

Chapter 16

KADE SUTTON

As a homeless person, you have two basic personas foisted upon you. The most obvious one is invisibility. People will absolutely treat you as if you are not there. It sounds like the easiest one to go for, but some people struggle with it and they handle that by doing the classic 'fake out'. They'll spot you, a tiny bit of conscience will prick at them and at the last minute they will fake looking across the road for someone or something, or they'll start fake digging round in their purses for something that they don't need and that urgent need to locate it miraculously disappears when they get past you.

The second one, which the majority of people feel at home with, is disdain. Some vile people, who dare to call themselves humans, find it easier to throw shade and scorn at someone who dares to be less fortunate than they are.

Anyone showing something different causes that moment of quandary within us street dwellers, where we may, for just a moment, get our hopes up about being treated better than something they've just stepped in.

Since my makeover, the difference in how people

treated me was the biggest issue I had. The miserable old cow on the front desk at the Double Days greeted me like a long lost friend. There was no haranguing or screeching about 'my type', and I was sure if I had asked her for a hug, she would have caved and given it to me. There was only a small spark of something in her eyes that indicated she'd seen me somewhere else before.

"And if you could look this way, Kade," the photographer requested and I did as he asked.

"And if you could give me just a couple of normal face poses, no smiling?" I granted him his wish and was rewarded with, "Perfect. Those are perfect."

Daisy had collected Brody and I during the morning and whisked us away to a photo studio where we were to start putting together some PR shots for the network's promo plan. The photographer had already received some directions via email.

"Why is it just me? No props or other people?" I shouted at the guy after changing clothes for the fourth time.

"The screen behind you is a blank so we can superimpose you over some appropriate scenarios," he told me, furiously flipping through the shots he'd already taken on a laptop. That explained why I'd been pictured in a very sharp business suit, some casual sports gear, a boating outfit, and now I was climbing into a tuxedo.

It was all part of the ruse.

"While you get yourself into that monkey suit, I'm going to take a few snaps of your dog."

The guy didn't wait for my answer. As with most people in this industry, time was money and as I wrestled myself into a shirt with cufflinks and then a goddamn cummerbund and bowtie, he got on with it.

I watched from behind a useless clothes shade that gave me about as much privacy as a hand towel as Daisy coaxed Brody into some sensible shots. Only when he started to misbehave did she get involved. That little dude knew what he was doing and before long, she was rolling around the floor with him having a ball. There was no direction from the photographer, just the constant clicking of a camera shutter.

She was a beautiful girl who had no idea just how appealing she was.

"Why the hell are you playing around with that mutt?" I heard from the side entrance of the studio, closely followed by two sets of clicking heels.

"I… uh… Brody was struggling with his shots, so I got involved to keep him on track," she told Meredith and the plastic fantastic who was glaring at Daisy so badly she could have been boring holes into her head. As I suspected, they hadn't spotted me yet.

"Where is he? Don't tell me you've lost him already."

"I'm here, Ms. Hennessey," I said, making her jump. Neither she nor the girl had seen me approach from behind them, and the looks on both of their faces were priceless.

"My, my, my." Meredith crowed. "I do believe I may actually pull this one off."

Her choice of words was not great. I sincerely hoped she was talking about the show and not me.

I moved into position in front of the blank canvas after helping Daisy off the covered screen floor and stopping to give Brody a scratch on his head. I heard the photographer get into position quickly and start taking shots before I was ready, and I knew he was taking some candid shots of me with Brody.

"Enough with the monkey suit. I want some different shots now. I trust you've done all the ones on my list?" Meredith asked the photographer, who nodded. "Kade, there is some swimwear in a bag on the back of the screen. Go and put it on. Now!"

Meredith used no pleasantries at all, and when I didn't move on command, the assistant with her looked up at me in shock, wondering how long I was going to defy her. My mind told me there was much worse to come and that putting on some surf shorts was not a real issue. Right now, it was a case of picking which battles to fight and I knew this wasn't it.

Meredith and the girl continued to ignore Daisy, who had been relegated to dog sitter, and wandered to the photographer to check out the rest of the shots from the session. I took off the tuxedo and left it in a heap on the floor. My patience was being put to the test, and I thought wasting even a few minutes hanging up some damn rental suit was a risk I couldn't afford to take.

Opening the bag to seek out the swimwear, I was shocked to discover a small pair of *Speedos* I was less than happy about. I knew I could pull the look off, but that didn't make me want to do it.

"Come on, Kadey," she jeered. "Let me see the goods."

I pulled the *Speedos* into place, snapping the elastic to indicate I was nearly done, and walked around the shade.

"No. Good God, fucking no. Daisy, explain this," she shouted, screaming in Daisy's direction but pointing at my crotch.

I looked down and then up, then down and over at Daisy, then down and finally up, shrugging my shoulders at the photographer in confusion.

"Why can I see hair? He was supposed to be groomed. Was getting him manscaped too much to ask?"

Daisy, forced to look at my crotch area, was opening and closing her mouth like a fish, and Meredith's assistant was clearly pleased that Daisy had screwed something up.

"This won't work. You're supposed to have money and portray that you care about your appearance. A guy of means does not neglect his grooming. Someone find me something else to work with?" Meredith bellowed.

Everyone began to look at each other, wondering who would be the lucky person who was carrying an alternative outfit for me. When no one else moved, one of the guys working the lighting for the photographer wandered to a gym bag and produced a pair of boxers. Throwing them at me, he muttered, "They're clean. Keep 'em."

I retreated back to the changing shade and got changed again, before presenting myself to Meredith.

"That's better, oh genius! Designer *Calvin Kleins*. Get into position please."

Somewhat taken aback that she seemed placated and she'd actually used the word please, I wandered back to the blank background.

"Okay, mate, you need to vary it up a bit, nothing too pornographic, and if you're lacking in any area, we can always *Photoshop* it in, if you know what I mean," he laughed.

Daisy suddenly seemed excessively occupied with Brody, barely glancing in my direction, whereas Meredith and the miniature witch with her were almost frothing at the mouth, until I changed position and put my hands on my hips, exposing my mother's name tattooed on my bicep.

"What...? Wait! What the hell is that?" She pointed.

"A tattoo," I replied, feeling my hackles rising.

"I can see that. Tattoos are part of the package that will appeal. You know what won't? A tattoo of some other bitch's name."

Anger ran through my body quicker now and I was unsure how to respond. Part of me knew to simply ignore her while another, fairly big, part of me wanted to punch her. Fortunately for Meredith, she moved on quickly.

"Lydia, create a person in his backstory with the name... What does it say?"

"Shelby," I told her through gritted teeth, trying to warn her that belittling that part of my history wasn't going to fly.

"Better yet, give him a drunken night at college with his frat house where he wakes up with that. I don't need a host of Shelbys turning up, claiming to be her and stealing my show's PR." Lydia was nodding and typing on her *iPad* at the same time

"I hope I can trust you better than this once you're in the house, Daisy. I don't like being let down."

Once again, the assistant smiled with joy at Daisy being told off, while Daisy continued to ignore us all and focus on Brody.

"For the sake of these pictures can you fold your arms, or even one arm and cover it up with your hand? No, wait," she squawked. "We'll cover it with make-up for now. I don't want any questions or paps digging around until filming is well underway."

This woman was working my last nerve, but both myself and the make-up artist did as she asked, and like the pretentious bitch she is, Meredith declared the shoot a success and left just as quickly as she arrived.

"That's a wrap," the photographer confirmed and I went back to the shade to put my clothes on. Daisy was astute enough to sense my bad mood, so we didn't really speak until she was dropping me back off at my motel.

"Are you okay?" she asked tentatively.

I'd had more than enough of being in the spotlight.

"Are *you* okay? That woman treats you like shit, Daisy." She flinched a bit when I verbalized the words and I immediately felt bad. "I'm sorry."

"No, you're right. Sometimes it's easier to just let her think she's won. Incidentally, she's in a bad mood because she knows I'm a better PA than contestant. It was planned that Lydia would be in the mansion with you. I think you get that she was going to run the inside action based on Meredith's carefully scripted wishes."

"Ah, and she can't do that now without an inside bitch to manipulate things," I replied, catching on quick.

"Exactly."

Feeling like I'd cleared the air a bit, I bid her good night and got out of the car, understanding that Meredith was going to do anything possible to make sure the show went in the direction she desired. Little things like me, my dog and Daisy weren't going to get in her way or there would be hell to pay.

Chapter 17

DAISY INGLES

It had been a couple of days since I'd told Mom and Pop about my 'new job' and Pop was still very quiet. I'd told him that everything was fine, it was part of my job and it really wasn't me escaping from them. It truly wasn't, but a little part of me couldn't help looking forward to the respite from worrying about them. Then I felt guilty and said I wouldn't do it if they didn't want me to. It was then that Heath, my brother, dragged me into the kitchen and had his say. His take on it was that I should go and have fun and not worry about our parents.

"You know, honey," he said with a stupid grin on his face. "Our kids are all grown up now, and we can really trust them to be home alone."

That earned him a smack on the back on the head, for which he pulled me into a hug and rained wet kisses on my cheek.

He was right, I knew, but Mom was still getting over a major operation. A kidney transplant wasn't like having a tooth extracted; she'd had an organ removed and a new one put in. It was no wonder I worried about her, but I decided to listen to my big brother for once. I had to admit it was kind of exciting yet absolutely petrifying all at the same time.

The thought of the cameras being on me was scary, but the idea of sharing a house with nine other women scared me so much more. I wasn't what you'd call socially inept. I could hold a decent conversation with most people, but I hated being around large groups of women. It reminded me of my high school days, and often saw me breaking out into a sweat. I had to do this, though. I needed the money and I'd promised Kade.

Yep, and then there was Kade. He was the one who provided the little fizzle of excitement about the whole thing. Spending time with him over the last few days had been really enjoyable. He'd had a hard life, yet he never spent time complaining. He talked about it, of course, but always with fondness, never with a hint of bitterness. Plus, there was the added bonus that he was looking amazing. I'd always thought that there was a handsome man underneath all the dirt and grime, but he was actually quite beautiful, or as my mom would have said 'swoony'. Just thinking about him made my heart do a little two-step jig, but then I remembered the tattoo. Whoever Shelby was, he obviously cared about her a great deal because he wasn't happy that Meredith wanted him to cover it up.

Pushing thoughts of Shelby to one side, my memory banks then flashed up images of Kade in those tiny swim trunks, and the heat started rising up my neck. I knew Meredith complained about him not being waxed down there, but my goodness, did she not see what the guy was packing? Let's just say there was no room for anything else in there. Then there were his abs; I still had to wonder how a guy who had lived on scraps and small offerings for the last three years could have such a great physique. He obviously hadn't worked out, or at least I didn't expect he had, so it must have been…well, just him.

NIKKI ASHTON & VICTORIA JOHNS

And, I had to say, 'just him' was freaking awesome.

"Daisy," a screaming voice shouted. "Get in here, now!"

I gave a weary sigh and rolled my chair back from my desk. The sooner I had time away from *her* the better.

"Yes, Meredith."

"You need to get yourself some decent clothes," she barked without even looking up at me. She was concentrating closely on a sheet of pictures.

"Are they Kade's pictures?" I asked, hoping to change the subject.

"Hmm," she muttered. "He's fucking magnificent. I'll give him that. Even those dreadlocks of his look good."

I smiled, doing a little dance in my head. She liked what she saw and maybe wouldn't give him a hard time after all.

"Can I look?" I asked.

Meredith lifted her head slowly and frowned at me. "Didn't I just tell you to go and sort your damn wardrobe out?"

"Yes, Meredith. I just thought-"

"I don't damn well pay you to think, Daisy. I pay you to be my PA, but you've fucking managed to get out of that one for a few weeks with your little plan with Kadey boy."

"It wasn't a plan," I protested. "I had no idea he was going to suggest it."

"He didn't suggest it," Meredith snapped back. "He held me to fucking ransom."

"I'm sorry."

She curled her lip and waved a hand at me. "Go and sort your clothes, and take Lydia with you. She may not have a brain, but she has style."

I groaned quietly. Going shopping with Lydia was the worst thing that could ever happen to me. I'd rather have spent a weekend locked in a room with Meredith than go shopping with Lydia.

"I can go on my own. I don't need her. I do know what sort of clothes to buy."

Meredith's gaze raked up and down my body, taking in my denim overalls, white tank and pink Timberlands. As she reached the messy bun on my head, with a scarf tied around it in a bow, she practically gagged.

"Lydia!" she screamed. "I need you to take Daisy shopping."

"You really are weird," Lydia said, turning up her nose that I knew cost her daddy almost six figures. "Who doesn't like *Hervé Léger?*"

"I didn't say that," I sighed. "I just said I'd feel like my insides were being shoved out of my back passage wearing something that tight."

"God, you're so crass." Lydia pouted, putting the yellow bandage dress back on the rack. "What *do* you want? Everything I've suggested you've rolled your damn eyes at."

I shrugged and looked around the store, turning in a circle. "I like that," I said, pointing to a dress behind Lydia. It was pale pink, sleeveless, had cut outs at the sides and had a flirty skirt. It was really pretty and I could wear it with the lovely cream wedge heels I'd got from a local flea market.

As she saw it, Lydia clapped her hands. "At last. Maybe you're not such a lost cause. *Zac Posen* I can work with."

She turned on her heels and started flicking through the racks of clothes, pulling things out and putting them back with an occasional cursory glance at me and then a shake of her head. Finally, she marched towards the dressing room and pulled the curtain to one side.

"Get in," she snapped.

"Lydia, I said I liked the dress, not any of that other stuff." I groaned, my heart sinking at the amount of outfits in her arms.

"Oh shut up and get in." She pointed her finger to the dressing room. "And puhlease tell me you have decent panties and a half normal bra on."

I tried to think about what I'd put on that morning and knew she would not be pleased with my panties that said 'Wednesday' on them. As for my bra, that was a little more grey than white, so I was sure she'd have a fit.

"Oh my God," she squawked. "I can tell by your face it's going to be bad, isn't it?"

"No one sees it except me," I objected.

"Shit, I hate Meredith for making me do this. And I fucking hate you more for taking my place in the mansion. I should be the one getting the air time, not some twinky little freak like you."

"I'm not a freak. I have my own sense of style. I just don't follow the masses and bow down to the latest trends or current favorite designer."

"Ah shove it, Daisy," she snarled. "Just try the damn clothes on."

When we left the store almost an hour later, I had to admit I had some really beautiful clothes, shoes and underwear, my favorite thing being a cute white, sleeveless shirt dress that I was darn well going to wear with my pink high tops, no matter what Lydia said.

"Can I go home now?" I asked wearily.

"No, you cannot. We're going to the optometrist." Lydia flounced past me, her hip knocking the mass of bags in my hand.

"Excuse me," I called, chasing after her. "But why are we going to the optometrist?"

She looked at me and grimaced. "To get you lenses of course."

"But I like my glasses."

"Well I don't, and neither does Meredith, so shove it again, Daisy."

With that, she was gone, stalking down the sidewalk as fast as her stick thin legs and skyscraper heels would let her.

Chapter 18

MEREDITH HENNESEY

With Daisy and Lydia shopping, I knew I wouldn't be disturbed. The two of them were the only ones in the entire damn office who had the balls to actually talk to me, and they were out in the city, forcing some fashion sense into Daisy, so I had some time.

I slammed my door shut and turned the lock before moving over to my desk. I reached inside my purse and pulled out a set of keys, unlocking the bottom drawer. When I opened it and looked down, I knew my eyes were shining with excitement because I could feel the wetness at the corners.

Hesitantly, I put my hand in and pulled out the large *Hershey's Special Dark*, the *King Size Caramello* and the *Reese's Nutrageous*. My stomach groaned at the thought of the pleasure the three bars of candy were about to bring. I thought momentarily about the cocktail dress I had to fit into tonight, but knew all I had to do was make myself puke a couple of times and I'd be good.

With twitching fingers, I opened the *Hershey* bar first, the back of my mouth tingling with anticipation.

Determined to enjoy every single bite, I didn't stuff it in as was my usual practice, but broke off a couple of squares and popped the bitter, dark chocolate on my tongue. As the taste flooded my mouth, I gave an orgasmic groan.

"Oh fuck," I moaned. "So good."

I was about to break off some more when my office phone trilled out. No one called that number, no one except Roddy. Quickly swallowing the remainder of the chocolate already in my mouth, I picked up the receiver.

"Roddy," I said, swallowing back some chocolaty saliva. "What can I do for you?"

"I'm checking on the progress of your next award winner," he said, his tone bored and distracted. "Actually, what am I saying? Your *first* award winner."

I let out a slow breath and flipped the receiver the bird. "It's going great, Roddy," I simpered. "In fact, we're going to be ready to interview the contestants tomorrow."

"Really? You need me to attend?" he asked, his tone much lighter at the mention of pussy.

"No. I have it covered."

"I may just pop by. So…" He sighed. "You got a suitable bachelor?"

"Yes," I said tightly, crossing my fingers and wincing. "Entirely suitable."

"Name," he commanded. "I may know him."

"Oh, I doubt that. He's not been around the scene much."

Fuck it. I didn't want him to find out about Kade until we'd already started shooting. That way he couldn't tell me to replace him if he found out he was a homeless guy. Too much money would have been spent and Roddy would not want to spend any more; he didn't damn well have it for a start.

"Tell me about him," he snapped.

I heard a chair scrape back and wondered whether Roddy's latest bimbo had just finished giving him a blowjob and he was moving to let her out. An off-the-wall thought, I know, but not unfounded. Roddy was known for asking his PAs to do some dick taking as well as dictation. When I heard his door close, I knew I'd been right. She obviously wasn't that good, or Roddy was a silent cummer. My money was on Roddy.

"Meredith, I'm waiting!"

"Okay, I'm just pulling his file now," I lied, shuffling some papers around on my desk. "Like I said, he's been off the scene for a while, but his name's Kade Sutton."

"Kade Sutton," he mused. "Nope, never heard of him. Send me a picture over. You do have pictures?"

"Yes, of course. We've already done the promo shots."

"Good. Now, tell me all about him. I want to know if my money has been spent wisely."

Thank God I'd already decided on Kade's back-story, because if I fumbled over any of this, Roddy would know there was a problem. He was like a fucking rat sniffing out shit when you tried to get one over on him.

"Well," I continued. "His parents died in a helicopter crash when he was twelve, leaving him with almost seventeen million dollars. His father was heavily into real estate, specializing in hotels. That was how he met the mother. It was the early eighties, and he was setting up a deal in Europe—Italy, I think. She was working over there through the summer."

"And he still has that sort of money?" Roddy asked, focusing on the money. "I can't believe someone didn't take advantage of him as a kid."

Yep, because that's what Roddy would've done.

"It was held in trust until he was twenty-one—watertight so no one could get their hands on it. He was brought up by a family friend who also died just after Kade hit twenty-one. Once she passed, Kade decided to go off travelling, ended up in the Caribbean, and has lived there ever since. He's been running a beach bar at an exclusive resort where only the mega rich can afford to vacation."

I'd looked into Kadey's background, so I knew there were no parents, just a mother and then a foster mother, who were both dead. That meant if Roddy did check up on me, my story would stand up, to a point.

"Don't fucking tell me he's been bumming around and spent it all," Roddy hissed.

"God, no!" I exclaimed, eyeing my chocolate hungrily, wishing Roddy would just fuck off. "He's been investing it and now has double what his parents left him."

I held the receiver from my ear as Roddy whooped down it.

"Good job, Meredith. Good job."

"Thanks, Roddy," I simpered. "It wasn't hard to persuade him to take part in the show either. He jumped at the chance. Now he's back in the country, he wants to settle down and thinks this is the ideal opportunity. The deal of the show is he has to live with the winner for six months, so who knows? He could find a wife out of this. I think that's what *he's* hoping."

"How old is he?" Roddy asked. "Are you sure he's going to take it seriously, because if he doesn't, the audiences will know. They'll fucking hate him and the show will bomb, which will be on your head, Meredith."

Thanks for the reminder, shit head.

"He's twenty-eight," I said, adding three years on to Kade's age.

"And the girls are going to like him?"

"Oh yes," I said, truthfully. "He's dark and tanned with amazing blue eyes, and he has real titled features. You know the kind—square chin, long nose. He's just oozes money, Roddy, and he's damn pretty with it."

It was true. He really could pass for someone who'd lived a privileged life. I didn't know how he'd done it, but three years on the streets hadn't harmed his physique or weathered him in any way. Lucky little bastard; it took me thousands of dollars every month to look good.

"Okay, so he's not going to back out on us then?"

Roddy asked, and I could hear the alarm bells ringing in his ears at the thought of losing any cash that had already been spent on the show.

"No," I said gravely. "Not a chance. He's signed the contract."

"Which he could easily buy himself out of," Roddy growled before pausing for a few beats. "Maybe that would be a good thing. We could take him for millions."

"Roddy, come on," I said, feeling my heart pick up its rhythm. "You don't want to do anything to make him quit. He's perfect and will bring millions of female viewers to the show."

Do not fucking mess with this, Roddy. Don't you fucking dare!

"Okay, he's probably got a shit hot lawyer anyway. One who could get him out of any penalty clause. These rich fuckers always do."

I breathed a quiet sigh of relief.

"Okay, tell me what you have cooked up for the show then," he said, changing the subject as quickly as he changed bed partners.

"There'll be ten girls in the house with him. For the first week he'll have a private date every night. They'll kind of compete for his affections and to get to know him better while we're showcasing the plethora of beauties he has to choose from. Right from the off, they'll be competing to get laid by Kade." I laughed.

"I like that," Roddy said. "That's the name of the damn show."

"Well, I'm not sure, Roddy…"

"My decision, Meredith. This fucking show is going to be called, 'I Wanna Get Laid By Kade'. It's a fucking winner. Now carry on."

"Okay," I sighed, making a mental note to try to dissuade him later. "So the viewers will vote for their favorite two girls for a private date that we'll film. All dates will be held somewhere in the house. We'll mock up a restaurant or they'll go on a boat on the lake in the grounds. At no point will they go out in public."

"Yeah, I like that. Minimizes the chance of any of them hearing rumors about what's going on behind the scenes. Okay, what else?"

"The two girls who come first and second in the vote will be who Kade has to choose from for his date. But," I said, with a laugh, "before that, he'll have to evict one of the other girls."

"Excellent. You got shit lined up for them, too?"

"Oh yes. We're going to get them to do all sorts of things to rock the boat."

I had no idea what yet, but it wouldn't take me long to think up some real nasty tricks to mess with them.

"There'll be so much shit, in fact, that they're all going to wish they'd joined an online dating agency instead," I said, breaking off another piece of chocolate.

Roddy's laughter on the other end of the line was low and chilling.

"Excellent," he said. "It sounds award winning."

And for once, we agreed.

Chapter 19

KADE SUTTON

My last few nights in the motel were a somber affair. I'd been living such a luxurious life while my transformation for the show was taking place. It was nothing special, but it was clean and warm. It was probably a good thing that Meredith had put me in here first. I felt grateful for the chance to acclimatize back to the basics of being a human with four walls to claim as his own. The problem with that was that I was starting to get a bit jumpy over what was to come, the house—fuck… mansion!—was going to be something my brain didn't have the capacity to dream up. My needs were so simple that I couldn't visualize the grandeur I knew I was going to find.

My back-story was simple enough. I'd spent a whole night going over it, and I could easily come up with enough conversation to talk my way around running a Caribbean beach bar. My frat days weren't a period of time I was happy remembering. It almost always led to me thinking about Cody, but it was probably the closest frame of reference I had to being around copious amounts of idiots who drank too much. And wasn't that what rich people vacationing in an exclusive Caribbean resort would be? Idiots who threw around money, enjoying the sun, sea and sex on a white sandy beach with strangers.

Just as I was about to get ready for lights out, the phone in my room rang. It startled the shit out of me and because I jumped so much, it put Brody on guard duty, too.

"Yeah?" I answered wearily.

"Kade? It's Meredith. A limo will be at your room at 10am tomorrow morning. We're transferring you to the mansion. Pack your... What am I saying? You don't have any stuff."

Even on the end of a phone she was a bitch. I imagined this to be her least favorite method of communication. Ms. Hennessey was the type of troll who liked to see the reactions she caused in people. Using common tech like phones removed that sadistic pleasure from her.

"Are you still there? You haven't said anything."

"Haven't had a lot of opportunity," I barbed back at her.

"Anyway, be ready for the driver. He's taking you there-"

"And Brody."

"Yes. You and your dog will be relocating and getting familiar with the place before the girls arrive. Ideally, I'd like you to know the layout and not make us all look stupid by getting lost. I've arranged for some media to be at the mansion gates. Please stay inside the limo and do not open the windows. I'm building up the intrigue. You will have a whole night to yourself to explore and get acquainted with your new house staff. The camera crew will also be there to set up the live TV feeds and whatnot. The show kicks off filming with the girl's arrival tomorrow night."

She kept on prattling, obviously not hearing or understanding my little jab from a moment ago.

"Now you need to remember this. All filming will take place as agreed in our contract, and then it will be edited to remove dull, non-essential activity. The final edit will be what is screened by the network. Ten girls, Kade, ten whole girls to have fun with," she suggested. "Once a week, the viewers will vote for their top two girls, based on your interactions with them. You, Kadey-boy, will then pick one of them to take on a date. Aside from that selection, you will also need to evict one."

"Right."

"I will have a line of communication with the on-set director, Carson. He will pass messages to me if you have any. Got it?"

"Yes."

My answers were short. I could tell I didn't have long to insert them between her commands while she took in more oxygen.

"Is that it? Right?" she shouted. "No questions? Just right."

I was over this. "Ms. Hennessey, this doesn't feel like a conversation. Conversations are usually where two people move words back and forth. What we have here is a dictation, so, I have heard your orders. Be ready for 10am, don't open the limo windows, go wander around my new home. Ten girls, the viewers pick two favorites, I select my favorite from the two, take her on a date and do something with her. Evict one. Find Carson. Am I missing anything?"

Meredith stuttered a little bit. I knew that people didn't serve her own shit back at her often.

"No. I think you have it down. We'll line up the actual date activities for you, and Carson will inform you of the details."

"Sure." I smiled. I was struggling to hide my glee at pissing all over her rampage.

"Good night then, Kade, and one final thing. If I get even the smallest hint that you are favoring Daisy or scheming, she will be the one who pays. I promise you that. After all, you have nothing to lose."

I was still gripping the receiver a long time after the dial tone told me she'd hung up. I wasn't sure how long I sat there contemplating throwing it across the room, but it was long enough for some kind of alarm siren to sound from it. In the end, I slammed it back on the handset so hard that I made Brody jump again. I needed to get some rest because for the next six weeks, I would be playing someone else's game and this could be my best night's rest for a long time.

The limo collected me and I had my own idea for a show. It was going to be called 'Live in a Limo.' It was that big I could have easily made it into a home. Life was crazy really. People were living on the streets without basic human amenities, and here I was riding around in a fucking box with a fridge and disco lights that was used to ferry the entitled back and to.

"We're ten minutes out, Sir," a voice sounded from a ceiling speaker close to my head.

I decided that would be the last rich versus poor comparison I would make. I had a privileged persona to get into and would never be able to fool anyone if I wandered around feeling growing distaste towards the world's wealthy.

Scarily, in about nine minutes, *I* was going to be one of the world's wealthiest singletons.

The scenery all the way from the motel gradually grew more and more rural. Wherever the mansion was, it was in the middle of nowhere. We'd stopped passing traffic a while ago. Every house I passed had no immediate neighbors. They were completely secluded and had acres and acres of fenced off garden space. I knew this place was going to blow my mind. When we rounded a corner, I felt the limo take a sharp right and then head slowly down a single track road covered in block paving stones with strategically placed palm trees and bushes on each side. After a few minutes, the view from the window changed, and I was shrouded by a brilliant white painted wall over ten feet tall.

My heart rate sped up as the wall continued on and on, and Brody began barking and leaping around the limo. I knew exactly how he was feeling—boxed in.

I felt the driver apply the brake as we slowed down, and then I saw them.

Dozens and dozens of guys with cameras and huge telephoto lenses.

As soon as they spotted the limo, they began to sprint across the curved courtyard driveway in my direction. My heart juddered a little faster and I began to push myself back in the leather seat. Meredith honestly thought I'd be tempted to open my windows to these people? There was no way in hell I was going anywhere near them. They were pushing and shoving, braying for the best shot. Camera lenses smacked against the windows in the frenzy, and Brody had had enough. The barking and growling coming from his tiny, furry frame was that of protection, and no matter how much I tried to calm him down, it wasn't working.

I knew they couldn't see me, but I still felt like hiding and when we finally came to a stop, I could hear them shouting to the driver whose arm I could see pushing an intercom button for entry.

"Just one picture!"

"Come on, open up!"

My fear ratcheted up a notch when I heard the door handle being tugged, but before I could completely freak out, the car sped forward and we were moving again. Looking behind me, I could see enormous wooden gates closing automatically, shutting out the craziness.

"Sir, are you okay?" asked the box in the ceiling.

"Fuck! I thought they were getting in here," I breathed out in relief.

"This is not my first rodeo." He laughed and I could tell it was the truth.

As soon as he drew to a complete standstill and I heard the doors unlock, I jumped out. I needed space and fresh air. Fresh air would be my salvation, and it was the one thing I could always depend on. Brody leapt out from behind me and was off, his nose to the ground, investigating our new surroundings,

"Don't get lost, buddy," I shouted and then turned to look at the house.

Fuck. Me.

"Because I might get lost myself," I whispered when I finally saw it.

The place was so big and white and grand that I wasn't sure whether I was shielding my eyes from the sunlight, the size, or my own shock. There was no way this was a house. It was a hotel. The only way this was a house was if someone had read the building plans wrong and built it to the wrong scale.

My feet were rooted to the spot, as I surveyed the windows and the little pointy tiled roofs. I was seriously considering having to tie Brody up somewhere. There was every chance we could get lost and not find one another for a whole week.

"She's something, ain't she?" said the limo driver, coming to stand beside me and looking up at the house. He was a huge black guy who looked like he should have been a quarterback for the NFL rather than folding his massive frame into the front of a car for nine hours a day. "Some Hollywood star used to live here."

"Who? Michael fucking Jackson?"

He bent double, laughing. "Hope not, although if Bubbles the monkey is still swinging around, you've got your answer."

"I'm Kade," I said, offering my hand.

"Clint. I'll be bringing your young ladies tomorrow and hanging around to help remove them as the weeks go on."

Clint's grin was wide and I felt relieved that I wasn't

alone right now. "Fancy doing the tour with me?" I asked.

"Yeah. I'm gonna live here, too. Every millionaire has their own personal driver so I already have a room and know my way around."

I watched as he lugged his tall frame from the parking courtyard and up the steps, and because Brody was never one to miss out, he appeared like a magician the minute we got near the front door.

The cool air conditioning hit me immediately. I could feel the breeze bouncing off the marble… well, everything. There was marble everywhere. The reception area was massive and all I could see were doors and hallways. The height of the ceiling was something else, and the chandelier that commanded the space above us was like something from *Dynasty*.

I didn't say anything as Clint started to show me around the various rooms. I was too awestruck to process that this level of opulence and magnificence existed. It was nuts. There were so many bathrooms that the running water available to the property would have been enough to solve the drought in some third world nation somewhere. There were powder rooms, luggage rooms, play dens and sitting rooms. TV rooms, closets and studies.

Occasionally, I would glimpse a member of the house staff who would nod at me, and when one said, "Welcome home, Sir," I nearly had to pick myself up off the floor.

"The staff have been recruited using your legend and the show's premise. If they think you're rich, there's less chance of them selling the real story on the outside."

"You know?"

"Well… yeah, I picked you up from the motel." He shrugged.

I was beginning to desperately hope that Clint could become a little slice of normalcy for me.

In each of the rooms we wandered round, there was discreet filming equipment. Someone had worked hard to turn the place into the ultimate filming location.

Clint led me down into the kitchen, which was four times bigger than the one at the shelter. "The kitchen staff will be here twenty-four seven. Everyone, including me, has been told to keep a low profile. We're not to get in the way of filming."

"Where's my room?"

"Follow me." We walked for what felt like miles and ended up at the top of a very large staircase with two routes leading off it. "Your wing is that way," he said, pointing to the side of me. "The girl's bedrooms and bathrooms are that way." Clint continued pointing in the opposite direction. "The TV crew are staying in the old staff block at the end of the garden. They'll work rotated shifts, and your house staff are all on the ground floor, behind the kitchen. Me included."

It was all starting to make my head spin a little. It was like being woken up from a nightmare and dumped in a make believe world. "I'm struggling with all this," I admitted.

"Anyone who isn't born and bred into this world does. How about I show you something that will cheer you up?"

"Does it pass a cold water fridge?" I asked.

"It does, and it's called your drinks room."

I let him lead the way again and grabbed a bottle of water from some cheesy bar that was inserted into a room built for entertaining. Brody slid passed me at one point. He was struggling with the marble floors. He was like some hyped up cartoon dog who had figured out the only way to slow himself down was to bang into the walls. After seeing him do it about twenty times, I began to use the sound of his claws on the floor as an early warning system and my cue to get out of his way.

Clint opened a door way in front of him. "This here is a half sized basketball court, and there's a fully equipped gym next door. You have a movie room in the house and I'm told that's like something from the fifties, although I haven't found that myself yet. There is a state of the art disco-slash-nightclub, but in all honesty, most of the rooms are wired for music."

We left the basketball court and cut through the mansion, and before I knew it, we were standing on a terrace overlooking an enormous swimming pool, surrounded by loungers and day beds. "I imagine most of your guests will spend a lot of time here. There's a *Jacuzzi*, too, and an outdoor grill kitchen just behind that wall."

It wasn't the ridiculous swimming pool that had my attention, though. It was the view. It rolled on for miles and miles. There was a lake and a track running through what looked like a vineyard. I seriously hoped there was somewhere out there I could escape to, just for a little slice of heaven and calm when the madness all got too much.

"All of this is yours, too. There's a garage full of mountain bikes, quads and dirt bikes should you feel so inclined. The lake is manmade and has a couple of those silly English rowing boats, too. I believe there is also a maze on the other side of the vineyard."

"Jesus."

It was the only word I could get out. There was no way I could form enough words to describe where I'd ended up.

"I know. My advice, stay on your toes. It's all just bricks and mortar, my friend. Don't let it change who you are deep inside."

I leaned forward and looked out over the vista; it was all so unbelievable.

If I closed my eyes and just stopped for a moment, I could believe I was the ruler of some kingdom, but that thought was interrupted by some Spanish screeching. I looked down to see what the commotion was as Brody appeared, lurching out onto the poolside with a joint of meat in his jaws, followed by some funny looking little woman in a maid's outfit. Clint was struggling to hold back his laughter, as was I, but it was all in vain as the dumb dog took a leap and plunged into the pool, never once dropping the meat, but drenching the maid in water.

Chapter 20

KADE SUTTON

My bedroom was as nonsensical as the rest of the estate. The bed was hand carved out of some poor tree, and because more is always more with rich people, it was a four-poster. It was so big that Brody was able to stretch out along the bottom and we never disturbed one another as we slept. The sheets were so luxurious and thick that, whatever happened, I was stealing as many as I could before I was kicked out. I was so impressed with them that I was considering having a toga party with the camera crew, just to see who had a sense of humor and who didn't.

Clint's words were wise, and the key to my survival would be figuring out who I could trust and who was here purely to manipulate me for Meredith's entertainment.

After the longest shower I'd ever had in my life, I dressed in casual swim shorts and a polo shirt, thinking I'd take a dip in the pool after breakfast. It took me some time to backtrack my way through the maze of hallways before I finally landed in the kitchen.

"Morning," I said, smiling as I walked into the middle

of some serious looking catering activity.

The whole place stopped dead. Someone amongst the ten or fifteen staff working in there dropped something that broke the silence.

"Mr. Kade, you should be in the breakfast room," an officious looking butler said, heading towards me.

"Why?"

"Because that's where you eat breakfast."

His attention was drawn to Brody, who was sat waiting patiently by my feet. The sneer on the guy's face was very telling, and I got the impression that my boy was lucky it was the little Spanish firecracker who had chased him and not this jail guard.

"And you are?"

"Mellings, Sir."

"Well, Mellings, me and Brody will take our breakfast in here if you don't mind."

I didn't wait for him to mind. This was my kitchen after all, and I was quite happy to sit here and make friends with the staff. In any case, the sooner Brody learned to trust them and stop stealing shit from the kitchen, the better off we'd all be.

A couple of younger girls fed me some scrambled eggs and toast, and after thanking them and putting my own dirty plates in the sink, which again shocked them, I wandered to the pool.

Twenty minutes after I sat down on a sun lounger, a chunky set guy in jeans and a bad taste Hawaiian shirt approached us and sat down next to me.

"I'm Carson. How are you settling in?"

"I'm Kade," I said and leaned across to offer my hand, figuring that was the quickest way to get an idea about his personality.

The guy didn't hesitate, which was a good sign. "The girls will be arriving at four. They'll be given two hours to select a bedroom and settle in. At around six-thirty, we'll be introducing you to them."

"Okay, thanks for the heads-up."

"The real heads-up is that my crew start filming you in less than an hour. We just need you to wander round and do stuff. We'll be using that as filler for the first show, so if you could look excited about having a harem of women delivered for your selection, that would be great."

And he just managed to effectively wipe out the good vibes he'd given me with the handshake.

After my nod of acknowledgement, he got up to walk away. "I'd also suggest letting the house staff wait on you. Millionaires don't tend to deal with their own dirty plates."

Finally, he turned and walked off. My mind was made up more than ever to find at least one member of the camera crew who would be a good link to the outside world.

I'd segregated myself away in my room with Brody. There was a big ass TV on the wall so I decided to sit and pass the hours until it was time to go and meet them all.

All I could think about was the fact that Daisy would be here soon. I desperately hoped she wasn't too nervous and if she was, I hoped even more that seeing me would help her feel better.

I took my second shower of the day and got ready for the big reveal, dressing in a simple white linen shirt and some cream-colored cargo pants. My plan was to portray a guy who had just stepped out of the Caribbean sunshine. Putting on a pair of Havaianas had me nearly convinced myself.

The phone by my bed rang and I reached for it, noticing that my hands were shaking slightly. "Yeah?"

"Sir, your dinner guests are all waiting in the formal dining room for you," Mellings told me, and I could hear the disdain in his voice. Why he chose a career in service, especially for the rich and famous, was just stupid when he didn't appear to enjoy it.

"On my way." Placing the receiver down, I looked at

my best boy. "Time to get this show on the road."

As soon as I opened my bedroom door, I was blinded by a camera light. There was one guy holding the camera, another holding a stupidly big microphone, and Carson rolling his hands indicating I needed to ignore them and roll with it. All of them had headphones on and carefully stepped to the side to let me pass.

Fuck. This was how it was going to be. The minute I stepped out of my bedroom, they'd be there.

Trying to hide some of the awkwardness I felt, I started to chatter and bend down to pet Brody. He was the key to helping me relax into this.

"Let's go meet our new friends. We have lots of new people for you to play with."

Brody barked and was on the verge of tripping me up in his excitement at my suggestion. The closer we got, the more he could smell those new people. Shit, even I could smell them. The combination of overpowering perfumes was like a lingering fog.

"Go on, find them, boy," I urged all of sudden and pointed down the hallway.

This would be an icebreaker. As I reached the hallway to the formal dining room, I could hear chatter and squeals from the girls, although at this point, I couldn't tell whether they were squeals of fear or happiness because Brody was hunting them down.

When I finally walked into the dining room, I was presented with a lot of faces and more camera crew.

"Good evening, ladies. I see you all made it. I hope you had a great journey. I'm Kade Sutton and I'm pleased to meet all-" I counted them "-nine of you. Are we one missing?"

Nerves shot through my body as I took in the faceless bimbos in front of me one at a time. Pretending to joke and count at the same time, I scoured them to recheck my math and search for the one face I was desperate to lock eyes on.

"Ten of us, I'm here," said the giggly voice I recognized, and as she placed a palm on the table top and tried to get up, I shot round quickly like a gentleman to help her.

"What's going on here?" I asked, but I knew before I got there and had no idea how to cover it up.

"Your dog seems to like my perfume." She laughed, embarrassed, and when I finally laid my eyes on her, she was being smothered by Brody, but she looked different.

Daisy was wearing clothes similar to the other girls in the room, she had painted nails and I could see her legs, but the thing that struck me the most was that I could see all her freckles as she had no glasses on to hide them.

"Brody, leave the young lady alone. Let me apologize," I said, offering her my hand. "My dog has this good people radar. I guess you passed his first test." I winked.

And then my acting had to kick in for real, because as soon as she placed her hand in mine, this zap of electricity charged up my arm and shot through my chest.

What was worse was that I knew she felt it, too.

Chapter 21

DAISY INGLES

Meredith had arranged for all the girls to be taken by two limos from the TV station to the mansion, and all of them, bar none, were high on excitement. We were told which cars to get in, and I had a feeling Meredith had already decided who the front-runners were.

I figured this because, in the first limousine, which I should point out I wasn't in, all the girls were absolutely beautiful—varying shades of blonde and most definitely surgically enhanced in the boobs department. In my car, while the other girls were still very pretty, they were exactly that—pretty, not beautiful. They all had long, silky tresses, like the first lot of girls, but in this car there were brunettes, red heads and one dirty blonde. I looked at the girl with the dirty blonde hair, whose name I thought was Mindy, and wondered why she wasn't with the other blondes, and then noticed that she was pretty flat chested, so there was my answer.

The noise in the limo was awful. It was like an aviary of birds on high alert. I hated being around large groups, especially of women, and I felt sick to my stomach. I had to think calming thoughts of sandy beaches and beautiful sunsets until my anxiety finally passed.

The other girls seemingly had no such worries. They all twittered at different pitches and varying speeds, their hands flapping around like wings. I simply sat and watched, my hands pressed between my knees when I wasn't tugging down the skirt of the dress I was wearing. It was the pretty pink one I'd chosen, with the flirty skirt, and while I loved it, it really was much shorter than I was used to. I'd teamed it up with my wedge heels, but as soon as Meredith and Lydia saw me, they both reamed me out and insisted I change them. Meredith practically ripped Lydia's bronze sandals off her feet and threw them at me. Thankfully, they fit, though I was sure Lydia wished we weren't the same size as she was now walking around in my flea market bargain.

Once we arrived at the mansion, the noise level increased with the girls hanging out of the car windows once the huge wooden gates were closed. Our driver pulled up behind the first limo and then one by one, we were instructed to get out, walk towards the house, stop, look over our right shoulder and smile. Apparently, the individual monologues about ourselves that we'd all done to camera earlier in the day would be cut in with the footage of us arriving. Meredith had told me to keep it simple and stick to the facts about my life, except for the fact that I worked for the station, obviously. Seemed I was some sort of aspiring romance author—go figure.

When we were shepherded into the dining room, it was evident that there were already divisions being formed. The blondes all sat together down one side of the huge table, while the non-blondes sat on the other. Little old me was left with the end seat, the one furthest away from the door that Kade would appear through.

We all waited in anticipation of his arrival, and I could feel my heart jumping around in my chest. I hadn't seen Kade for a couple of days, and I was real excited to see him, to see how he was looking in all his new duds. Mostly, though, I was anxious to see that he was okay, and not too stressed out by everything.

The inane chatter soon turned to squeals and Kade was here. I caught a brief glimpse of him before Brody came running around the table and launched himself at me. His paws landed on my chest, and his long tongue came out, licking and slobbering all over my face.

"Good evening, ladies. I see you all made it. I hope you had a great journey. I'm Kade Sutton and I'm pleased to meet all..." I heard Kade say as I wrestled with Brody.

"Get down, boy," I whispered, remembering not to say Brody's name. "Please, go. Go back to...your master."

"Nine of you. Are we one missing?" Kade asked, a slight edge to his voice.

Brody finally jumped down and started to lick my feet, leaving slobber on Lydia's sandals.

"Ten of us, I'm here." I giggled, slamming my hands onto the table to push myself up and away from Brody, but he was on his hind legs again, sniffing me.

Kade came around to my side of the table and moved towards me. He asked what was happening, and I gave some stupid answer about my perfume. It was all I could think of to explain Brody greeting me in such a way. Kade commanded Brody to leave me alone and made a comment about him having good people radar, echoing my words from the shelter and making me smile. Thankful that we appeared to have got over our first little hiccup, I relaxed but then Kade held out his hand to me by way of apology. Oh geez, I was suddenly as wound up as a clockwork soldier. The thrill that shot through my body was instant the moment we had skin on skin contact. Goosebumps erupted over my body, my knees wobbled and I do believe I got a little bit wet in my panties.

"Hey," I breathed, my boobs straining against the pink silk bra I was wearing. "I'm Daisy."

Nine other heads shot around to look at us, and there

were lip curls and furrowed brows all round.

"Pleased to meet you, Daisy," Kade said, smiling widely, his eyes bright. "I hope Brody didn't hurt you."

"N-no," I stuttered. "I love dogs."

Kade swallowed hard as his hand lingered in mine before giving it a squeeze and taking a deep breath.

"Okay, ladies," he said, letting go of me.

I didn't want him to let go, not just because of his soft hand but because his touch had jump started my heart that stuttered as his hand left mine. I felt the connected energy leave with him.

"Let me welcome you all to my home," he said, turning to the other girls. "Well, mine and Brody's home."

As he walked away from me, I let out a breath, and watched him walk around the table, greeting each girl individually. I could see that they were all in awe of him as they took in his long, lean frame, startling eyes set in a smooth tanned complexion, and that wispy hair, floating round his sharp facial features, now looking clean and cool. Each girl flirted and fussed over him, but I could see in his eyes that he was feeling a little uncomfortable as they all crowded around him.

He wasn't used to so many people in such an enclosed space, and he certainly wasn't used to all the attention. As one hand fisted at his side and the fingers of the other rubbed hard at his temple, I knew that Kade's anxiety was getting worse. I had to do something before he got too upset, but I had no idea what. Looking around, I spotted Carson standing next to the cameraman, whispering in his ear and telling him what to film. Maybe I could catch his attention, get him to wrap things up for a while and then take Kade away for a break.

I edged myself around the back of the table, moving slowly towards Carson. At just a couple of feet away, I cleared my throat loudly, but with the noise the girls were making, I couldn't be heard. I coughed again, louder, and then banged one of the chairs against the table. Carson's head shot around to me and he gave me a narrow-eyed stare.

I pointed at Kade with my hand close to my body, and then mouthed, 'he's getting stressed'. Carson shrugged his shoulders, and it took another couple of attempts until he realized what I was saying.

"Okay, ladies," he called. "Let's leave it at that, shall we? We need to film you all choosing your rooms now, so, Kade, if you'd like to step over here."

Kade moved over to Carson and heaved what I knew was a huge sigh of relief. He rubbed the back of his neck under his hair and let his hand drop, feeling for Brody. As soon as the soft ears of his hound were beneath his fingertips, he visibly relaxed.

"Now, girls," Carson shouted above their noise. "On the count of three, I want you to go find yourself a room."

As the girls all gave squeals of excitement, I saw Kade shrink back, and knew then that I'd been right in getting Carson to stop filming.

I moved towards the back of the shrieking, excitable crowd as Carson counted down, then with a fleeting smile at Kade, I slowly followed after them, knowing that I'd be getting the leftover once again.

Chapter 22

KADE SUTTON

"You okay?" the guy called Carson asked, his eyes on all the girls.

I blew out a breath, inflating my cheeks. "Fine, just a bit..."

"Good, good," Carson said distractedly, moving away from me. "I thought Daisy was being a bit melodramatic, but that's women for you."

As he disappeared through the door, I pulled out a chair and sat down, Brody flopping down at my feet, wondering what he meant about Daisy.

"Shit," I muttered, reaching down to stroke my dog. "That was crazy."

I was still sitting there when an older lady came into the dining room, carrying a solo cup and a huge smile.

"Hey, honey," she said, holding her hand out. "I'm Bessie Winters. I'm the on-set counselor, and this is for you."

She pushed the solo cup towards me. "What is it?" I asked. "Because I don't drink."

I didn't have a problem with alcohol as such. It just

reminded me of a time when drinking had caused the death of my best friend. Not a drop of liquor had passed my lips since I'd found myself on the streets. It was just safer that way, and I wasn't going to start now.

"It's diet coke, honey." She smiled warmly and cupped my chin. "You okay? Was it a bit much for you?"

I stared into her eyes. If living on the streets had taught me anything, it was to look someone dead in the eye. If they were trustworthy, they wouldn't flinch from your gaze. Thankfully, Bessie held my stare.

"It was hard," I said on a long exhale. "It's been a while since I was in a confined space with that many people."

"I know it must have felt suffocating."

Bessie pulled out a chair and moved it to sit opposite me so that our knees were almost touching.

"You really a counselor?" I asked, before taking a long drink of the deliciously cold drink.

Bessie nodded. "Yes, I am. This sort of show can be extremely stressful, pushing people beyond their comfort zone and bringing to light issues that they thought were deeply hidden. Plus, ten women all under one roof for six weeks, think about it, honey. That's an awful lot of hormones and an awful lot of tears."

"I guess so." I laughed. "Thanks for the drink. It's thirsty work chatting to ten women I've never met before."

"You know Daisy."

I couldn't help the smile that broke out. Just the sound of her name made me feel better. The reminder of the connection from our touch earlier made me look down at my hand to check it wasn't scorched in some way.

"Yeah, she's good people," I said matter-of-factly.

"I believe so. She was the one who asked me to come see you. Once the girls had picked a room, the crew went in to film their individual reactions to you, which from the few I heard were very favorable."

She grinned and winked at me, but I had no fucks to give about what a bunch of money grabbing women thought of me. Just the few minutes I'd spent with them had been enough to tell me it was my 'money' they were interested in. One, whose name I had totally forgotten, had even asked me what number I was on Forbes List.

"Daisy took that opportunity to find me. After getting Carson to halt the filming, she was really concerned about you," Bessie informed me.

Christ, Daisy was so fucking adorable and I was right; she really was a good person.

"Would you like me to give you some coping exercises?" Bessie asked.

"Sorry?"

"Coping exercises for stressful moments like that one."

I looked at her kind eyes and soft grey curls, and was glad there appeared to be someone else looking out for me.

"Please, that would be great."

Bessie smiled and patted my hand. "No problem, honey. Okay, sit back, kick off your flip-flops and we'll get you relaxed."

Almost an hour later, I was so relaxed I was practically floating. Bessie was really good at getting me to visualize a place of serenity and then take myself to that place in my head. Weirdly, my place was Dominique's, having the sweet smelling oil rubbed into my hair. Even more weirdly, in my mind's eye, it was Daisy rubbing it in.

Once we'd finished, Bessie was called away to talk to one of the girls, leaving me alone in the dining room, with Brody flopped at my feet. Apparently, the girl had been traumatized by the fact that there was only a shower in her bathroom and, shock fucking horror, no tub.

I was wondering whether I should go and find someone from the production company when Daisy popped her head around the door.

"Hi," she whispered, stepping inside. "Are you okay?" I nodded and grinned. The sight of Daisy always brought a smile to my face, but to see her in what was obviously an expensive dress and a pair of camel colored, soft sheepskin boots made my smile even bigger.

"Nice footwear," I said, pointing at her feet.

"Oh gosh, my feet were killing me. It felt like I was walking on hot coals and having my heels pricked with thousands of needles."

"I have no idea why women do that to themselves."

"Ugh, me neither. Thank goodness I managed to slip these into my case without Lydia finding out. She'd go crazy, especially if she realized they're fakes."

I furrowed my brow and shrugged. "I have no idea what's fake about them, but they look okay to me, especially with that dress."

Daisy's cheeks reddened and she lowered her eyes. "I know. I don't really do high fashion. I just do what I'm comfortable with. When you look at the other girls, I guess I'm kinda weird."

My heart thumped at the thought of embarrassing her.

"God no, that's not what I meant. They look cool with the dress, and well…" I paused as I looked her up and down. "You look really beautiful in it."

Daisy slowly looked up at me, and I could see that she was holding her breath. My heart was sending my blood around my body at lightening speed, and as Daisy sucked in her bottom lip, that same blood rushed its way to my dick.

"Daisy…" I whispered, pushing up from my seat.

"There you are!" a booming voice sounded.

It was Carson and he looked ready to blow a gasket as he thrust his hands to his hips.

"The fucking crew are waiting on you, Daisy. We're ready to film your monologue about Kade."

"Oh, sorry," she gushed, pushing a hand to her neck. "I-I'll get up there now."

"Good, and hurry up. We need to film Kade walking the grounds before we lose the light."

"Okay, see you later, Kade," she said as she moved past Carson.

Carson caught hold of her elbow. "Oh, and Daisy, Meredith said you're to appear underwhelmed."

"I'm sorry?" she asked, blinking rapidly.

"About Kade," he replied. "You're to appear underwhelmed. Meredith's orders. She said she'll be checking the dailies closely."

"Fucking bitch," I muttered under my breath.

Daisy gave me a quick glance, nodded at Carson and then disappeared.

"What is her damn problem?" I asked Carson, pushing my chair back into place alongside the others with some force.

"Daisy?"

"No, Meredith. Why is she so intent on getting Daisy out of here? She knows if Daisy shows she doesn't like me the public won't vote for her."

Carson shrugged. "She's the boss, Kade. I just do as she asks. She's not a lady you want to get on the wrong side of."

She didn't scare me. I'd faced up to a knife wielding, ex-wrestler, homeless guy high on heroin before now. Meredith was small fry.

"Yeah, well tell your boss to cut out the shit with Daisy or I'll walk."

"Ah c'mon, man," Carson said with an empty laugh. "As if, when you could be staying here instead of on the streets."

"I would," I replied, my voice calm and low. "I fancy my chances more on the streets than I do in here. So, like I said, give Meredith the message."

Carson shook his head and wandered out, leaving just Brody and me once more. As I looked around the room, wealth and opulence oozing from every fixture and fitting,

I began to wonder if I'd made the biggest mistake of my life.

Chapter 23

DAISY INGLES

My first night in supposed luxury was just awful. The joy I felt at seeing Kade again was killed by the panic I recognized in him at being swarmed by my bitchy sorority sisters.

As I left him to go and do my monologue, I felt my insides scrunch with fear. It was bad enough that I was already lying to the public and pretending to be someone I wasn't, but now Meredith expected to me become a second character I really couldn't resonate with. My boss was a bitch and if I didn't keep my feet on the ground, I was in danger of having some kind of identity crisis.

All I wanted to be was myself.

All I wanted to do was spend some time with Kade and get to know him away from the office building wall, because he really was making my heart flutter and my private parts quiver.

Once upstairs, I was sidled into a makeshift interview room and hustled towards a stool.

"Hi, guys," I said and no one replied. They all looked at each uncomfortably and then pretended to check the equipment that was clearly still fine and set up from talking with the other girls. "Really, this is how we're going to be?"

Before they could answer, Carson came stomping into the room. "Let's get this done. We're behind schedule and I need to get some shots of Kade. Remember what I said downstairs. Toe the line, otherwise this is uncomfortable for all of us and they don't need Meredith kicking their asses because you've gone off script."

I felt my mouth gaping open as Doug the cameraman started to zoom and focus the camera lens. He'd just confirmed that they were all following Meredith's instructions to the letter and I knew that a couple of them would be genuinely scared about being fired. I had enough on my shoulders right now; worrying about their careers was something else I didn't need.

"That gaping fish look you've got going on isn't going to work. Say your piece and fail to impress, please."

I was going to come out of this looking really bad, and even though I always knew the production crew would select someone the public could hate, I never thought it would be me. While I tried to pull myself together and beat back the tears I was sure were on their way, Carson looked over at me, tilting his head expectantly.

I knew how these things were done. They were just segments so the subject had to work an inferred question into their answer, otherwise they'd need an interviewer and an interviewer could go off script and cause more problems. More problems caused extra editing time and that was a big no-no.

"Yeah, I'm a little unsure about things right now. It was lovely to meet him and I'm super pleased to be here in the mansion, but, well, he wasn't what I was expecting." I tried my best not to grimace as I told a partial lie. Kade wasn't what I was expecting, because he was so much more.

When I failed to come up with anymore, Carson

stopped filming in frustration.

"Meredith underestimated your natural ability. It seems you do underwhelming really well. If I was watching you with that disinterested attitude, I'd be throwing my weight behind the other contestants, too."

A couple of the guys looked at me with pity and that just made the prospect of crying a more real possibility, so I stood up and walked past them all, heading for the first doorway I found. When I flipped the lights on, I was in some storage room packed with cases and boxes of filming equipment. Shoving them angrily to the side, I found one sturdy enough to sit on and slumped on top of it.

This was going to be a nightmare. I was the most transparent person in the world and worked hard to avoid confrontation, but I knew that was exactly what was expected of me. I heard the camera crew wander off to look for Kade and decided to brave the bitch brigade and try to remember which room I'd dumped my case in.

I opened a number of doorways and was screamed at to get out before I'd even wandered in. Some of these girls were not ladies. They had the manners of alley cats and I knew that Kade and even Brody would hate spending time with them.

When I made it to the final bedroom, there were two girls inside already, and a small spare bed was stuffed in the corner with hardly any room to move round. They were girls I recognized from my limo ride in. It still shocked me a little that the segregation we'd started at the beginning of the journey was still in full force and it was all based on looks.

"Sorry, you've ended up with the worst bed. I'm Natalie and this is Jess."

At least they were talking to me. They didn't appear to want to poke my eyes out just yet, but it was early days and I was useless with people. Unless I was dealing with something that had fur, four legs and fangs, I wasn't sure whether they were friend or foe.

"I'm Daisy."

"Can we help you finish unpacking? We figured this was your luggage. It was already dumped in the room."

"I don't have much to unpack. I think I'll just visit the bathroom and turn in for the night." I looked around the small room that was about as luxurious as a public swimming pool changing cubicle. It didn't feel like the rest of the mansion. "Uh... where is the bathroom?"

Jess squinted her eyes and answered, "*We* don't have one. We have to use the main bathroom down the hall, although good luck getting in. I figure this room is temporary. As soon as girls start leaving, other rooms will become available for us second class sisters."

I was suddenly exhausted and desperate to sleep. I figured this was how I was going to feel each night I went to bed, and in order to be ready to fight the next day, I needed rest. Grabbing my favorite Little Miss Sunshine PJ set, my lens case and my glasses, I wandered off in search of the bathroom.

When I finally located it, there was a hive of activity. Girls were running around in lacy thongs and bras, their hair in curlers, painting toenails or tweezing already non-existent eyebrows. The work surface by the sink looked like someone's make up bag had exploded; there were creams, potions and lotions everywhere. They were messier than the dogs I cared for at the shelter. It was disgusting. I walked in and was glared at for simply being near them so I walked out and slumped down on the floor to wait my turn.

My eyes grew heavy as I listened to the asinine chatter about products and beauty regimes, and after what felt like forever, I was allowed my time to wash my face and get changed. When I was finally done, the hallway had gone quiet and I welcomed the silence. As I passed a window that looked out over the back of the property, I was drawn to the pool lights. It all looked so pretty. A scamp of activity caught my attention and I could see Brody sprinting back and to across a manicured lawn. When he retrieved a ball, I followed him with my gaze to see who was playing fetch with him. I wasn't surprised to see it was Kade. As he bent down, his frame seemed relaxed, like he was at peace spending some quality time with his buddy. All the doubts about why I was doing this were replaced with that satisfied feeling of helping someone worse off than me. Kade needed the money to make a better life for him and Brody.

As I continued to watch, I saw a reflection appear and distort in the pool water. The splash that followed confirmed that he was no longer alone, and as a body glided through the calm water to the opposite edge of the pool, I waited to see who it was.

Like a *Baywatch* babe without the swimsuit, a blonde appeared from under the water and climbed out. Kade launched the ball for Brody again without taking his eyes away from his late night guest, and I watched as she sashayed her way over and stood in front of him, dripping with water in what seemed to be just a pair of panties. She was so close to him now that I couldn't see his face or how he felt about being joined; so close they looked like they were inseparable and I hated it.

Feeling sick and unable to watch how it panned out, I turned away and trudged to my little closet of a bedroom, knowing that the much needed sleep I was desperate for was further away than ever. Kade was about to be seduced by a beautiful girl, someone far prettier and braver than me, and there wasn't a damn thing I could do about it.

Chapter 24

KADE SUTTON

This was how it was going to be. I was going to be hounded permanently by these wannabe porn stars.

"Go out for a walk around the property," Carson had said.

"Take Brody and throw a ball by the pool," Carson had said.

"We just need natural footage of you at peace with your dog in your big ass home so we have some shots to overlay the interview stuff from earlier onto," he had explained when I didn't seem keen.

And it was a big fucking set up.

I'd berated myself earlier for over thinking everything, but I now realized I had to. I had to be three steps ahead of these fuckers in order to beat them at their own game.

The girl—her name was something foody like Cherry, Peaches or even Apple—was just stunning... if you liked that kind of thing.

Her hair extensions had survived the underwater *Baywatch* scene and she'd even managed to get out of the water gracefully. I won't deny that her near naked body was perfect, toned and smooth, and the water was running down her body strangely so I knew she'd oiled herself up before coming out here. She had a scrap of cloth covering her pussy, and even thinking of it in feline terms made me want to burst out laughing. It probably had claws. Her tits were upright and honestly, if the program advertising some plastic surgeon in the Hollywood hills, he was about to get a chunk of business. When I looked at her face, she was trying to do a pouty, seductive look but it just wasn't working. It was more like an oxygen starved grouper fish.

As she took a step closer to me, I felt Brody prod his nose into my leg. Not knowing what the hell she was planning, I reached down and took his ball without losing her from my vision. In the back of my mind, I knew that there would be cameras somewhere and this was heading for the show tomorrow. The one thing I didn't know was how far away the sound gear was, and if I didn't play this correctly, the footage would end up on the cutting room floor and Meredith wouldn't allow that. She'd be persistent and keep on pulling strokes like this until she got exactly the footage that she wanted.

"Shouldn't you be in bed?" I asked.

"Shouldn't you?" she breathed back.

"Aren't you cold?"

"Are you?"

Was she going to repeat everything I said? Or was the one brain cell rattling around inside the head of that hard won gym body asleep?

I needed to stop thinking like that. It was making me giggle, and while I didn't think I should be throwing shade on her efforts to seduce me, I didn't want to come across as too happy. I knew she'd be bragging about this to the rest of them and then I'd be faced with a parade of oiled bodies night after night.

"How can I help you…?"

"Honey." She filled in the gap and I was mentally high fiving myself for at least getting the name category nearly right. It was food, just not fruit.

"I figured we didn't get the chance for a proper introduction, with all the other girls in the dining room."

"So you came for some one-on-one time?"

"Mmm," she replied coyly, squeezing her forearms together so her tits looked like balloons on the verge of exploding.

"Well, it was nice to meet you, Honey." I smiled, forcing myself to clasp her upper arms.

She took this as a green light, and wrapped her oily self around me.

Pulling back, I kissed her on the cheek before turning and leaving. "Brody! Let's go, buddy."

As we wandered back to the main house, I waited until I was underneath an ivy-covered pergola and stood to the side, shaking and anxious. As soon as they'd assumed I was out of eye sight, Carson came sprinting from the pool house with a bath robe and towel for Honey. I couldn't tell what they were saying, but he seemed pleased with the footage he had. His nodding and smiling was emphatic as he helped her into them, but from the look in his eyes, he was also pleased to be so close to a half-naked woman.

I thought I'd handled it well, and I knew from the vantage point of the pool house, they would have only seen her back and my face, so I did the best I could to show some kind of surprised pleasure at being presented with such a forward gift.

The next morning when I woke up, I took my breakfast in the kitchen with the staff. Mellings had got bored of trying to get me to conform. He now had a house full of guests to fawn over and if he wanted to pander to the whims of those women then he could knock himself out trying.

Carson came through as I was eating the last of my poached eggs and told me that today was a pool day. The girls would be spending time with me and we'd play a little volleyball in the pool, have some champagne and generally live it up like the rich and famous were used to doing. The only thing I heard in all he said was that I was going to see Daisy again, and somehow that made it all worth it.

I could hear music by the poolside the closer I got, and as the cameras followed me down to the waiting crowd of women, I did my usual talk to Brody and tried to ignore them. Bursting through the doors was like time warping back to a frat party from my college days. Girls splashing in the water, some on loungers, a few of them drinking something sugary with a cocktail umbrella sticking out of it and some dancing on the side of the pool like there was a pole in front of them.

The girls had already grouped themselves into what would no doubt become their cliques and battle teams, and I was nervous that the phone lines would be opening soon so the public could pick their two favorite date potentials. Unfortunately, the girls also knew this and the small swimsuits they were sporting were an indication of just how seriously they were taking it. I grabbed myself a can of *Cherry Coke* and made my way around the pool, stopping and sitting on the edges of the sun loungers, making chitchat where possible. I could talk for hours on end, but not with some of these girls. Conversation was not a skill they had mastered.

My ultimate destination, though, was Daisy. She and two other girls were furthest away from me and seemingly content in their own spaces. That wouldn't work, though. They needed to be involved or they'd alienate themselves from the public. If I could sneak a word with Daisy and tell her that, I had to. It was going to be difficult to justify keeping her in the house if we didn't have some interaction.

When I finally made it to her gathering of friends, I could see that they were different. They didn't have the standard issue hair weave and barely there two piece swimsuits on. These girls were wearing strapless, simple block colored swimsuits, and one girl even had a wrap around her middle to cover her butt and thighs. Daisy, who was gazing in the opposite direction, was hiding behind oversized sunglasses, and looked so uncomfortable that I wanted to bundle her up and run for the hills.

"Good Morning, ladies. Did you all have a good night's rest?"

"Yes thanks. I'm Natalie, this is Jess and the girl who is catching up on her zeds is Daisy. She had a restless night."

At the sound of her name, she jolted awake and realized she'd been dribbling from the corner of her mouth. It was cute and I couldn't hide the smile that was rocking around my cheeks.

"I hope you'll all join me for a friendly game of pool volleyball later." I smiled.

"Sports aren't my thing," Daisy finally said, her mouth tight and strained. I wanted to ask her to remove the glasses but couldn't. I felt lost not being able to see her eyes, especially when I knew something was wrong with her.

"Brody! Come here, boy," I shouted, and the dog scampered towards us at full speed, knocking a couple of girls dancing pool side off balance and sending them into the water.

I saw the faint flicker of a smile on her lips and genuinely hated that she was unhappy.

I knew the cameras would be lurking, and I was nervous about spending too long lingering in her space without it looking odd. "I'm going to go and get my best boy some water. It's hot out here. Talk later."

The pool volleyball was as expected—bodies everywhere and all of them clambering to touch mine. I was praying for time to speed forward so it could be over. Lunch finally arrived, and we had a magnificent picnic on the lawn. With all of them lounging around me and eating grapes, it really did look like I was some Middle Eastern

NIKKI ASHTON & VICTORIA JOHNS

Prince collecting women like valuables. The music started up again and the girls began to disperse to go and clean up after they'd eaten. I rolled over onto my front and Daisy was inches away from me. Propping my head on my arms, I took a chance and whispered, "You okay?"

She looked looked away from me. "How was your late night rendezvous?"

"My what?" It took me a moment to realize what she was referring to. "What did Honey say?"

"*Honey* said nothing. I saw you. It looked very... cozy."

Before I could conjure up a response, Natalie and Jess came back and lay down beside us.

"Excuse me, I think I'll go and freshen up like the other girls. Gotta pull myself together and win some public votes," said Daisy sarcastically, and I watched, feeling my frustration grow as she climbed up from the picnic blanket, stumbled over her own feet and then pushed her sunglasses up her cute button nose before leaving the garden and disappearing inside the house.

Chapter 25

DAISY INGLES

Slamming my bedroom door and flopping onto my bed, I groaned, wondering once more what the hell I'd let myself in for. I knew it shouldn't have, but watching Kade and *Honey* last night had made me angrier than a swarm of hornets. My lips felt as though they were glued together whenever Kade came near me. They couldn't lift into a smile and could barely open to speak to him.

"Oh fudge it!" I cried, throwing one of my pillows across the room. "I hate this place."

I knew what the show was all about, what Kade was supposed to do, but knowing it and seeing it were two different things. Besides which, when I agreed to this I wasn't as attracted to Kade as I was now. Yes, I'd liked his company and felt some sort of connection, but now he sent me into a tizzy with just one look or one of his beautiful smiles. It was all too much to cope with, and I wasn't sure my heart or my nerves were going to last the distance.

As I contemplated my fate, the door pushed open and Natalie and Jess trooped in. It had to be said, they both looked as dejected as I felt.

"Hey, what's wrong?" I asked, pushing up onto my elbows.

"This is such a fix," Natalie moaned, collapsing face down onto her own bed.

"Why?"

Jess gave me a resigned smile and perched on the end of my bed. "You know that girl with humongous titties?"

"Which one?" I giggled. "They've all got humongous titties."

"Hmm, true." Jess laughed. "The one with the bigger rack than the rest. She had a gold bikini on today."

"Oh, her." I scoffed, remembering how she'd walked out of the pool like a Bond girl, just as Kade was walking by.

"Yeah, her, well she got called into the study."

I groaned. The study was where we were summoned to talk to the production company, either to talk about ourselves, the other girls, or to simply relay messages back to the mansion about any tasks. I had a feeling that Bond Girl's visit to the study had been to relay a message. There was no way Meredith would allow us to get too comfortable.

"What do we have to do?" I asked, lying my head back on my remaining pillow.

"We don't have to damn well do anything," came the muffled reply from Natalie.

Jess glanced over at her and sighed.

"Titty Galore, or whatever her name is, had to pick one other girl to go and give Kade a relaxing massage before dinner."

My heart clenched and dropped along with my spirits. This had Meredith written all over it. If I didn't think I'd hid my attraction to Kade well, I'd have said it was to mess with me, but I was sure it was more to do with ratings. I knew that every day she'd be poring over the daily results, and if they weren't where she wanted them to be, someone giving Kade a massage would be the tamest thing to happen.

"Who did she pick?" I asked, dread threading through my veins.

"Honey." Jess's lip curled as she said her name with utter distaste.

Natalie rolled over onto her back and kicked her legs up in the air, pushing her hands under her lower back.

"It's obvious to me," she puffed out, "that Honey, who is a fucking bitch, and Vanessa aka Titty Galore, are the production team's favorites on this show. Not only were we held back while they got to pick their rooms first, but," she said, dropping her legs back to the bed, "Honey was *told* to go and swim half naked in front of Kade. I overheard that Carson guy tell her when I nipped back outside for my wrap I'd left out there. Then, of course, Vanessa was given the massage task."

"If you can call it a task," Jess grumbled. "I'd gladly put my hands on that mighty fine tall drink of water."

I turned to watch Natalie bring her knees to her chest.

"What are you doing?" I asked.

"Stretches. I used to be a gymnast so like to keep supple."

"Oh shit," Jess said. "That means if you ever get laid by Kade, it's going to be so damn spectacular he'll never look at the rest of us again."

"No one will have sex with him," I protested, feeling uncomfortable with the crass way they were talking about getting laid and hoping to God I was right. "Surely not on TV."

Natalie stopped her stretches and gave me a weird look.

"You do know that's the whole point of the show? Didn't they tell you that in your interview?"

I felt the blood draining from my cheeks as Jess and Natalie exchanged glances.

"No," I breathed out.

NIKKI ASHTON & VICTORIA JOHNS

"Well *yeah*!" Natalie sat up and pushed herself up the bed, crossing her legs Indian style and stretching her arm behind her neck. "Anyone who goes on a date with Kade gets to spend the night in his bed with him. So come on, Dais, what d'ya think is going to happen? He's young and hot, and will have a willing female in his bed. I reckon it's safe to say there's gonna be a lot of hoochy coochy going on in this house over the next few weeks."

Jess nodded sagely. "She's right, and look at the name of the show. That tells you everything."

I had no idea what the show was called. Meredith didn't even want me in here, so she wasn't going to give me any help or information.

"I fucking know, right?" Natalie cried. "I Wanna Get Laid By Kade. I mean, come on, Dais', really?"

"I-I-I just didn't think about it," I stammered, feeling a little sick to my stomach.

"Oh, Daisy, are you a virgin?" Jess asked, sympathetically rubbing my knee.

"No!" I said indignantly.

I wasn't, well not officially. I'd had sex once when I was seventeen with my then boyfriend, Dennis Morley. It really wasn't good. For the first couple of minutes of him thrusting in and out, his penis wasn't even inside my twinkle—damn it, I had to remember I was now twenty-two and should not call my vagina a twinkle any longer. Anyway, once I managed to tell Dennis that he wasn't actually in, things did not improve, believe me. I'd had dates since then, but I'd always been so busy helping to look after Mom that sex wasn't something I had time for.

"So what's worrying you?" Natalie asked, now off the bed and touching her toes.

"Well, I don't want to be on TV having sex, if in fact I ever get picked."

There were two things worrying me actually. No, I didn't want to have sex on TV, but I also didn't want anyone else to have sex with Kade—on TV or otherwise.

146

"Oh, they're not allowed to film that," Jess announced as she got off my bed and went over to our shared closet. "It was in your contract. I know because my dad's a lawyer and he checked mine."

"They might put a mic' outside the door." Natalie was now doing the splits.

"They shouldn't do that either, but if you do have sex with him, it is in the contract that you tell the truth when questioned. Although, being a drama student, I think I could quite easily lie," she said, flicking through various outfits. "Hey, you think this is okay for tonight's barbeque?" She held up a pale lemon dress with barely there straps. It looked awfully short.

Natalie lifted her head from her knee and grinned. "Yep, perfect. What are you wearing, Dais?"

I shrugged, unable to speak, as I was still worrying about someone enjoying Kade's body.

"Well, I bet Titty Galore and Nasty Bitch are wearing very little at this moment." Jess groaned as she flounced out of the room clutching her shower caddy.

"True story," Natalie said nasally as she stood on her head.

I simply wanted to cry and wished I had a pair of sparkly red shoes that would take me home.

Chapter 26

KADE SUTTON

When Carson told me I was going to get a massage from two of the girls, I nearly peed my pants. Call me a pussy, but it appeared that most of these women were practically feral when it came to men.

I wondered whether it would be too much to ask that one of them could be Daisy, and yeah, it was definitely was too much to fucking ask. I swallowed hard when Honey and another girl, who I thought was called Virginia, came sashaying towards me wearing just underwear. I mean, I think it was underwear… Their bras barely covered their nipples and the panties made it quite clear they both waxed thoroughly down below. Personally, I thought it looked more like something you'd wear in a porn movie—and a bad one at that. I was sure there would be a few guys at home jacking off to this clichéd trash, but it wouldn't be stirring my dick any day soon.

Yeah, they were good-looking girls, or they could have been if they wiped off some of the shit on their faces. What was it about women who thought the more make-up they wore the more attractive they became? Give me

Daisy and her cute freckles any day of the week. Shit, yeah, please give me Daisy. Thinking of Daisy massaging me in a bikini created a definite twitch in my dick, and in the grey sweat shorts that Molly the wardrobe girl had insisted I wear—without underwear—there was no hiding it.

"Hey, you seem pleased to see us," Virginia purred.

Knowing that I had to do a good job, I grinned and winked. Oh my God, I was turning into the biggest prick known to the Universe. I was becoming the sort of guy I actually hated at college, all for a damn TV show.

"Well, it's always lovely to see you beautiful ladies."

Yep, I'd just puked in my mouth.

"Vanessa and I are here to give you a massage," Honey said in a sultry tone. "You ready for us?"

Woah, Vanessa not Virginia. *Vanessa, Vanessa, Vanessa,* I chanted in my head.

"I'm sure I'll cope," I replied, which was a total lie.

"Let's do this then."

Vanessa caught hold of Honey's hand, gave her a wink and then licked her lips. I'm sure she thought it was sexy, but it made me want to snort with laughter. Lipstick lesbianism was never my kind of porn, especially when it was done badly.

"After you, ladies."

I stood to one side and waved them towards the door of the 'playroom' as it had been named. Apparently, this was where I could spend time alone with any of the ladies, *if* I wanted to. There would be no camera crew, just the static cameras that had been set up in various places around the mansion. As for spending time alone with the girls, I had no doubt the ladies in question would not be my choice, but that of Meredith, the old witch. She definitely didn't want me and Daisy getting friendly, but if she didn't stop pulling the strings on how Daisy was to behave, I would be walking.

I'd thought earlier that maybe she'd told Daisy to be

offhand with me, but after speaking to her, I had a feeling it was more to do with my little meeting with Honey by the pool last night. That thought fucked with my head. I hated to think that Daisy was upset, but I kinda liked the fact that she was jealous. Maybe she was attracted to me as much as I was to her.

Following Honey and Vanessa, I took a deep breath, the sight of their ass cheeks rubbing against a thin piece of string making me clench my own buttocks. It must be real uncomfortable; no wonder they always had pouty lips, they were obviously in pain.

"Okay, Kade," Vanessa said. "Take your shorts off and put this towel around your waist."

I took the white towel she was offering, held it in front of me and studied it.

"I think you gave me the wash cloth," I said with a forced grin.

"Oh come on, Kade," Honey gasped. "Don't be shy."

I smiled and shook my head. "Okay, ladies, but if you don't mind." I twirled my finger in a circle, indicating for them to turn around. "I don't want to show you the goods just yet. Anticipation and all that." I felt like puking. These bitches wouldn't understand the allure of anticipation if it smacked them around their food starved cheekbones.

They both giggled and turned around. With a sigh, I whipped down my shorts, quickly covering myself with the towel when I saw one of the ceiling cameras move towards me. While I wasn't small in the dick department, I wasn't huge, maybe above average, but I swear to God, my schlong was almost hanging below the towel. There was a definite blast of air getting to it.

"Ready yet?" Honey asked, glancing over her shoulder.

Thankfully, I was. "Yep, so where would you like me?"

The tall bed that had been put up in the middle of the room was really well padded, covered in white towels and looked a lot more comfortable than the one at the beauty shop I'd visited with Daisy. I got on, lay down and adjusted the towel as best I could.

"Wow," Honey whispered. "You kind of look like Tarzan lying there with your little towel."

"Oh my gosh," Vanessa gushed. "He so does. You so do."

"Who's Shelby?" Honey asked, somewhat sulkily, as she pointed at my bicep.

"Just someone very special to me," I replied, giving a little tug on the towel. Then remembering what I was there for, I said, "No one you ladies need to be concerned about."

"I wasn't worried." Honey's pouty lips told me she was lying.

"Oh my gosh, we weren't worried," Vanessa chirped. "Not worried at all."

Fuck me, please beam me up *now*, Scotty.

Honey took my top half and Vanessa my legs, slathering oil on to me, and their hands, before they began their massage. I was not experienced in having massages, but I was pretty sure rubbing their tits along my skin was not exactly the way it should be done—again, unless it was in a porn movie.

"So, what if we need to get under the towel?" Honey asked with a little giggle. "Are you going to let us take it off?"

"Oh my gosh, are you-"

"Erm, no," I replied, before I had to hear Vanessa parrot Honey once more. "I'm good as I am, thank you, ladies. Your moms could be watching this."

Honey just snickered as they both continued to rub the oil into my skin.

"Your skin is so soft." Vanessa slid her hands up my legs, yep, followed by her tits. "You can tell you really look after yourself."

I almost choked at her blatant lie and unbelievable ass licking. I'd lived on the streets for three years, in all conditions, so I knew that my skin was by no means silky fucking smooth. These girls were so vacuous, all they could see were dollar signs, and their only thoughts were probably how to get their hands on it.

"I'm not sure that's entirely true." I couldn't help but call her out on her lie.

"Oh you are, don't be coy." Now it was Honey's turn to allow her nipples to skim my chest. Problem was, they were so fake and solid that it was more of a drag than a skim.

Christ, this was torture and I found myself praying for divine intervention to stop it. Then, as if the Gods above had been listening to me, a loud, obnoxious alarm started blaring.

"Oh my gosh, what's that?" Vanessa shouted, thrusting her oily hands against her ears.

"An alarm," I replied a little sardonically. "I think we should go. There may be a fire."

Both girls screamed, which was more ear-piercing than the alarm, and ran towards the door as fast as their high heels would allow them. Jumping down from the bed as they ran through the door, I scooped up my shorts and dragged them on before slipping my feet back into my flip-flops and going after them.

Out in the hallway, there was panic all around. Girls in various stages of dress were screaming and waving their arms around, while Carson and his crew were hurriedly pushing past them with their equipment as members of the household staff were trying to direct everyone outside. The problem was clear. It was a huge melee of people who just weren't listening.

Amid the chaos, there were two things that fogged my brain: Brody and Daisy. I had to make sure they were both out. I was just about to double back to the kitchen, where I'd left Brody sleeping in a basket, when I spotted Daisy coming through its door.

"Thank God," I breathed, pushing through the girls

towards her.

When I reached her, I saw that she had Brody on a leash, and was looking distinctly calm. She was standing and watching with her hands in the pockets of a pair of real tight pants that I knew would show her ass off perfectly.

"You okay?" I asked, glancing down at Brody, who suddenly flopped to the floor, totally disinterested.

"Yeah, I'm fine."

She looked up at the static camera that was pointing away from us, and indicated with a tiny movement of her head to move back a few steps, out of its range.

"Daisy?"

"I lit a match under the smoke alarm in our bathroom," she hissed. "I knew how much you hated it that day at the beauty shop, so I figured you'd be hating every minute of your massage. I got rid of the match, don't worry."

She looked up at me and nibbled at the corner of her mouth. When I didn't say anything, her mouth dropped into a perfect, pouty little O.

"Oh fudge, I'm sorry. Were you enjoying it?" She clapped a hand to her mouth. "Oh, Kade, I'm so sorry."

I burst out laughing. She was so cute it was unreal. "Fuck, Daisy, I could kiss you."

"You could?" She swallowed hard and her eyes widened.

Shit, I really could, but in the hallway with everyone running around would not be where we had our first kiss.

"Yep. It was horrible."

I made a gagging sound, which made her laugh, a beautiful, tinkling sound that was the sweetest music I'd ever heard.

"They kept rubbing their tits up my body, and made me wear the tiniest fucking towel I'd ever seen. I think they were considering de-robing and defiling me when you saved the day."

She started to laugh a little louder, and her whole face

lit up as she looked up at me. Shit, she was pretty. No, actually, she was beautiful. Those damn freckles of hers just did something to me.

"I'm sorry I was off with you today," she said, glancing towards the open doorway. "I was being a bitch."

From our vantage point in the shadows, I could see that we were pretty much the only ones left inside.

"We should go before they suspect something. You go first," I said, glancing up at the camera. "Run and they'll think you went to rescue Brody. I'll skirt around to the door from the games room and it'll look like I was checking in there."

Daisy nodded. "Okay, I'll see you out there."

"Okay, we'll try to talk later."

I gave her a gentle push and she was off running, adding in a little scream for good measure. And Brody, like the champ that he was, started barking. Meanwhile, I stood there like a love-struck idiot, gazing at her with a huge ass grin on my face.

"Yep." I sighed. "I was right about those pants."

Chapter 27

DAISY INGLES

I shouldn't have been as happy as I was about the mayhem I'd caused last night. Meredith would have an absolute meltdown if she knew I'd interrupted it all, and I could only hope that the unpredictable prospect of a fire made good TV as a consolation prize for her.

The chaos was hilarious. The brunettes were pleased that the massage had been stopped and were muttering that it might actually bring the odds back in everyone else's favor. It was hilarious, like a half-naked and hormonal version of *The Hunger Games*. The blondes were more concerned that their clothes and shoes were going to catch fire, which was just hysterical. Most of them should have been more worried about themselves going up in flames; there was enough plastic, fake hair and hair spray between them to make a Disney firework display look dull.

I did my best to look as traumatized as the rest of them, but I had to work seriously hard not to break out into fits of laughter. I spotted Kade consoling a girl who was concerned that her hair irons might have been the cause. Apparently, she'd left them on before in her own place and had to call the fire department. Kade was doing a good job of placating her until she told him that it all ended well, though, "Like it was fate or something." Apparently, she'd hooked up with two of the firemen so it had been worth it in the end. Watching his jaw hit the floor in astonishment nearly tipped me over the edge, so I made a conscious effort not to look at him for the rest of the night.

I didn't get chance to talk to Kade again, but I slept better than I had for the last couple of nights. Some of it was sheer exhaustion, but a lot of it was relief and I wasn't afraid to admit it. I was completely relieved that Kade was no longer being pawed at by two blonde girls who could have been mistaken for Afghan Hounds if you squinted at them from far enough away.

Jess and Natalie were just as pleased with how it all turned out. There was a certain amount of camaraderie between us. It was clear the cliques and groups were forming, and I needed to keep in with my own roommates who were quickly becoming friends and allies. At breakfast the next morning, we were celebrating at one end of the table, while Honey and Vanessa looked like they'd been told acrylic manicures had been outlawed.

It was going swimmingly until Carson and Doug appeared with the cameras. "Ladies, apologies for last night's disruption, but at least we got some good footage of you running around in a panic in your underwear."

The guy was such a sleaze. The sneer on his face said it all really; when life gives you lemons, you make lemonade. And the lemon that sent their massage plan awry gave him jugs and jugs of lemonade in the form of pretty women running around half naked, which had, no doubt, all been captured on camera.

"Today is going to be as exciting as yesterday. The public's first vote closes in a couple of hours, and later we announce the lucky top two. One of you will be getting your first date night with Kade, and from where I'm standing, he's a lucky, lucky guy."

The look of excitement was nearly identical on most of the faces around the table, until Carson continued and indicated to Doug to switch the camera on. "And for one of you, Kade will be sending you home. We'll be filming his decision, and the unlucky lady will be expected to leave immediately. Clint, Kade's personal driver, will be waiting so I'd suggest each of you pack up this afternoon, just in case."

The smiles had vanished, all eyes were wide and Carson was loving every minute of being the bearer of bad news. He turned and left as soon as he'd finished his delivery, and Doug stayed to capture the aftermath on film. Their reactions were ridiculous. One of them started to sniffle, desperately urging tears forward. Another actually adjusted her inflatable breasts in their too small top, as if the tease of reminding the audience they existed would earn her some extra votes. Another girl had her head in her hands, like she was praying for help—no, scratch that, there was actually a girl praying. What the fudge?

"Are they for real," I said without thinking, and it was the straw that broke the camel's back.

"Yes, this is real. *I* don't want to go yet," one whined in a horribly nasal tone.

"Me either," another one hissed. "Other people deserve to go before I do."

They all started calling one another names and the room descended into a high school catfight. The camera kept rolling as a girl called Dolores stood up and pointed her finger at another girl, threatening to take her outside and, "Go all Tennessee on her ass."

Jess seemed immune to most of it. "Pass up the jelly," she asked Natalie, who stopped spreading stuff on her own bagel and handed it to her. In the midst of all this craziness, my new friends just carried on, and that level of bizarre made me laugh. I couldn't help it. It felt so good until Tennessee Dolores noticed my undeserved reaction and threatened to take me out, too.

Hating the tension and feeling slightly threatened, I snuck out to go and pack my case, feeling sure Meredith was going to take this opportunity to be rid of me when Carson stopped me in the hallway. "Nice little touch. Didn't figure you'd be the riot starter of the bunch. This should get us some good footage."

"I-"

"And because of that, I'm going to convince Meredith that she's wrong and you weren't behind last night's fire drama."

"I-"

"You scratch my back and I'll scratch yours," he suggested and then let me pass.

We were all lined up outside by the pool. The production crew had gone to town on the place and even I had to admit it looked impressive. There were tiki torches everywhere so they'd been able to ease up on the lighting rigs. The pool had a few lily pads floating around and giant palm bushes in brightly colored tubs had been brought in. There was an ornate chair sat at one end of the pool, and it didn't take a math genius to figure out that was where Kade would be sitting.

As we all nervously waited, wearing our best eviction outfits as Natalie had suggested, a big man with more muscles than Hulk Hogan appeared wearing a grass skirt and a lei, carrying a drum. After he'd got himself set up and began beating out a tune, the tension really increased, and then Doug began a slow walk down our line, filming each of us for some kind of reaction. When Hulk Hogan's drum tune changed, we knew Kade was coming.

Brody appeared first. He was wearing a lei like a collar and he trotted down in front of us, stopping by me to give me a sharp head butt in the leg before I heard, "Brody," grumbled in admonishment from behind him.

When I swung my head up to look at Brody, I felt my

legs go weak and it had nothing to do with the bump I'd just been given. Kade was bare-chested apart from a white flower lei around his neck and a few leather bracelets tied around his wrists. He was wearing the simplest white linen pants that hung off his hips, leaving his good physique on show. He had the tiniest smattering of wispy dark hair just above his waistband and it made my mouth water like someone had switched on a faucet inside. The linen pants were baggy and just about see through. You could see a hint of his underwear, but more than that, you could see the strength in his thighs and butt cheeks as he moved. His feet were bare and he moved with assured grace as if everyone around him was in the palm of his hands.

And we were.

The girls in the line were swooning so much we could have been physically swaying as we catalogued every delicious thing about him. Kade's hands hung limply and swung as he walked to the big seat, and I watched as he lowered himself into it, looking like a king getting ready to survey his subjects. His fingers flinched ever so slightly as he gripped the arm of his chair and that was the only sign I spotted that he was as nervous as the rest of us.

"Ladies, you all look stunning this evening. There is much business to attend to. The public have decided who I must consider for my date tonight, and I have the unpleasant task of asking one of you to leave."

The production team had been busy. While we had been pondering appropriate outfits and trying to calm our nerves, someone had been schooling Kade in the procedure for tonight.

At that moment, I felt like crying. This could be the last time I saw Kade in the flesh, and leaving him there, knowing he looked so devastatingly handsome with all of these vultures was going to play havoc with my mind. I was no longer avoiding my feelings. I wanted Kade. I had deeper feelings for him and the man I'd grown friendly with before we entered this charade, and in some cruel twist of fate, I was going to end up losing him when Meredith got her wish.

"When your name is called, please take a step forward from the line. I will call three names, and one of you will be asked to collect your bags. My driver is waiting to take you home. Thank you for your company in my home. Of the two remaining ladies, one of you will be joining me for a night of tiki enjoyment where we'll have some fun and have the whole night to get better acquainted. The lady left standing will rejoin the others and have to try harder next time to win an exclusive evening with me."

I could feel myself shaking like the other girls, but they were shaking with fear that they may be asked to leave. I was feeling angry. I wanted to be the one to get to know him better and help him through this God-awful experience.

The drumbeat changed and he began. "Dolores, please step forward."

I looked down the line at Tennessee Dolores and wanted to stomp over to her and unleash some Hollywood on her ass, show her how we local girls did things when we were cheated.

"Honey, please step forward." She sashayed her ass out from the rest of us, the breeze catching the edge of her flimsy, floaty dress and revealing her bare ass to the camera.

"Oopsie," she faked, doing a pathetic job of slowly trying to smooth it down her thighs.

"The last girl is Jess. Please take your place in front of the other girls."

What?

What the fudge had my roomie done to attract the viewer's votes?

Honey, I understood; she was like a soft porn film waiting to happen, and would be securing the lecherous votes of the college boys and desperate husbands. Dolores was volatile; voting for her was clever. She was already hated in the mansion, and she could clearly be counted on for some future bikini brawl action, but Jess? Her time had been as uneventful as the rest of the brunettes.

"Unfortunately, the lady leaving tonight is..." The drumbeat grew more intense and ferocious... "Dolores."

"What the fuck?" she yelled in a crass manner I knew Carson would have to beep out.

"It was lovely to meet you. Clint, my driver, is waiting outside."

"Y'all motherfucking set me up." Dolores stomped off, very unhappy, followed closely by a second cameraman and sound guy, who were busy catching all her unladylike phrases that would no doubt please Meredith.

"On to the more pleasant part of the evening, my date for the night."

Jess actually portrayed nervousness and shock that she'd even been selected above some of the others, and Honey widened her stance like she was getting ready to sprint in his direction.

"Jess, please join me this evening. I'd like the opportunity to get to know you better."

Honey looked shocked that she'd been turned down, and Vanessa moved over to her and rubbed her arms in a consoling manner. Once again, it was bordering on ridiculous.

Me, though, I nearly puked up everywhere. My roommate was going to do the one thing I wanted more than anything—spend alone time with Kade. The possibility of what they might get up to was eating away at my insides like a parasite taking over my body

I hated how this whole experience was making me feel, but even more, I hated how much I hated Jess right now.

Chapter 28

KADE SUTTON

My pre-eviction-slash-date selection meeting with Carson had not gone well.

I was told who the date choices were, and I knew it would be a rehash of the massage menagerie from yesterday. No way was I going to put myself through that again.

I'd been planning on evicting either Honey or Vanessa until Carson reminded me that life would get uncomfortable for Daisy if I didn't toe the party line.

That would be Meredith's party line.

In the end, we managed to agree on who should be evicted: Dolores. She had that odd glint in her eye that spelled trouble. I'd spotted it easily, and I had enough snakes slithering round in the form of Meredith and the production team that I didn't need them amongst the women, too.

I then told that the public had voted for Honey and Vanessa. This show was so rigged it was unreal. So after pointing out that the public would never believe it and that if it got anymore x-rated Meredith would risk it being cut from prime time altogether, Carson agreed to a deal.

He would pick one of them for the final two, I would pick the other girl, and the choice of date was up to me. His only caveat was that the other girl could not be Daisy. I could live with that, plus it meant Daisy wasn't being evicted.

I complied and followed their directions after some negotiation.

I complied and followed their scripted bullshit wording.

In the end, I complied and followed their date plans and actually had a nice time.

But I knew, deep down, it was because Jess reminded me of Daisy.

And that led us to now… We'd had some one-on-one time in front of the camera, and now they were expecting me to big this up, so the public were in no doubt that we'd be having a lot more one-on-one time away from the camera.

I'd stood up from the garden bed we'd been lounging on and, like a gentleman, offered her my hand. In my mind, I was simply helping her up so she wouldn't expose herself to the public and cameras. In the viewer's eyes, I knew it would be viewed as entirely different, as a simple gesture that was laden with promise.

I didn't drop her hand as I made my way back through the gardens. My fur ball best friend sensed just how nervous I was about what was coming next and came to see if I was okay. Only then did I release her from my grasp so I could squat down to scratch Brody,

"You can sleep in the kitchen tonight, pal. Stay out of the refrigerator and don't get under Mellings' feet," I told him, trying to delay the inevitable for as long as possible.

As if he was telling me to man up and get on with it, he barked and headed for the kitchen where no doubt Mellings had a member of staff on 'Brody guard' over both the refrigerator and pantry.

"He's a loyal dog," Jess commented.

"That four legged fur fiend is the best friend I've ever had."

"I bet he enjoyed his travels with you."

I nodded and reached for her hand again, feeling melancholy because she had no idea just what my 'travels' really were. I missed the simplicity of that existence. Just me and Brody, looking out for each other and living from day to day. Find food, find shelter and watch the world go by until Daisy came along and became the part of my day I really enjoyed. Then I remembered why I was doing this. I'd picked Jess to save Daisy and selfishly keep her in the house, and it was starting to fuck with my mind that they looked similar. Maybe that was how I would get through tonight, close my eyes and imagine she was Daisy.

I could see Carson on the far side of the lawn getting antsy. He was completely over my internal battle and wanted me to do as I'd agreed and take her upstairs to my bedroom.

I knew I had to get my head in the game, so I pulled her to walk alongside me. My nerves were going crazy. I convinced myself that if it felt like she was walking willingly rather than being dragged behind me to her doom, I might be able to see this through.

Jess got closer and ran her other hand up the inside of my bicep, dangerously close the tattoo of my mom's name. Would she be disappointed in me for doing this?

I had to put that out of my mind. It was enough that I knew Daisy wouldn't like it, Adding my mom to that equation was a sure fire way to kill the mood.

"I'm a little nervous," Jess whispered in my ear.

I stopped and looked at her, aware that the cameras weren't far behind. Running my thumb along her jaw, I looked into her eyes.

"Me too, but you know… we'll figure it out."

I started to walk again, finally reaching my hallway and turning down it to head towards my door. Carson agreed that the cameras wouldn't follow me here. They wanted my pick to be less nervous, but what my pick didn't know was that there was a single hidden camera and mic right outside the door.

What about my nerves? I hadn't so much as kissed a girl since I'd hit the streets.

The door loomed closer and closer.

My choice was becoming clear: either hyperventilate, grab Daisy and Brody and run out of this zoo, or get the fuck on with it.

Taking in a secretive breath of courage and resolve, I stopped Jess in front of the door and maneuvered her into the wall so I was just in reach of the door handle. I stepped up against her body and prayed with all my might that I could see this through. I needed to reassure myself that I could handle this now, and more importantly, I could handle what was going to happen as soon as I shut that door on the rest of the people in the house.

"I'm going to kiss you now," I whispered, taking her face in my hands.

I noticed her breath hitch and her pupils dilate just a tiny bit. She was excited. This was what she'd come for.

Me. Millionaire, Kade Sutton.

Her lips parted in anticipation, and I placed a testing gentle kiss on the very edge of them, just to see how they felt. They were soft and warm, and her tongue darted out to meet me as I made the journey to the centre of them. There was no room between us now. We were up close and personal, the only sound that of our lips gently meshing.

After a few seconds of pulling my shit together, I dived in, getting more involved, and took her mouth in the first real kiss I'd had in forever. My head was not in the game but worrying whether I would remember how to do this. Would my old skills come back to me, because call me a dick, but I use to have great skills. Jess reciprocated with fervor and compliance, her hands reaching up to clasp the back of my head. We stayed like that under the hidden camera, giving Meredith what she needed to confirm what would be happening behind the door.

When I finally broke the kiss, it was obvious that we were both anxious. I won't deny it, it felt amazing to be desired and kissed like that again, but I'd hoped that first kiss would be better.

"Come on, let's go inside," I said, reaching out to turn the door handle and pulling her inside.

I closed the door on the cameras and sound team, finally getting the privacy this situation deserved.

After all, no one should see Kade getting laid, let alone for the first time in forever.

Chapter 29

DAISY INGLES

Watching Kade and Jess from my bedroom window had been absolute torture. When he held a hand out to help her from the day bed...well, he may as well have torn open my chest and ripped out my heart with his bare hands; that's how painful it was. I knew the deal when I agreed to this, believe me I did, but I had no idea that my feelings for Kade would become so intense. I don't know, maybe it was just being trapped inside that house with a bunch of hateful people causing my feelings for someone I cared for to become heightened. Let's face it, as nice as Jess and Natalie appeared, they weren't the usual sort of people I mixed with, yet they were becoming friends—Sisters in Arms. So perhaps that was it with Kade. He was a friendly face in a swamp full of piranhas, so I was clinging to him like a life raft.

I lost sight of Jess and Kade as they moved into the house, and I knew that I thought of him as much more than a friendly face. The idea of what they would be doing in his room later caused tears of despair to crawl down my cheeks. I wanted to break down his door and tell him to stop, forget the money and leave with Brody and me. We'd be okay. We'd look after each other and he could come and live in my apartment with me. I would do anything to stop him doing something he could never take back. Something that I would never be able to forget.

"Hey, Dais," Natalie said as she pushed into our room.

"Hi, Natalie," I replied, moving away from the window and surreptitiously wiping my wet cheeks. "So good for Jess, hey?"

I tried to bring some lightness to my tone, but all I really wanted to do was curl up into a ball and cry.

"Yeah, how the fuck did that happen?"

I looked up sharply and Natalie flashed me a grin.

"Just jealous," she chimed, sitting at our vanity table and watching me through the large mirror. "Come on, I like Jess, but don't tell me you weren't wondering what she'd done to get the votes."

I had wondered, it was true, and if she hadn't got the votes, I doubted Meredith would have fixed it for her to be in the top two. She wasn't one of the blondes obviously being favored by production.

"My guess," Natalie sighed, "is that Kade has obviously said something to camera about her."

"L-like what?" I placed a palm against my stomach, trying to quell the nausea that was rolling around it.

Natalie pulled a brush through her long dark hair, her eyes still on me.

"That he likes her. The world is full of romantics, Daisy. If he's said he has feelings for Jess then they'll vote for her. Everyone loves a fairytale, Dais. Never forget that."

I swallowed back the lump in my throat as Natalie's gaze left mine, and wished that I had a room of my own, because all I wanted to do was get into bed, pull my comforter over my head and sob.

With emotion tickling at my nose, I put a hoodie on over my sleep shorts and top, and decided to go for a walk.

"Where you going?" Natalie asked as she wiped her eye make-up off.

"I just need to…erm, I just need some fresh air."

As I opened the door to leave, Natalie caught hold of my hand.

"You okay?"

I gave her a watery smile and nodded. "Yeah, it's just been a bit emotional, you know with Dolores leaving and all."

"Okay," she said with a squeeze of my hand, definitely not believing my lie about the wonderful Dolores. "But don't stay up too late, big day tomorrow."

"We do?" I had no idea what the itinerary was. I wasn't exactly on Meredith's list of people to keep in the know.

"Yeah," she cried, grinning huge. "We gotta make sure those viewers get to see us and like what they see. You and me, Daisy, we'll get one of those date nights. You see if we don't."

As I wandered past all the girl's rooms, I was surprised by how quiet they all were. It was only just eleven-thirty and they all appeared to be sleeping. I guess they all had the same idea as Natalie: get some beauty sleep to make a better impression tomorrow.

Reaching the top of the stairs, I stopped and looked down the hallway towards the end of the house where Kade's bedroom was. We weren't allowed down there, unless invited by Kade of course. The masochist in me, though, wanted to sneak down and listen outside his door., but what would I do if I heard Jess's moans of pleasure? What would I gain? Absolutely nothing, except more shards of my heart breaking off.

Padding down the thick, carpeted stairs, I looked up at the static cameras and so wanted to flip them off. I didn't, though, because that wasn't what good girl Daisy Ingles did. Instead, I smiled graciously and gave a little wave.

Meredith would no doubt ensure that didn't make the show, but I was betting a flip off would have done. I was beginning to hate her more each day, and wished I'd never stopped to talk to Kade that day. Then she would never have seen him and he would still have just been my friend, Kade with his dog, Brody.

That thought made me feel terrible. How selfish was I being? Kade deserved this and the benefits that came with it. He was a good man and deserved this break.

When I reached the downstairs hallway, I could see a light shining from the door that led into the kitchen. Maybe someone pleasant would be in there, or maybe it would be Carson filming some poor girl who hadn't been picked, comfort eating.

Pushing through the door, I was surprised to see Clint, Kade's driver, sitting at the table tucking into a huge bowl of spaghetti and meatballs.

"Hi Clint."

"Hey, little lady," he said, his fork pausing at his mouth. "Whatcha doing up? Everyone else seems to have turned in early."

"Can't sleep." I shrugged.

As I moved towards the fridge, Brody suddenly appeared at my side, nudging at my hand with his wet nose.

"Hey, Brody," I exclaimed, crouching down to give him a scratch and a hug.

As Brody pushed into my embrace, I breathed him in and laid my cheek against his soft coat. Tears pricked behind my closed eyes as I took comfort in his familiarity.

"He's been relegated to the staff quarters tonight," Clint said with a deep chuckle. "Kade obviously doesn't want him in on the action."

Clint's words were like a knife, stabbing into my chest, and without warning, I let out a huge sob as I clung to Brody.

"Oh shit," Clint muttered and pushed back his chair.

"Hey, Daisy, come on now."

Brody gave a little whine and shifted, starting to lick at my bicep that was wrapped around him.

"I'm sorry," I cried. "It's just…"

Clint dropped to the floor next to me, gently released my hold on Brody, and then pulled me into his hard chest.

"Hey, come on, shush now," he soothed, rubbing a huge hand over my hair. "Don't cry, sweetheart."

"I'm so sorry," I hiccupped.

Brody pushed his nose between us, and his tongue came out to mop up my tears. Clint just held me, rocking me gently.

"It's all getting too much, hey?" he asked.

I nodded. "I can't stay here. It's too hard."

Another great sob erupted from my chest, and Clint's hold got stronger and Brody's kisses sloppier.

After a few minutes, Clint slowly pulled me to my feet and helped me over to the table. He pulled out a chair and sat me down before crouching in front of me.

"You want a drink?" he asked.

I shook my head. "I'm so sorry, Clint. I interrupted your supper." I made to stand up, but he gently pushed me back down.

"I'm good, sweetheart. Now, why don't you tell old Clint what's troubling you. And," he said with a deep chuckle, "I want the truth, not some BS about missing home, 'cause I know you ain't missing that old buzzard you work for."

I looked up at him wide-eyed, and then looked around for any cameras.

"There ain't any in here," he said. "Who wants to see what the hired help do? No, the only time a camera will come in here is if there's some titillation going down. So, whatever you tell me is strictly between us."

He reached behind him and taking hold of a chair leg, dragged it forward before getting up and sitting on it. He leaned forward and took my small hands in his huge ones.

"Okay, shoot."

I looked down at Brody, who had his head resting in my lap, and then gave Clint a smile.

"I think I love him, Clint," I whispered, chewing on my lip.

He let out a laugh and shook his head. "Oh, sweetheart, tell me something I didn't know. I've seen on the dailies how you look at him. I see how he looks at you."

"I don't understand," I gasped. "How...?"

"What the hell do you think I do all day. I ain't driving Kade around, that's for sure. I'm part of the production team, too."

"You are? I had no idea."

"Well, if I said, 'Tell me what you think of Kade, Daisy?' what would you think?"

"Oh my goodness," I gasped. "You're the voice who asks the questions for the monologues."

Clint nodded and gave me a teeth-baring smile. "That's me. I also do the voiceover for the show, so I get to see all the dailies, not just that shit Meredith puts out."

"Wow, you must be really busy. No wonder you're eating your supper at almost midnight. And I'm keeping you from it."

"Take no mind, I've told you it's fine. Yep, I have busy days. Meredith sure does like her pound of flesh."

I looked at his kindly, round face and a small sense of calm wrapped over me. I'd just found another friend in this hell hole.

"I don't know what to do, Clint," I whispered, reaching down to pet Brody. "I need this job. I need the money that Meredith has promised me. Well, I don't need it like Kade does, but I need to help my folks."

"Don't ever tell her that. She'll hold it against you. Damn bitch," he growled. "Listen, you want my advice, Daisy?"

I nodded.

"Stick it out, sweetheart. That boy cares a lot for you. I see it. Now, he'll do what he has to do, but remember even if you have to be apart for the six months he's contracted to date the winner, it don't mean you have to be apart forever."

I'd almost forgotten the six month 'dating' clause, what with Jess being holed up in Kade's room at that very moment.

"What if he falls for her? What if he's doing things with Jess at this very minute, and he ends up liking her? He might decide to distance himself from me, and then the next six weeks in here will be hideous."

"Well," Clint said, taking a deep breath. "I'm not sure that will happen, but if it does then he ain't the guy for you. Just try to remember one thing, and you should know this working in TV: What you see ain't always the truth. Okay?"

He squeezed my hands again and looked at me expectantly.

"Okay," I breathed out.

"Good, now go grab a bowl and help me finish this spaghetti and meatballs. I think the cook thinks I need building up. She left me enough to feed an army."

Feeling a little better, I went and got myself a bowl, and as we tucked in to our food, I tried not to think of Kade and Jess upstairs.

KADE SUTTON

Leading Jess out of my bedroom, I took a deep breath, wondering what shit storm would be about to meet us. Gripping her hand tightly, I paused outside my door and pulled her to me, kissing her gently on the forehead.

"Thanks," I whispered. "I had a great night."

Jess giggled and rolled up on her tippy toes to kiss my lips. "No, thank you."

She let go of my hand, and walked away, giving me a sweet smile over her shoulder. Once she had disappeared out of view, I blew out a breath and dragged a hand through my already unruly hair. Now it was time to face everyone. If I was honest, I had no fucks to give about what the girls or the crew thought of me, but facing Daisy was a different proposition. I really didn't want to hurt her. I fucking cared about her. She brightened up my day with a just a small smile for God's sake, but I had to do what I had to do to get through this next six weeks. To get us both through this.

I made my way down the stairs, and hearing noise from the dining room, guessed that breakfast was already in progress. Pushing open the door, I was surprised at how many of the girls were in there. A quick head count told me there were eight of them. Knowing Jess was upstairs, that meant all the girls were there.

My eyes sought out Daisy, and there she was, sitting with her head down, looking at her cereal. My heart lurched as I saw the stoop of her shoulders and the way she was playing around with her breakfast, stirring her spoon around and not eating any of it. I needed to talk to her. Damn it, I needed to touch her.

Taking a determined step towards her, I felt myself suddenly pulled back by my arm.

"Kade!" a voice shrieked. "Come sit with us. Tell us all about your night with Jess."

Everyone's head shot up or swiveled around to face me. Everyone, that is, except for Daisy. She carried on creating a whirlpool of milk with her spoon.

I turned to see a girl called Suki had a grip on my arm. She was beautiful, with coffee colored skin and an amazing bleached blonde Afro, but she'd already proven herself to be a bitch. She seemed to have tagged on to Honey and Vanessa's little group, and last night I'd seen her put her foot out to try to trip Jess after I'd announced that she would be my date.

"I'm good thanks, Suki," I said, gently pulling my arm from her stealth grip. "I need some fresh air so I'm going to sit over there."

I nodded towards the open patio doors that, coincidentally, Daisy was sitting in front of. Suki's lip curl quickly morphed into a smile.

"Sure, maybe we'll catch up later." Her long fingernail ran down my forearm as she moved away.

"Suki!" I heard Honey hiss. "You were supposed to get him over here. God, if you want a job doing properly, do it yourself."

So, Honey was head mean girl then. With a shake of my head, I quickly moved towards the buffet, put some fruit and a cereal bar onto my plate and then moved with speed towards the empty seat next to Daisy.

"Morning," I said, as I flopped into the chair.

Daisy looked up at me and I wanted to pull her into my arms. Her eyes were red and puffy, her cheeks were blotchy, and her beautiful plump lips were determinedly downturned.

"Hi," she whispered, and then went back to her cereal.

"Daisy," I pleaded. "Please look at me."

She looked up at me, but there was nothing behind her eyes. The welcoming twinkle I was used to was gone and there was no sweet little smile, absolutely nothing.

"You know I have to do this," I whispered, leaning a little closer.

"I do, Kade. So don't worry about it."

Her bottom lip trembled slightly, and it took everything in me not to reach over and caress it. She was so damn beautiful and being here was making her miserable. I should never have asked her to do it. It was totally selfish of me.

"I do worry, though," I said. "I know what you think about me spending the night with Jess, and I know it's hurt you."

Her eyes took on a steely glare. "Why would it hurt me?"

I inhaled deeply, wondering if I'd got this totally wrong. I could be about to make a huge dick of myself, but somehow I didn't think so.

"Because I know you like me."

There, I'd said it, and she wasn't laughing. I had to be right, unless I'd totally misread all the signs. The things she'd done for me, the way she looked at me. The way she looked now, which was killing me. I'd really hurt her.

"Yeah, you know I do. You're my friend," she snapped, turning back to her breakfast that was fast becoming mush.

"You know it's more than that, for both of us."

My hand went to her knee under the table, startling her. "Please, Daisy," I pleaded as she looked back up at me. "What, Kade? What do you want me say. You're in a game show where you have to spend the night with different girls. I understand. I knew the deal."

"But you're so hurt, I can tell. That's the last thing I wanted. You know I *had* to do it."

She gave me a short nod. "Yep, I do. But just one thing."

Her eyes narrowed and her grip on her spoon tightened.

"What?" I asked, my pulse quickening as she licked her lips.

"Did you say or do something to get Jess into the top two?"

"I'm not sure I know what you mean," I replied, wishing she'd asked me anything but that. I couldn't lie to her, but Carson had sworn me to secrecy or Daisy got the push.

"I think you do. Jess is a great girl, but she's not exactly lit the show on fire, so I have a theory that the viewers took notice of her for another reason. She got into the top two for another reason, and I'm wondering whether you had something to do with it." She flashed me a smile, one that barely moved her lips. "Just curious is all."

My eyes went to my untouched breakfast and suddenly, I really wasn't hungry.

"Well?"

Looking back up at Daisy, I nodded. "Yeah, I think the viewers voted for her because I said I liked her. And I do, but not like I like you, I swear."

Daisy pushed back her chair. "It's okay, Kade. I really do understand. You like her, and spending the night with someone you like is good. I want you to be comfortable doing this so it's fine."

"Where are you going?" I asked as she stood up to

177

leave.

"I have a migraine coming on. I'm going to ask Carson if I can duck out of filming today."

"Daisy…"

"It's fine, Kade. You have fun with the girls."

With that, she was gone, pushing past some of the girls at the buffet. I wanted to rush after her and tell her I was sorry, but for what? I was just doing what I was told, and unfortunately, she was getting caught in the crossfire.

Chapter 31

KADE SUTTON

Walking around the house was slowly draining me of all my morals, and pretending to be someone I'm not was exhausting. I mean, look around me. The place was full of freak women who thought this was the way to meet a husband. As if that wasn't bad enough, they were prepared to do it in front of millions of viewers. The only one who was seriously struggling with it was Daisy, and although part of that was because she was being forced to live a lie, a bigger part of it was because of her disappointment in me.

The longer the day went on, the more I could see how affected she was by it. Little things were starting to concern me—what if she never spoke to me again after my night with Jess? What if the cameras were picking up on all of this and she was hated on the outside? Daisy helped so many people at the shelter, and now I was worried that she would never be able to go back to the place. Another frightening thought I couldn't shake off was what would happen if her parents were watching and she disappointed them.

All because of me.

I tried my best to engineer some way I could get her alone and just tell her to go back to acting and faking it, praying that I'd be able to undo all the damage I was doing now once we were on the outside.

After lunch, I went over to sit with her, Natalie and Jess. A few of the blondes were following me around like lost puppies, and the minute I sat anywhere near Jess, they spotted the threat and came to intervene and remind me they still existed. It was pathetic, and as I sat and listened to the conversation, I knew Daisy was struggling to be civil with Jess. It was obvious to me, and I'm fairly sure Jess too, but like a trooper, she carried on. When more blonde leeches joined our party, it tipped Daisy and the other brunettes over the edge. Trying to concentrate on more than one person's chatter meant I missed my chance to speak to her again, but as she rose to leave, Brody, my fucking amazingly intuitive friend followed her.

"Ladies, I must go and make sure my dog isn't being a nuisance. Keep my seat warm," I crooned and leapt up, timing my attack perfectly. As she was walking past a bathroom door, I crowded her back and pushed her inside.

"What the fudge?" she protested.

"I thought you weren't filming today?"

"Carson pulled rank and threatened me, so yeah, I'm having a ball watching you and your harem."

There was an edge to her that I'd never seen before, and it worried me that I was having this effect on her.

"Daisy, please, you just need to hold it together for a few more weeks," I pleaded.

I watched as she dropped her head back and looked at the ceiling, desperately trying to find some divine intervention. When she righted her posture and faced me again, I knew she was doing her best to maintain her composure.

"I won't ruin this for you."

I took a step forward. "I'm not bothered about that.

You're my friend-" I halted my words when I saw that they didn't help the tenuous grip she had on her control.

"I know I'm just your friend. Thanks for pointing it out."

I took another step forward and pushed a loose piece of hair behind her ear, feeling her shiver as I made the tiniest bit of contact with her. The zing of emotion coming from her was undeniable. As her lips parted, I saw the briefest glimpse of her tongue up close and leant in, desperate to find out what she tasted like.

Our eyes were open and our faces close, and she didn't push me away, so I tilted her chin towards me until her lips were ready for me to move in. When her eyes drifted shut in contentment, the rest of the madness outside the bathroom door ceased to exist. Daisy didn't change her stance, and I knew if I let go of her chin, the spell she was under would snap and disappear. With her lips barely a hair's breadth away, I whispered, "I'm sorry."

That admission was enough to bring her back to the here and now.

"You're breaking me, Kade. I'm not this girl. Have you forgotten who you were with less than twelve hours ago?"

A quick kiss and heart to heart in the bathroom was never going to be enough to get her to forgive me for spending the night with Jess.

"I'm only doing what's necessary, Daisy. Can't you see that?"

"I can. It doesn't mean I have to like it."

With a gentle shove, she pushed past me and left the bathroom, leaving me alone with a reflection in the mirror that I didn't recognize. It wasn't just the change in appearance and haircut; it was the sins I could see in the back of my eyes.

I heard the bathroom door close. "Daisy, I…"

When I turned to talk to her again, I was faced with Carson, and the displeased look on his face told me he knew who I'd been in here with.

"You know the deal, Kade. Meredith will not be pleased."

His words were like pieces of broken glass teasing open an already bleeding wound, and in an effort to maintain my control and not punch the fuck out of his smug, overweight, bad-breathed face, I gripped the edge of the sink.

"She's my friend and this process is hurting her."

"If I'm to believe Meredith, that's your fault. You insisted she be in here."

"Believe me, I'm regretting it."

"Great job with Jess by the way. The footage from outside your bedroom door is excellent."

Having him remind me of that only jabbed the open wound more.

"I need you to make sure Daisy is in the top two tonight. I have to put things right with her."

"Not happening," he laughed. "The public votes how the public votes, and Meredith will kill me." It was unbelievable how all of sudden he seemed to forget the previous night's vote rigging.

I had to get some alone time with Daisy and put our friendship back on track. Another night in my room with one of the other girls and it would be beyond tenable.

"It wasn't a request, Carson. Make it happen."

I watched as he folded his arms over his chest, trying to suck in the beer belly he'd acquired over the years. The sleeves on today's pick from his never ending tasteless Hawaiian shirt collection were straining, just like the tiny grip I had on my nerves.

"I'll repeat. It wasn't a request. You don't do this for me and I walk, and the first thing I do is get an interview with NVTV."

His eyes squinted at me at the mention of the TV network's biggest rival.

"I'll tell them how you engineered this whole shit trip

to make those beauty queens out there look bad. Then I'll go back to my cardboard carton outside the building and remind Meredith publically how she fucked this up."

"Don't push her, Kade."

"Do this and no one is pushing anyone."

We were squared off, facing one another, and I wasn't going to back down. "You think money is keeping me in here then you've underestimated me. With the behind the scenes stories about this lot, I could make as much in interviews."

"Not with the contract you've signed." Carson smiled smugly.

I finally dropped the eye contact and burst out laughing,

"Really? And where will you send the lawsuit? 1027 Cardboard Carton Avenue on the corner of homeless and don't give a fuck? You people with everything seem to forget, I came in with nothing and I can go back out with nothing."

I continued chuckling as he thought my threat through. After what felt like forever, he turned and stormed off.

"I'll wait to hear from you then."

Hours later, when it was getting dangerously close to recording the date selection and eviction part of the show, I was outside throwing a ball for Brody, giving him the chance to enjoy the space and freedom before it was no longer available to him. My time here had taught me a few things, and one of them was that my buddy needed to roam free. When we were back to normal and we had the chance, I'd spend more time at the park with him. He was a dog and that meant running around and playing fetch. I'd been selfish all these years, keeping him next to me at my begging post.

The girls were long gone, getting themselves spruced up and packing their things ready for the big reveal. The production team was busy setting up the scenery; it looked like we had a medieval theme tonight. Sconces and flags like those carried in front of Kings and Queens on horseback were being set up.

"Kade," I heard, after launching the ball as far as I could for Brody. I knew it was Carson, and this could be the moment it all came to an end. "I can't get hold of Meredith so I've made an executive decision. Do it. Put Daisy in the top two with Honey. In return, you'll evict Vanessa."

I didn't understand his request at first, but then it hit me. If I picked Daisy over Honey, the blondes would hate it. It would be my second night with a brunette, but after evicting Vanessa, the chaos that followed would be camera gold and at the centre of it all would be Daisy. Once again, she would be responsible for throwing the mansion into turmoil. This was his way of making it up to Meredith, of salvaging his ass instead of forcing her to rip him a new one because he had gone against her express command of not letting Daisy win a date night with me.

"Brace yourself, Kade. There will be repercussions, and when they come, remember you asked for this."

I should have heeded his warning. I have should have back pedaled and told him to forget it, but I couldn't. I needed to make things right with Daisy before things got too fucked up and out of control. I hated myself enough for my night with Jess; feeling the weight of Daisy's disappointment was just too much right now.

Chapter 32

DAISY INGLES

This was like that ridiculous film, *Groundhog Day*.

Everything was just ridiculous. That was my favorite word today.

My roommates had been giving me a wide berth my mood was that bad, and no matter what I did, I couldn't shake it off. The impending doom of an eviction did nothing to help improve it, either.

This time, I was already packed and waiting to go. I was so distraught after Kade had spent the night with Jess that I never unpacked.

Here we all were again, like meat selections at the market, waiting to be chosen. The whole premise of this show was seriously degrading, and it was unbelievable that we didn't have feminist groups protesting outside.

Kade had walked past me, once again hurrying Brody along. He seemed to have taken to following me around the house. The dog knew I was upset with his master and was doing his best to try to bridge the gap. It was a shame the fur-baby had no clue that things were so broken it would take more than some wooing by a cute dog to put it right. I was like a bear with a sore head—completely unapproachable. I did my best to ignore Kade. He was dressed in some kind of olde worlde peasant shirt and pants. The neckline of his shirt should have been tied up with the crisscross laces, and its sleeves were long and dangled past his wrists. The pants looked soft and comfortable, and in my eyes, with his disheveled hair that always looked in need of a trim, he looked more like a pirate or ship's deck hand. A court jester wearing one of those ridiculous harlequin outfits had replaced the Hulk Hogan drummer tonight, and he was playing some old fashioned instrument that just irritated me. Kade made his way to what was definitely a throne and sat down. It was all just ridiculous. They basically dressed him up like a pauper and put him on a throne, and I found the likeness offensive, seeing as he was a poor man in a mansion.

"Ladies, welcome to my court," he began, and the tut of annoyance I felt escape my lips did not go unnoticed by Natalie who was stood beside me. "By now you all know the drill, so let's get down to it. There is much merriment to be had this evening."

For fudge sake, he was even talking in a ridiculous manner.

"Let's get the unpleasantness out of the way. For one of you, your time here is at an end. My driver is waiting to escort you home… Vanessa."

The blondes all gasped in unison. This was not part of their plan. She'd been involved in everything she possibly could be, and in some cases would have gladly split herself in half just to spend more time with him. An ugly, high-pitched wail left her body through badly inflated lips and she collapsed to the ground. Another tut left me involuntarily.

Some of her fake friends dived to help her up, but their self-preservation was kicking in and it was clearly proving hard to stop smiles of relief from striking their faces. As soon as they'd shoved her in the direction of the exit, they resumed their places in line, smoothing down their nearly non-existent dresses and forgetting that Vanessa was ever part of it all.

"The public have cast their votes for tonight's date selection. When I call your name, please step forward." Kade paused for effect. "Honey," he said, and if I hadn't been on camera and could have gotten away with jutting a hip and slamming a hand on it in sheer attitude, I would have done. I imagined he had a good time with Jess, but when he got Honey behind those closed doors, they'd be re-writing the Kama Sutra. I was that incensed, I nearly shouted at Carson to have an interior designer on standby. Furniture was bound to be broken and light fittings would need replacing after a night of getting to know Honey better. While I was busy trying to bleach visions and thoughts of them having sex from my brain, I felt Natalie jab me in the side.

"Ouch! What was that for?"

"Step forward," she hissed.

"What? Why?"

"Step forward and stand with Honey," she repeated, this time giving me a bit of heave-ho.

When I looked at Kade, he seemed amused. When I looked at Honey, she seemed unconcerned, like I was a fly she was about to swat. When I spotted the rest of the blondes, they seemed angry.

"My date for the night..." another irritating pause, "...is Daisy."

Honey started to fake sniffle beside me and the rest of the blondes rushed to her. Apparently her acting was good enough that they all believed she required consoling.

I stood completely stock-still. This was not part of my plan. Natalie placed her arms around me.

"Now maybe you'll cheer up a bit."

I couldn't answer as she sauntered off with the rest of the girls, and Jess was quick to follow her, only turning to give me a quick wink and smile as she passed me. One by one, the girls left me standing there. Some undoubtedly left feeling genuinely unhappy that they hadn't been selected to get to know Kade better. Most of the blondes left looking angry, like I shouldn't plan to be alone with them anytime soon.

I was still stood in front of the pool alone after a short while, with the camera crew watching in anticipation. This was TV gold. Kade had his eyes on me warily, wondering whether I was going to blow this whole thing apart and throw a huge hissy fit.

As soon as Kade rose from the throne, Brody came to greet me, closely followed by the King himself.

"Daisy, it's going to be nice to get to know you this evening. Would you follow me please?"

My feet stumbled blindly as I followed his command, more than keenly aware that I'd been able to hide in the background of filming up to now. That was all about to be thrown out of the window. I'd been selected for his date and this segment of filming would form the main part of the TV show's transmission. My parents would be seeing all of this.

When we made it down to the lawn, a medieval banquet table had been set up with plush, high-backed chairs and full of food. The immediate area was lit with more flaming sconces and as he filled a plate full of food for me, a royal court of entertainment started. Jugglers and dancers, mime acts and musicians all trotted out in front of Kade, Brody and I as the date was filmed. As I picked up the odd bits of food on the plate, I kept catching his eye and I knew I had to play the part as well. If we didn't, this would turn out to be the world's weirdest date.

"I'm sorry, I'm a little shy," I said.

Kade breathed out in relief. "Well, I hope I can make you feel a little more comfortable. Would you like to learn how to juggle?"

I was shocked at his crazy suggestion, but we needed to

do something and it seemed like the best plan at the time. As we both stood, a lady dressed in an acrobat's leotard appeared and proceeded to school us in the art of juggling. I was hopeless at it, and every time I dropped a ball, Brody would run off with it.

"Would you mind if we took a walk with Brody? I'd like to walk off some of that wonderful food we've just ploughed through."

"Of course, what a lovely suggestion." Kade thanked the lady but retained a couple of balls so we could keep his dog amused. We walked for over an hour, taking in the scenery and rolling hills, fully aware that the camera crew was never far away. After a while, he took the ball I'd been using to occupy my nervous hands and dropped it on the floor, taking my hand in his as we continued to stroll.

It felt amazing to have my tiny hand wrapped in his strong one. Every so often I kept looking down, just to check it was real. The connection I felt between us was ever present, and I felt slightly morose that I was probably reading more into this than he was. Kade had made it clear that he knew how I felt about him, and this was all part of what was expected of him during his date filming. The simple gesture of walking hand in hand caused my nerves to jangle and bubble, and I felt confused at how much I really liked it. I was a hopeless pretender and the fact that Kade had read me so easily at breakfast the day before was a sure sign that I wore my heart on my sleeve.

"It's getting late. We should head to bed."

When he finished that sentence, I felt the hairs on my arm stand up. I'd been jealous of Jess's time with him, and now I had my chance, I was suddenly afraid of what was going to happen.

Kade kept hold of my hand as we took Brody to the kitchen and left him there for the night. Clint was passing through with a wrapped plate of cold cuts. Having just got back from depositing Vanessa at her home, he'd missed dinner with the rest of the production team.

I tried to delay Kade for as long as possible by making sure that Brody was comfortable, but the cough from Carson, who was stood beside Doug the cameraman, indicated we should get on with it.

As I trudged up the huge staircase behind him, still connected by a single hand, I felt my legs tremble. When we arrived at the top and turned in the direction of his living quarters, I heard him whisper, "Stay with me, Daisy."

My first thought was that he was asking me to spend the night with him, but that was a given requirement of the date. Kade just needed me to hold onto my nerves a little bit longer until we got rid of the cameras.

As the door got closer, Kade slowed his pace and stopped, waiting for Doug and the sound guy to finish his segment outside the door.

"I'm going to kiss you now," he said, raising his eyes towards the ceiling. Glancing up, I spotted the discreet camera that had been installed.

I stepped back, knowing what was coming next and needing the wall to keep me upright. As Kade licked his lips and moved into my personal space, I felt mesmerized by the action of his tongue. His beautifully handsome face came closer, and I could see his stubble was heavier than it had been when we'd argued at breakfast. His lips were so plump and slightly parted, and I could feel the anticipation in his breath as he edged towards me. In the shortest time, we were connected and I wasn't sure whether the murmur of pleasure I heard came from him or me. It didn't take long for the kiss to deepen, and as his tongue touched mine, I was pretty sure my legs turned to jello it was that good. When I felt his hands reach up and take control of my head, slightly tipping it to the side so he could delve deeper with his tongue, it felt like I was floating. I knew kissing him would be something special.

I felt the urgency in our embrace, and when his hands ran down my sides, cupping my butt, I instinctively raised up to my toes to take it further. Kade understood what I wanted and picked me up so I could wrap my legs around his waist. Feeling him lean into me and push his hardness against me set off a reaction that threatened to set my panties on fire.

As I grabbed the back of his shaggy hair and directed his mouth down to kiss my neck, I opened my eyes briefly, spotting the camera above me.

I'd got carried away, swept up in the decadence of being wanted by the man I was falling for.

Remembering my parents would be watching this, along with millions of other viewers, I moved my mouth to his ear. "We need to stop."

Kade came back to face me, his eyes fogged with the lust of the moment, and remembered that all of this was being captured. Agreeing with me, he pulled us away from the wall with my legs still wrapped around his middle, and took us into his room to spend the night together.

Chapter 33

KADE SUTTON

"We need to stop," Daisy whispered against the shell of my ear, and for one awful moment, I thought she was going to let go and run.

When I pulled back and looked at her, thank God, I could see that she wanted this as much as I did; she just had a little more decorum than I did. I pushed away from the wall, and leaving her hanging on to me like a spider monkey, I pushed open my bedroom door.

Once inside, I kicked the door shut and reached behind me to lock it. Meredith would surely know soon, if not already, that Daisy was who I'd picked, and I wouldn't have put it past that bitch to come storming in.

Pushing thoughts of *her* from my mind, my concentration went back to the beautiful, hot girl wrapped around me.

"Daisy?" I asked, breathlessly.

Biting on the corner of her lip, Daisy looked up at me with huge eyes and nodded. That was the green light I needed, so I crashed my lips to hers. As my tongue slid into her mouth, between her soft, plump lips, the ache in my dick intensified. I didn't think it possible but I grew harder as Daisy moaned. Sliding one hand into her hair and leaving the other firmly on her ass, I walked us towards the bed.

Bending at the knees, I gently lay Daisy down on top of the thick comforter, not once breaking our connection as I climbed onto the bed, straddling her. Daisy's fingertips dug into my shoulders, and the pain was amazing—it meant that this wasn't a dream, that she was really here.

Pulling away gently, I reached over the back of my head and dragged the stupid ass shirt I'd been made to wear up and off my body, throwing it to one side.

"Kade," Daisy whispered, her hands coming up to pull me back into a kiss.

Her mouth opened, inviting me in, her tongue welcoming me with abandon. "Jesus fucking Christ, Daisy. You taste so damn good." I groaned as she began to fumble with the buttons on my pants, her fingers skimming against the rock hardness of my throbbing dick.

Once my pants were undone, I gasped as Daisy's tiny hand inched inside and took hold of my erection. Her fingers wrapped around it and started to pump me, eliciting another guttural moan from me.

"You need to be naked," I whispered as I rained kisses on her neck. "Now."

Daisy paused and stared up at me, and the look in her eyes was no longer desire but trepidation. Me, I had no nerves whatsoever; I was reawakening bit by bit.

"Hey, what's wrong?" I asked, cupping her chin.

"I'm scared, Kade. I'm...oh fudge." She closed her eyes and slapped her hands over her face.

Gently prizing them away, I kissed her gently. "I won't hurt you. I'll take it slow."

She stiffened beneath me. "How did you know?"

I shrugged a shoulder. I had no idea how, but I'd guessed she wasn't very experienced. I wasn't sure that she was a virgin, though. I mean, fuck, did virgins know how to kiss like that, bringing a man to his knees?

"I'll make you feel good, I promise," I said, kissing the tip of her nose.

"But this isn't me. I don't…you and Jess."

Self-hatred bubbled in my gut as I thought about my night with Jess, and the loathsome person this damn show had turned me into. Resting my head against Daisy's, I took a deep breath.

"I'm so sorry," I whispered. "But I had to do what I had to do. If I don't toe the line, Meredith will kick you off the show and I really don't think I'd survive in here without you. I really care about you, Daisy, more than you can ever imagine. If you're not comfortable or don't believe how much I care about you then we can stop this now."

With tears lapping at her lashes, Daisy watched me for a few moments and then dragged me back down to her. The kiss was long, hard and full of raw desire.

As we continued to kiss, we rid ourselves of our remaining clothes, adding to the pile on the floor until I was naked and Daisy lay there looking more beautiful than the sunset, wearing nothing but the blush in her cheeks.

Sitting back on my haunches, I lazily ran a finger down the center of her body, between the valley of her plump, pert breasts, past her ribs, along her taught stomach, and over her neat patch of pubic hair. There was nothing fake or enhanced about this gorgeous woman.

I brushed my fingertip down the center of her folds, parting them to give me access to her clit. As I ran my finger over it, Daisy moaned out my name and lifted her back from the bed, her legs bent at the knees and dropping wider. This was how I knew we were right together; she was inexperienced but her body's reaction to me was natural and instinctive.

"You're beautiful," I said, leaning down to kiss her as my finger pushed inside. "So fucking beautiful."

My mouth found Daisy's and I devoured her with

kisses, and with each thrust of my finger, my need to be inside her grew worse; it was the only thing I was certain of. I wasn't even sure of my own name.

Daisy's hips moved with my hand as she gripped the cover beneath us in her fingertips, and when I rubbed my thumb over her clit, she cried out.

"Oh my God!"

Her back arched and her nipples budded as she grabbed at my hand, gripping it in place.

"Kade," she whimpered.

"Let go, Daisy. Just let go."

She did, and it was the most beautiful thing I had ever seen in my life. She was the most beautiful thing I had ever seen—flushed cheeks, hair sprawled across my pillow, eyes half lidded and her beautiful breasts heaving with exertion.

Reaching over to the nightstand, I opened the drawer and pulled out a condom. Still watching Daisy come down from her orgasm, I quickly ripped the foil open with my teeth and sheathed myself. Leaning down between Daisy's legs, I kissed her lips, which were even plumper than usual from our kissing. She whimpered against my mouth and then smiled.

"Oh, fudge," she said, lifting a hand to cup my face. "That was amazing."

The cute way she said fudge instead of cursing made me smile. Fuck, she made me smile, period.

"You were amazing, and this is going to be even better. It might not last too long this time, but it'll be good." Smiling, I ran a fingertip down her nose. "Okay?"

She nodded and lifted her head to kiss my chin.

With my eyes on her, I slowly slid inside her. The agony of the slowness and the ecstasy of feeling her pussy clench around me was the most amazing mixture of feelings I'd ever had.

"Daisy."

She let out a little moan as I moved, causing me to

pause, but as her hips lifted and her fingers dug into my ass, I knew she was okay and started to move in long, languorous strokes, taking my time to savor every damn moment. The insides of her thighs were soft and warm against me, and her little gasps of pleasure made my heart race faster. Daisy lifted her head, her mouth searching for mine, and I was more than willing to accept her hot, sweet kisses.

My hand skimmed down her side and reached for her leg, lifting it higher, and as I increased the speed of my rhythm, Daisy matched me. My breathing was hard as my cries mixed with her moans, and each thrust became more demanding. When I felt the walls of Daisy's pussy start to tighten around my dick, I felt the ball of electricity start to form, sparks going off all over my body.

"Oh God, Kade!" Daisy's cry was loud as her hands gripped my shoulders and her legs clenched around me.

With her pussy pulsing, I groaned out her name and stiffened as my own release came with my hand fisting in her hair. Euphoria and pleasure buzzed around my body and I knew that I would never get enough of Daisy Ingles.

Because of that, I owed her the truth, the whole ugly mess of my life and what had happened to put me on the streets.

Chapter 34

KADE SUTTON

No one ever wanted to use the words 'we need to talk', but I'd already taken liberties with Daisy and not been entirely open about all that I was. I'd gotten so caught up with having her in my arms that I'd pushed telling her the truth to one side. She'd been nothing but open and honest with me about her mom and dad and the reasons for the show from the start, and I'd held back.

I'd faced drug dealers on the streets and alcoholics trying to shake me down, I'd broken into places for survival, and yet telling this girl I was responsible for someone else losing their life seemed like the toughest thing yet. I'd been so content with her in my arms that the longer I lay there building up the courage to actually say the words, the sicker I felt.

"Baby, let me visit the bathroom," I whispered in her ear and felt the gradual loss of her warmth as she started to unravel her limbs from mine. When I'd seen to business, I pulled my shit together and headed back to her, gearing up to spill my guts. I halted at the open doorway and watched her from afar. Her body was wrapped like an Egyptian mummy in my bed clothes and her hair looked like she'd had her fingers in the power sockets.

It was fucking crazy beautiful.

I'd done that to her, and if she hated me after what I was about to tell her, that image would be burned into my retinas for the rest of my days.

"Come back to bed," she mumbled, completely aware that I was daydreaming, lost in the image of her.

"We need to talk," I blurted out.

I saw what that phrase did to her. It started a chain reaction of awareness through her body. I could tell when her brain had computed it by the way she bolted up in the bed. Her beautiful bed head was now upright and she looked more 'crazy scientist' than sex kitten.

"Wha...? Wha...? I...I..."

And here came the panic I'd caused by just fucking blurting it out. "I'm an idiot. I didn't mean to just say it like that," I told her, rushing to the bed, but the closer I got to her, the more she shuffled away from me, grabbing at the sheets to cover her naked body.

"I know I'm no romance expert but those words-"

"Were the wrong words," I interrupted. "What I should have said is, I need to talk about me. You know nothing about me and you deserve to."

Daisy stopped backing away and cocooned her frame in a sheet big enough to make a parachute. "The things I'm going to say about my past, it would be easier if I was in touching distance of you. You give me so much courage to see the possibilities of life, but this is hard for me. I need your strength, baby."

She shuffled sideways until we were side-by-side, opening one side of the sheet so I could snuggle underneath it. Her anticipation hung heavy in the air and it was as loud as my silence.

"I killed my best friend."

I heard the inhalation of shock and waited for her reaction. There was no screaming in disgust or the expected tears of disappointment. Daisy sat patiently, waiting for me to continue my sad, regrettable story. When I didn't continue, I felt her hand breach the non-existent void and clasp mine.

Why wasn't she running?

"I never knew my dad. It was always that simple, too, and I think that's because my mom gave me all the love and support I could ever have needed. Some kids had a dad and some didn't. That was just life. We lived in a little place and our next door neighbors, Paighton and her son, Cory became our family. We all relied on each other and at one point, we spent so much time together that I actually convinced myself that he was my brother."

I chuckled, remembering good times. We didn't have a lot of things, but what we did have was each other.

"Anyway, my mom fell ill. I spent more and more time with Paighton and Cory, not understanding what was going on, only that I was spending less time with her."

I dropped Daisy's hand and rubbed my tattoo gently with my fingers. It was like thinking about her and talking about her made it pulse and vibrate, as if it contained her heartbeat.

"Is that her? Your mom, I mean, Shelby?" Daisy asked, finally breaking her silence.

"Yeah. She passed away alone in hospital while I was excavating fucking dirt with Cory's *Tonka truck*. It's funny the shit you remember. Cory had gone inside to get us a couple of juice boxes—earth moving was thirsty business—and when he came back out, he told me his mom was crying. Later that night, she told me that my mom had gone to heaven and a lady would be coming by to pick me up. That was the first of many homes I went into, Bernadette's being one of them. The best one and I never wanted to leave."

Daisy's head was resting on my chest now. It felt odd to have her so close to my tattoo and my heart at the same time. My story was already causing an emotional overload, but I knew when she heard the horrid details and how it ended, seeing the look of disdain on her face might just kill me for good. Like I deserved.

"What? That's awful."

"It was at the time, but Larry was heartbroken when Bernadette died. He couldn't cope without his anchor and most of his family lived over a thousand miles away so he went to join them, which was why we had to go back into the system. Looking back, I know he did what he had to do to survive. So, to cut a long story short, I reconnected with Cory at college. I went on a scholarship and was determined to make something of my life. I didn't expect that my quest to do that, to fit in and be a part of the in crowd meant that he would lose his life."

Telling my story was getting harder and harder. I never said these things out loud, and I was able to compartmentalize when I was on my own. I didn't have to force myself to reflect on my actions. It wasn't working right now, though, and I hadn't realized that my breathing had become heavy and my body strung tight until Daisy climbed on my lap and took my face in her hands. "Please breathe, Kade. If it's too much then stop."

"No. I can't stop. Don't you see? I owe to it you. You trusted me."

"You don't owe me anything, and not being able to talk about something so painful doesn't mean I think you don't trust me."

As always, she was the voice of reason I was starting to rely on to soothe my soul. I knew I was crying when I felt her tiny, soft thumbs sweep under my eyes and wipe the tears away.

"I got so drunk, so fucked up that I couldn't get myself home from some irrelevant party. I called Cory and he agreed to come get me. When he was late, I text him and never got a reply." I was sobbing now, and as Daisy didn't try to stop me, I knew she understood that I was searching for something cathartic from this moment.

"I didn't know Cory had been drinking, too. He was over the limit and was texting my impatient ass back when he got in a car wreck. They told me he died as he was getting in the police car, and it was all my fault. I killed my best friend and sentenced his mom to a life of sadness and loneliness because I got too fucking wasted to sort my own ride home."

I didn't know how long she held me, but Daisy didn't interrupt my crying, and as I started to calm down, I heard her whisper, "I'm so sorry you suffered like that. I can't tell you not to blame yourself. Everyone has a cross to bear and only you can decide how heavy that burden is. What happened to Cory is something you need to come to terms with in the same way you've dealt with everything else in your life. That weight will be lifted when the time is right for you. I don't blame you, though."

"But it *was* my fault."

"You weren't driving the car. Cory was. You didn't decide to text while driving. Cory did. Actions always have consequences, and in this case, they were devastatingly final."

We continued holding each other for a long time.

For the first time, I was able to seek comfort from someone who didn't judge me but just accepted that there were reasons for my purgatory. This was Daisy Ingles at her absolute best. Her compassion was off the scale and as much as I needed to feel it, she needed to give it. Her caring for others, that ingrained part of her DNA that drew me to her like a moth to a flame, was devouring my guilt and slowly chipping away at the internal disgust that had been swirling inside me for years.

Chapter 35

DAISY INGLES

To say that Kade was amazing was a like saying Mark Zuckerberg was doing okay for money. He was more than anything I could imagine. He'd made my first real experience of sex beyond anything I could have dreamed. All I wanted to do was stay holed up in his room for the next six weeks and ignore everyone else in the damn mansion, Brody aside, of course.

The way he'd opened up to me made it all feel so much more special. It was just so sad to think how much he'd suffered growing up. It all made sense now, why he continued to punish himself and stay on the streets, the solace he was desperately seeking by living his life that way, and yet he still signed up with the show to help me to give my parents the gift of a lifetime. The distress I felt in my own heart when he cried last night was breaking me down inside, but I knew he needed to say the ugly words that had so clearly shaped his life. I truly didn't believe that he was to blame for the death of his friend, but those words were empty and meaningless if he wasn't yet ready to receive them. I wanted him to know that although I couldn't feel his pain or heartache, I did understand how something that tragic and dark could affect someone so deeply. My mission was to try to show him he wasn't alone and that I'd be by his side as he worked through his own deep-seated guilt and self-punishment.

"Hey," Kade whispered, pulling me against his chest. "You sleep okay?"

I gave him a sleepy grin and nodded. "Hmm, when we finally got to sleep."

Kade hadn't been a one-time performer, and each performance had been better and better. Was he making up for lost time? But then, how long was his 'lost time'? He'd been alone in here with someone else only the night before.

That thought of Jess in here with him soured the beautiful pictures that were flashing through my brain. Had he done all those sexual things with her, too? Had he carried her into the shower and taken her against the cool white tiles while water rained over them? Had he taken her from behind while they watched themselves in the dresser mirror? And worst of all, had he held her in his arms all night, sending her to sleep by stroking her back in gentle circles.

Unable to stop the vile images invading my headspace, I pushed away from Kade and threw the comforter back. No matter what I'd learned about him last night, it didn't stop me feeling stupid. He could still have shared his most painful confession with me, but I should have told him straight from the off that nothing could happen between us. But no, I'd let my damn hormones and Kade's magical penis sway me into doing something I was sure my parents would be ashamed of. The idea of my parents seeing our kiss sent my pulse racing. I just hoped that Kade pinning me against the wall didn't come across on TV as hot as it felt.

"Where you going?" Kade asked with a cheeky smile. "I thought we could have a little snuggle time. It's still early."

I glanced over at the silver clock next to the bed. He was right; it wasn't even seven a.m.

"I…I should go back to my room," I said, glancing at the door.

"Like that?" Kade asked, throwing his legs out of the bed.

I looked down at myself and realized I was naked. He was pretty familiar with my naked form by now, but I still grabbed a throw from the back of a wing-backed armchair.

With his brows furrowed, Kade walked towards me, gently pulled the cover away from me and threw it on top of our clothes that were still piled on the floor.

"Daisy, sweetheart, please don't hide from me, especially after everything we shared." His hands went into my hair, pulling me forward and resting my forehead against his. "Please, tell me what's wrong. Have you finally seen the light, that I'm tainted by my past?"

My chin trembled as I looked up at him through my lashes. He was so beautiful. His unruly, dark hair was hanging into his chocolate brown eyes that were full of worry, and I really wanted to kiss him. I had to be strong, though. I could not let my heart push me into doing something stupid that would ultimately lead to its own demise.

"No, it's not that and I don't want you to think that, but what we did last night was wrong."

Kade took a step back, his arms dropping to his sides.

"No," he said, shaking his head. "Absolutely everything about last night was right. Every damn bit of it. It was tough and fucking hard but it was right, and it was perfect."

"No," I whimpered.

He turned and walked away from me, taking just a couple of strides before turning around and storming back to me.

"How can you say that?" he demanded. "Tell me,

Daisy. How the fuck can you say that?"

"Because you were with Jess only the night before. She was in *here!*" I wailed, wrapping my arms tightly around my waist.

"You know the rules, Daisy. You know what I have to do. I have to pick a girl."

"So is that what I am, just another pick?" My question was anguished and I wasn't sure I wanted the answer.

"No, you know you're not. If I could have you in this damn room every fucking night, I would do."

"But you can't, can you?" I cried around the lump in my throat. "And you and I both know that Meredith will never allow you to pick me again."

"She can't fucking stop me," Kade growled. "I'll walk and she knows it. There is nothing she can say that would make me do or think anything differently."

"You can't." I gasped, shaking my head furiously. "This is your chance at a future, Kade. You can't walk and be left with nothing."

"I wouldn't leave with nothing. That's the point. I'd have you."

His words cut straight to my heart, filling it with warmth and tenderness. Maybe I was being a fool, but I believed him. He *would* leave this house for me. He was unbending

He laid a hand on my shoulder, his eyes pleading with me. "Please, Daisy. Believe me and stay in this room with me. Let's forget everyone else for just a little while."

He truly believed his own words, I was sure, but there was still the fact that I wasn't the first girl he'd had in here. I trusted that he wouldn't give any future girls the same sort of night he'd given to me. I believed him to be an honorable man, but Jess had been here before me.

I opened my mouth to ask him if he'd slept with her, whether *she'd* cried out his name when he'd brought *her* to orgasm, but I just didn't have it in me. Call me a stupid fool, but I didn't want to know. The pain of finding out the truth would be too excruciating. I was a coward and preferred to live under a cloud of ignorance than have my heart ripped to shreds.

Looking at Kade, his eyes begging me and his amazing, naked body enticing me, I really had no choice. I'd never had a choice really. Kade Sutton had always had me. I'd given him food because something about him drew me in. I'd come in here because he'd asked me to. I'd have done anything for him because I was totally smitten.

"Okay." I nodded.

"You'll stay?" he asked, smiling shyly like a small boy.

"I'll stay."

"I swear to you, Dais', I'll do everything in my power to get you into tonight's pick. Even if the public don't vote for you," Kade said earnestly, threading his fingers through my hair. "I promise."

"I know you will," I whispered.

He dragged me against his naked chest and kissed me thoroughly. "Fuck," he sighed out on a heavy breath. "You are so good at that, you know?"

I giggled and snuggled against him, holding on tightly as he lifted me up and carried me back to bed.

When we eventually emerged from Kade's room a little after eleven, we were both grinning and had a little bounces in our steps as we went outside to join everyone else by the pool.

"Ah, Daisy," Natalie cried, running over to me, her hands flapping wildly. "How was it?"

I glanced over at Kade, who had been surrounded by some of 'the blondes', and felt all warm inside when he gave me a warm, secret smile over the top of Honey's head.

"We had a nice night," I said distractedly.

"Nice!" said Poppy, a short, dark haired girl, who weirdly looked a lot like Justin Bieber. "He picked *you*— someone who says that they had a 'nice' night with that hunk o' love. Fuck me blind, sugar, that's just a darn waste."

A few of the other girls who were milling around trying to get gossip started to whisper amongst themselves. Natalie, meanwhile, grabbed my hand and pulled me to the shaded cabana bed over by the hot tub.

"Okay," she demanded once we were lying down with our faces being warmed by the sun. "Spill it."

"I told you, it was a great night."

"Ooh, a great night, that's a step up from nice." She kicked at my calf with her foot.

"That's all you're getting." I sighed, reliving the night before in my head.

"God," she moaned. "You and Jess are so boring. She wouldn't tell either."

My heart thudded at hearing Jess's name. I didn't want to feel jealous. I had to remember that he had a part to play. He had to do what the show required.

"Maybe tonight's pick will be a little more talkative tomorrow," Natalie moaned.

At that statement, my resolve started to disappear, but then I looked over at Kade settling himself on the day bed, unfortunately surrounded by 'the blondes'. He looked tired but beautifully handsome, and I knew that I had to try to work through it, for him and for us. Feeling more determined and hopeful, I closed my eyes to try to catch up on some sleep in readiness for the pick coming up later. A pick that, for once, I wasn't dreading.

Chapter 36

KADE SUTTON

The last thing I wanted to do was let Daisy out of my sight. I desperately wanted the world outside to cease to exist but we had to be realistic. We were stuck in the middle of this process, and even though I didn't care about the legalities of my contract, it would be a different story for Daisy. She was a real person with a real address who could end up on the rough side of a lawsuit.

"Hey, dude," I smiled, crouching down to scruff the fur on Brody's back. "You behave last night?" He barked at me and tilted his head sideways, helping me to interpret his response.

"Me? Oh, I was a really good boy last night." I laughed, unable to hide the happiness I felt from having that quality time and mind blowing experience.

"Sir," Mellings grumbled from behind me. "Your lady friends are having *another* pool day. I've been instructed to make… cocktails." The way he said it, with a distinct sneer, would normally have rubbed me up the wrong way, but nothing was going to dampen my spirits today.

"Best get my pool pouch on." I smiled widely at him,

waggling my eyebrows knowing it would irritate him more.
The camera crew followed me back to my bedroom, and I walked a little quicker than usual. I was keen to get back outside and lay my eyes on Daisy again. When I opened the door, my senses were assaulted with a fantastic reminder. The bed sheets and pillows were strewn everywhere, as if I could still see her fists gripping them and the imprint of her luscious body she'd left behind. The air was thick with her scent, and my cock jerked immediately at the sweet sensation my own imagination was causing. I wondered if I could ban housekeeping from cleaning it. Never mind. We'd just do it all again tonight, only this time, I'd try to retain a little memento from her— maybe her bra or panties.

As I reentered the pool area, I was greeted in the same the way as always. The brunettes shouted hi from their side of the battleground and the blondes tweaked and adjusted their nearly non-existent bathing suits before cat-walking their way over to me.

"You need to sit with us today," Honey demanded. "We've missed you," she continued, rubbing her top row of teeth suggestively with her tongue—either that or she needed to floss from breakfast.

I knew she thought I was taking her in and gaining pleasure from her appearance. She was wearing some crocheted woolen two piece that looked like it was made to fit a nine-year-old girl. Her fake tits were fighting against the design, and we'd be lucky if her nipples didn't make an appearance by the end of the day.

All I could see behind her, though, was Daisy. She was sitting with Natalie on a shaded cabana bed, talking about something that made them giggle. She looked so beautiful and carefree, and there was nothing provocative about her swimsuit apart from the vibrant fire truck red color of it. The simple strapless bathing suit screamed classy temptress, exactly what I now knew she was.

The camera crew had already set up for filming as some

of the house team delivered cocktails to girls on inflatable pool beds and sun loungers. I had to give it to the production team; if I'd been watching this through a TV screen, I too would have been convinced that the guy who lived this way had the best life ever. I mean, come on, a hot sunny afternoon, waiters, cocktails and women on tap. I looked like bachelor royalty.

Honey brought me back to reality as she took my hand and dragged me behind her to the blondes. As we walked past Daisy, I slowed to say good morning but the ass wiggling witch was not taking any chances.

"You lot had your turn. It's our turn now," she said sweetly when I knew she was anything but. Playing my part for the cameras felt like some kind of betrayal now.

"Sorry, ladies, I'm a guy in demand." I shrugged.

Most of Honey's friends vacated the four-poster day bed they'd acquired, parting the billowing sheets swathing the sides and greeting me like I was entering Caesar's bed chamber for group sex.

The chatter was inane and annoying. They all seemed to have this nasal pitch to their voices, and I began to consider the very real possibility that it was linked to plastic surgery. After a while, I zoned out. My night of activity was catching up on me, which was an odd concept. I was used to having little or no sleep and even more used to half sleeping so I could stay safe on the streets. It must have just been the sheer satisfaction and exhaustion from my love making with Daisy.

Love. Making.

That was exactly how I saw it. What happened last night was just the beginning. If I could keep things real while we were in here, there was a real chance that we could make something of this.

Not realizing I'd drifted off to sleep, I heard a man give one of those fake coughs to get someone's attention, and shielding my eyes from the sun, I was able to make out the shape of Mellings stood at the end of the bed. "Yes,

Mellings?"

I was surrounded by blonde women. They had all joined me on the bed while I was having my forty winks. There were limbs everywhere and I felt irritated that I'd let it happen with Daisy just on the other side of the pool. They all began to titter and giggle like high school girls as I shuffled to the end of the bed.

"You're presence is required in the study, Sir."

"Now?"

"Now, Sir. Might I suggest a towel for your walk back to the house?" He handed me one and as I loosely swung it onto my hips, I noticed the reason for the giggling.

Someone had scrawled, 'I Wanna Get Laid By Kade' across my abdomen in red lipstick, and when I turned to look for the culprit, Honey was sat, like butter wouldn't melt, raking the offending lipstick over her lips.

I followed Mellings, only wondering what was going on for a brief second. The closer I got to passing Daisy, Natalie and now Jess, the more bothered I was about what was written on my body. As I drew level with them, Daisy glanced at the scrawl and pivoted to lie on her front before I could make any further eye contact.

Her reaction made me want to scrub at my skin with a pan scourer but I couldn't. The cameras were lapping up the unhelpful body art.

As soon as we got to one of the studies on the ground floor, Mellings swung the door open before me and ushered me in, closing it behind me, leaving me looking at Meredith. On the way here, I was mentally preparing for a Carson conversation not a showdown with her. What am I saying? That's utter bullshit. I couldn't shake the feeling Daisy's reaction gave me. She knew the game we were in. We'd spoken about it, so if it wasn't the lipstick love letter, it must have been what I'd told her last night. It was a big fucking deal for me to tell her about my life and it had backfired. She'd finally realized that I was toxic and didn't deserve her love and compassion.

The sight of Meredith trussed up in some kind of tight dress and knee high boots was not welcome, almost as unwelcome as the smile she gave me when she spotted the lipstick graffiti.

"Kade, how are you?"

"Cut the chatter. What brings you here?" A personally delivered Meredith message was never a good thing, and like Carson had warned, she wouldn't have been happy about last night.

"I thought we agreed you wouldn't manipulate my show."

I didn't answer her. What she was saying was true and I had manipulated things.

"That will be the last fucking time you threaten to leave my show. Are we clear?"

"No. Not really. Did it somehow make bad TV?" I said, gripping the towel at my waist harder in annoyance. It was that or step closer and throttle her.

"On the contrary, it made excellent TV, like your footage of the previous evening." I hated that she reminded me of what had gone on with Jess. "Enough chatter, as you say. Tonight you will evict Daisy."

I could only respond to those utterly unacceptable words with a growl. This fucking cow needed to see just how I felt about that.

"It's my show and I will do what is necessary to stop you making it a fucking farce, Kade. You will evict Daisy and pick Honey tonight. I was going to compromise and let you have another bite of Jess, but now I've seen the endearing love note that Honey has left on your midriff. It's a brilliant idea even if it's not my own."

I was having enough of a trauma responding to the first part of her request about kicking Daisy out. Adding the Honey part was just beyond anything my sanity could comprehend. If I didn't say something now, I knew I was going to punch her squarely in her face instead.

"That's not going to happen, Meredith," I replied,

forcing some calm into my body.

"It is. Daisy will still get her money. After all, she's been evicted fair and square."

"There's nothing fucking fair and square about this," I roared back at her. The idea of telling Daisy to leave was making me feel more ill than I'd ever felt since... since I realized I was responsible for the death of my best friend.

Meredith stood up, or rather squared up to me, grinning like she was going to get her way, when in reality she was going to get exactly the opposite.

"I'll walk, you fucking bitch." She threw her head back, laughing at me. "There's nothing funny about this."

As her laughter came to an abrupt end, her demeanor turned serious. "On the contrary, you'll do no such thing. You walk and this goes public."

Meredith spun her cell phone in my direction and there, in full color view, was Daisy riding me.

"What the fuck?"

As I began to protest, she hit the volume button and all I could hear was Daisy breathing heavily and me grunting through each down stroke she made on my dick. The public wouldn't know it was Daisy, but I was clearly in view enjoying every moment of it. The viewpoint was from directly above my bed. The fuckers had put a camera in the four poster canopy, and seeing my hands reach up to grab Daisy's plump tits did nothing but tarnish my memory of it.

"You fucking bitch. I'll-"

"Wait," she urged, holding up a finger. "It gets better."

I knew what was coming. It was Daisy nearing the end of her enjoyment, and I watched as she thrashed about quicker, impatiently chasing an orgasm. I saw my right hand drop from her tit, remembering how I pressed my thumb to her clit in order get her there as I was struggling to hold off my own orgasm.

And like a car wreck that you couldn't look away from, I waited for the wail and outburst of Daisy, her orgasm complete as she dropped her head back in satisfaction, facing the camera that neither of us knew was there. Up until now, it had just been a faceless brunette. Now, it was very clearly Daisy Ingles. The smile on her face was radiant, like the sun breaking through the clouds, and this bitch had fucking destroyed it for me.

"The camera has already been removed. You will evict Daisy tonight and pick Honey, or this goes viral."

"Do it."

I watched as she scrunched up her face and her bottom lip pouted and wobbled, pretending to be a petulant toddler.

"Oh, baby, don't cry," she mocked. "You were warned not to piss me off. Evict her. She gets her money and you get this recording when your commitment to my show and your contract is over. If you tell her or anyone else about this, I release it and destroy her. Don't try calling my bluff. You played your hand last night. Would fast forwarding and playing the footage of your little confessional heart-to-heart help convince you? I know you care about her, and I'm willing to bet it's enough to make you do what I fucking say. So man the fuck up and be a fucking convincing playboy millionaire, Kade." Her tirade came to an abrupt end but the sparkle in her eyes was that of a victorious villain.

I was speechless.

I couldn't decide whether I felt sick with fear or anger.

The horrors of my past were now in the possession of this monster. It wasn't just about the sex she'd filmed anymore; it was that she held the very essence of who I was and how I came to be this Kade Sutton in the palm of her hands.

She didn't give me the chance to counter her insane request. She just strolled past me like she'd won.

And she had.

That video would destroy Daisy. The thought of her parents and friends at the shelter seeing it would kill her, almost as much as it was killing me.

That video would destroy Paighton, who didn't deserve to have the tragic events of her only child's death blasted round the media circuit.

I knew I was going to have to do it. I couldn't see a way around it.

Yesterday had been the start of something amazing. For the first time, I opened my heart and shared my darkest secrets in an effort to see what the possibilities of life could feel like.

Today, I knew without a doubt I was falling in love with Daisy Ingles.

Tonight, I knew I was going to rip her heart out and slice my own open in the process.

DAISY INGLES

It's a game. It's just a stupid game. He has to act this way. Everything he's doing is all part of it and I have to pull my big girl panties up and accept it.

I was still on the cabana bed by the hot tub. Most of the girls had left to get ready for the eviction/selection filming but I stayed put.

Watching Honey touch him when he entered the pool area was like someone pouring petrol in my eyes. It took a certain amount of restraint not to shout at her to get the hell off of him.

I thought I recognized the actor in Kade, but if my brain thought long and hard, he acted the same way with us all. What if he treated Jess and I the same way once we were behind closed doors with him?

When he lay down on the bed with all the blondes, it felt like someone was stabbing sharp needles in my eyes on top of the fudging petrol from before. Kade looked at ease with them, like he was enjoying the attention. Was it unacceptable for him to actually enjoy the attention after spending years being a nobody on the streets? Definitely not.

Natalie was whining about never getting her turn in the spotlight, and it must have been the way a lot of the girls were feeling. I was just starting to get through my oversensitivity to the situation when I saw the look on Jess's face. She looked like I felt.

The crushing blow that Kade might have been utterly convincing in his bedroom the night before with her was a feeling I was struggling to dismiss.

"Honestly, what's she doing?" Natalie hissed, and both Jess and I snapped out of our reverie to see Kade looking completely content and Honey writing on his body. How the fudge did he not feel that?

"Oh… interesting," Jess whispered, and when I braved a further look at the porn cabana, I saw Kade getting up to leave with Mellings.

The blondes looked disappointed and irritated, and so did Kade. When he got closer to me, gripping a small towel around the six-pack I had explored the night before, I could see what she'd written.

I Wanna Get Laid By Kade. She'd even kissed him on the chest and left lip marks.

As he walked past us, following his butler, the words also strutted closer and I couldn't not see them. My breakfast started to regurgitate in anger. The possessiveness I was experiencing was something I'd never felt before. Before I could let him see what all this was really doing to me, I spun over to lie on my front, hoping the world would just disappear while I got my head straight. I told myself I was waiting until I was in the right mindset to go and get ready, but I wasn't. I was waiting for Kade. I was desperately hoping he'd come back to the poolside, minus the body inscription, and tell me it was all going to be okay.

He never did, and after waiting as long as I could, I wandered back inside to get my game face on.

I dressed in a simple black maxi dress. It was long, floaty and completely different to the dresses everyone else was wearing. They'd all gone for maximum flesh exposure and I hated the pressure to comply and compete with them. I was feeling so far out of alignment with myself that I just needed something that would help me feel like the old Daisy Ingles. This dress was the closest thing I could find to me. I left my hair down and hadn't dried it after my shower. It was now wavy and wispy and moving in the breeze the same way my dress did. I over accessorized, adding lots and lots of leather bracelets and a few round my neck. Lydia had chosen them so they were longer than I normally wore and hung suggestively between my cleavage. When I walked out into the pick area, the rest of the girls all looked at me with no regard. Dressed like I was, I was no threat.

The costume department had been busy. The theme of tonight's date appeared to be video games. The pool had some inflatable *Pac-Man* characters and a donkey from *Donkey Kong* floating around, and Kade's chair seemed to be constructed out of blocks like it was something from *Minecraft*. The garden was littered with video game machines from an arcade and it looked cool. It was nothing, though, compared to the lawn behind the pool that was littered with characters from *Super Mario* and a makeshift racetrack had been constructed. At the start line were two little go karts, all set and ready for Kade and his date.

I was looking forward to kicking his ass on those video game machines and then beating him on the Mario Kart circuit. Maybe the long dress hadn't been such a good idea. Never mind, a little bit of fun might help take my mind off all the lipstick antics from the pool.

Like every other time, we lined up. Things had changed slightly though we were still standing in our allotted social circles, and some of the girls, like Jess, Natalie and I, held hands in some kind of solidarity. Brody trotted along the line first, and in a change of pace, he actually stopped this time and sat in front of me. His tail was wagging and it was so cute. Tonight, I was going to tell Kade he could spend the night with us—well, maybe some of it. If the Brodester didn't want to see his owner intimate with me, he could retreat to the bathroom. That was as long as the public had voted for me. I was hoping that our hot kiss last night had opened their enquiring minds and they wanted to see if things between us got even hotter. And if they didn't…well, Kade had promised he'd try to fix it, whatever the result, and I trusted him to do that.

I let go of the other girls' hands and squatted down to pet him. His tongue lolled out to the side. "Hey, buddy, you ready for this?" I mumbled.

"Brody!" Kade growled sharply. "Keep it moving."

The sharpness of his tone made me jump and stand up. The last time I'd heard that undertone from him had been during his negotiations with Meredith. As Brody carried on, Kade followed without so much as glancing at any of us, including me. He was wearing jeans and a collared polo shirt with white *Converse*. The material of the pants clung to the shape of his butt and it brought back memories from last night, of watching him walk naked to the bathroom after we'd made love and admiring the strength in his frame.

As he sat on the throne, Brody trotted off and left him. He clearly wasn't happy about being barked at and showed his contempt with his absence.

"Ladies, once again we've arrived at the part of this experience that brings both pleasure and sadness." Kade seemed to take a huge deep breath in as he continued. "I will call three names. Two of you have been chosen by the viewers as worthy of my singular attention and one of you will be asked to collect your belongings and leave my mansion immediately."

My knees began to tremble in anticipation of sex and a

repeat performance, although I thought we should probably get some more sleep tonight.

"Jess, please step forward." I watched as my friend rushed to stand ahead of the line and began to feel nervous that I would be facing a past conquest in this pick. "Honey, your personal tattoo services from earlier seem to have won you a space," he said, smiling for the first time that evening. I was suddenly glad I'd worn the long dress as my knees had moved from trembling to definite knocking.

"And Daisy."

On a sigh of relief, I took my place, knowing that when Kade had to choose between my roomie and me it would probably affect our friendship.

There was no music man tonight, no drum or piped tunes to create atmosphere, which meant the production team would be overlaying it during the editing process. You could hear everything so clearly—crickets rubbing their legs together in the grassy lawns, birds chirping before they settled down for the night and the girls shuffling impatiently.

"The girl leaving the mansion this evening, the girl who needs to gather her belongings and make her way outside to my personal driver is…"

Honey looked at Jess and I, and we returned her glance with slight smiles. Jess and I may have been about to suffer the consequences of being separated by selection, but without a doubt both of us would be glad to see the back of that troll.

"Daisy."

On hearing Kade say my name, I felt Jess squeezing my hand.

"Fuck, Daisy, I'm so sorry," she whispered, and before I had the chance to register the enormity of what had just happened, she was wrapping her arms around me.

There was some mistake. There had to be. He'd promised he would make sure we had more time together.

He'd said he'd fix it. My confusion was multiplying by the second as my brain tried to figure out whether I'd missed who'd been evicted and he'd made me his pick for the night again, but that couldn't be because Jess was consoling me.

Natalie, too, stepped forward and joined our hug. I couldn't return the affection as I hadn't even blinked yet. My heart was stuttering and stumbling in an unhealthy way, and if I'd had pains down one of my arms I may have been convinced I was having a heart attack.

"Daisy, thank you for your time here," Kade repeated, like he was slowly dragging a serrated knife out of my chest and sinking it back in, repeatedly. As I looked over at him, his face was like stone, emotionless, like he needed me out of the way so he could go back to the rest of his business.

Jess and Natalie released me from their hugs and resumed their places, Natalie in the line of faceless wannabes and Jess to go and stand next to Honey.

I urged my feet to move. I begged them to turn and walk away from this horror show, but I couldn't take my eyes off Kade. He needed to see what he was doing to me. This was no longer an entertainment spectacle. This was him cutting me off at the knees and towering above me, sneering at me with an evil grin.

There was a commotion in the bushes and trees by the pool then Brody appeared. He sauntered over to his master, a rumbling whine, which quickly became a displeased growl leaving his four-legged frame.

Suddenly aware that the cameras and film crew were waiting for me to make my dramatic exit so he could get on with selecting Jess, I did the opposite. My world had just fallen apart and I would not give them the satisfaction of seeing just how much.

"Good luck, ladies," I whispered bravely, forcing a small smile for Jess and Natalie before turning to Kade. "Thank you for the opportunity to get to know the *real*

Kade," I bit out, spearing him with my eyes. I needed him to know that he'd had me fooled. He had been the cute guy who needed support and a sandwich here and there, but this experience had changed that. I'd seen someone who had embraced the luxury he'd missed out while he lived rough. I'd seen a guy who was doing all he could to earn a large paycheck and worse than that, I'd uncovered a guy who had missed out on the attention of women and sex, and now he was doing all he could to make up for it.

Kade's face didn't change apart from a split second where his eyes widened in hurt at my words, but I was hurting too much myself to care.

As I spun away from the others, I remembered my parents watching this show and tried to remain dignified. Within a minute or so, I looked down to my feet and saw Brody trotting beside me. In a break from his normal behavior, he'd come to make sure the evicted girl was okay.

"I'll miss you, buddy," I told him quietly, well aware that the camera crew would be following me right up until I climbed in the back of the limo.

The door to the main house came into view, and I heard Kade begin again. "Ladies, tonight's date will be... Honey. It's time to see if she's really as sweet as that tempting name of hers."

My feet stumbled and caught on my dress, and I rushed to put my hands out to brace my fall. The first few tears had already started to streak down my face. This felt like the ultimate betrayal. Kade had cut his teeth on Jess the night before, ticked me off his bucket list then moved on to the real bedroom entertainment.

Brody nudging my arm reminded me that I was still on my hands and knees on the concrete just outside the house. Everyone was going to see what this experience had done to me and how broken I was. My parents would be distraught, and they didn't need this with everything else they were dealing with. The production team would make the most of the footage, slowing it down and zooming in on my unhappiness. Clint would give some lame but accurate narration about how the heartbreak became too much and it brought to my knees. Meredith would oversee it personally, having the final say on just how awful this would be. It stuck in my throat that I could end up playing such a fundamental part in her tactless and degrading show, winning her the award she so desperately coveted.

I would never work for that horrible excuse for a human again.

Gathering some resolve, I stood up and robotically moved to my room, gathering up the luggage I'd never unpacked after the heartbreak of knowing he'd spent a night of passion with Jess.

No one helped me carry it down the stairs. Carson and Doug the camera guy followed on like bloodthirsty leeches, desperate for more heartbreak and despair. It was truly degrading. I knew these people. We'd worked together for a while now, but that didn't stop them reveling in my sadness.

Clint was the only one who showed any compassion. As I arrived at the limo, Brody was still at my side, following me round like he could somehow stop me leaving. The guy who had shared his dinner with me came and took my belongings before helping me into the back of the car.

The last thing I heard was Kade's voice coming towards the entrance, shouting in panic for Brody. Of the two of them, the animal and the human, the pet was the one with whom I could most associate. It had always been that way for me. Human nature always let me down; animals didn't.

The last thing I saw before closing the limo door was Kade rushing forward and pushing the camera team to one side. My heart started to beat again, hoping and praying that he'd finally seen sense and decided to walk from the show and come with me, but that wasn't the case.

He ignored the limo as Clint turned over the engine.

He ignored Doug the cameraman as he warred between following my departure filming what Kade was up to.

And he ignored me, never once looking in my direction, only concentrating on his dog who was steadfast in his efforts to try to follow me out of this hellhole.

Chapter 38

KADE SUTTON

Five Weeks Later

Well, this was it, my final day in that fucking hellhole of a prison. Luxurious it might have been, but it was still a prison and my cellmates weren't murderers, thieves or rapists but a bunch of vacuous, materialistic women.

I hated it there. I hated what the show had made me do. Okay, so everything I'd done, I'd done for Daisy but I'd still allowed myself to be bullied and manipulated by Meredith. If I'd been any sort of man, I'd have stood up to the fucking bitch and supported Daisy through the shit storm, but I hadn't. I'd gone with my heart's reaction to her plan. I couldn't let Daisy be hurt so had conceded to Meredith's manipulations. In hindsight, I realized that if that film had got out, the studio would have been in huge trouble. We'd all signed contracts that agreed no sex scenes would be filmed, and they'd reneged on that. They'd broken an official contract. There was no way she could leak that footage and she damn well knew it. Meredith had been at her manipulative best and fooled me because my heart, my feelings, and my love for Daisy were clouding my judgment.

It was almost a week after Daisy had left when I realized Meredith couldn't show the film and demanded a meeting with her. I told her that I was leaving and where she could shove her damn show, but she had me again. She agreed that the studio couldn't film the sex scenes, so she had no problem whatsoever with holding an 'investigation' and laying the blame firmly at Clint's door. I laughed in her face, but then she told me what I'd already guessed—that he was part of the production company so would have had the necessary access. Meredith then told me that her 'investigation' would reveal that he'd sneaked a camera in because he wanted to make some extra money, selling it to the highest bidder. Apparently, we had good viewing figures and were causing a stir with the press, so there'd be plenty of takers. The damn bitch even showed me footage of Clint entering my room with a black backpack that 'obviously had the camera and equipment in it'. It didn't matter that the backpack was mine and the footage was Clint bringing it to me because I'd left it in the limo on the first day. She'd even changed the date stamp on the footage. So, I was royally screwed. If I walked, two good people would be hurt by my actions and I couldn't do that.

Today, though, I would finally be free. I had one last pick to make—who I would date for the next six months.

Thankfully, the public had taken a shine to Jess, so a lot of my nights over the last five weeks had been spent with her. Meredith didn't dare to risk rigging every vote. She wasn't that stupid. A couple of nights had been with other random girls who had done something during the day to catch the public's eye, but for the vast majority I'd had to choose between Jess and Honey. If Honey was in the pick, Meredith had sent a message of who should be picked, like I needed to be told.

Now here we were, just Jess, Honey and me left in the

house and it seemed empty and cold. Hell, it had seemed empty and cold since the day Daisy had walked out of it. That had been the worst night of my life. Telling her she was being evicted and seeing her try to be brave, while I knew she was breaking inside, had felt like my heart was being crushed by my own hand. I couldn't look at her because I knew if I did, I'd break—I'd beg her to stay, tell her that I was falling in love with her and fuck the consequences. I knew my face was hard and emotionless, but that was the only way I could get through what I had to do.

If that hadn't been bad enough, when Carson, the evil bastard, showed me the footage of her falling to the ground, it didn't just crush my heart, it fucking obliterated it to tiny pieces that pierced every part of me.

"You ready?" Sam one of the runners asked, poking his head around my bedroom door.

I blew out a deep breath and nodded. "Yep, as I'll ever be," I said, straightening the designer tie I was wearing with the crisp white shirt and perfectly cut midnight blue suit I'd been instructed to wear.

"Oh, and Meredith said you've to pick-"

"Honey, yeah, I know."

"Actually, no," Sam said, sounding a little shocked. "You're to pick Jess."

My eyes widened as I stared at him.

"Are you sure?"

"That's what she said," he replied with a shrug and a shake of the head. "I'll see you down there."

"Thanks, Sam," I said distractedly, wondering what on Earth Meredith's game was. She'd been championing Honey all along, so why was she changing her allegiance now, at the final pick.

While I was glad it was Jess I would be spending time with over the next six months, something didn't feel right. My gut was telling me that this shit storm was far from over.

227

Tonight, the show was live, which considering Honey wasn't going to be picked, was a brave decision. I wasn't sure her reaction would be totally sane. It was Meredith's funeral, though, and she'd evidently decided it was worth the risk. I personally would have been worried about tonight's set, which they'd obviously shelled out some major cash on.

My seat for tonight looked like a real, honest to God, throne. It was gold and jeweled, with real thick red velvet cushioning, and next to it was a smaller version, evidently for my chosen one, and leading up to them was a lush red carpet. Fairy lights had been strung all around the place, along with huge, badass fire lanterns. The pool held hundreds of lit candles and lilies floating in it, and on the patio were red velvet high-backed chairs, for all the original contestants who were returning for tonight. Yeah, I'd already asked Clint if Daisy had been with the girls when they'd arrived earlier in the day, but he shook his head and walked away. Clint loved Daisy, and he was as fucked off with me as I was. He had no idea what hold Meredith had over me. All he could see was that I'd fucked Daisy over.

No matter, I thought. As soon as it was possible, I'd be going to find her and tell her the truth. I'd tell her how I felt, that she was fucking mine and that I couldn't be without her a minute longer. I just hoped that she was on board with that.

Sitting on my throne after being primped and pampered over by hair and make-up, we were ready to start. There was a drum roll and then some fancy ass classical music was played, which if I remembered correctly from my college days was called 'Pomp & Circumstance', and on to the patio walked our host for the evening, Daniel Driscoll. He'd once been a real heavyweight in the TV hosting game, but after hosting an episode of American Rock Star while drunk, he'd been sacked, falling very quickly from grace.

"Hey, everyone," he smarmed to the camera, flashing glowing white teeth against his orange skin. "How ya all doin' tonight? So, it's the big night, ladies and gentleman. The night that Kade gets to pick his true love…"

It was at that point that I tuned out, dropping my hand down to my side to feel for Brody, my trusted buddy, who I knew would be there, and he was, lifting his head for me to ruffle his ears. I instantly calmed and watched the show playing out in a daze. Daniel introduced all of the ex-contestants, making no mention whatsoever of Daisy's absence—that much I did notice—and then he explained what would happen. I would pick Jess or Honey and we would date for six months.

The drum roll started again, and out walked the two ladies in question. Jess looked sexy but demure as she sashayed in on black and silver sandals. She was wearing a black, knee length dress that clung to her body but had a killer neckline that was slashed almost to her naval. Her hair was a little fuller than usual and her make-up was smoky eyes with rose pink lips, and she looked really pretty. Then there was Honey, and what could I say about her, other than she looked like a cheap tart? Her gold dress just about covered both her ass and nipples, and when she turned to wave to her bevvy of blondes, I could see her ass crack. Her shoes were the same color as the dress, and would have looked more at home wrapped around a pole in a club. Her hair was even blonder than usual and her lips were covered in the same red lipstick that she'd used on my body—the lipstick that I now fucking hated. I could not believe she was here in the final two. How did the public keep voting for her? But then, of course, the vote had been 'helped' by Meredith who, I was led to believe, was in the gallery directing things, which must have pissed Carson right off.

Finally, Daniel turned to me and gave me my cue.

"Okay, ladies," I said, forcing a smile. "We've had a

long journey, but we're finally here at our destination."

Fuck, who the hell wrote this fucking shit script, some five-year-old?

"So, before we disembark this train of love, I need to let one last person off."

As instructed, I paused for effect and for the girls on the patio to 'ooh' and 'aah'. Then a sound like a heartbeat echoed around, adding to the tension. I tried to look contemplative, shaking my head and looking from one girl to another. Finally, Doug my cameraman gave me the thumbs up. The heartbeat stopped and I stood up.

"Tonight, I evict..." I paused for ten seconds. "...Honey."

There were gasps from all the blondes. The brunettes and redheads cheered and Jess gasped. Honey shocked me. She smiled sadly, hugged Jess and then gave me a little wave and blew me a kiss. That was it, and then she walked over to the patio to be engulfed in a group yellow-haired hug. What the hell had happened to her? Had she been given a sedative of some kind?

Looking back at Jess, I smiled and gave her a wink. She was a nice girl, and if I had to be with anyone over the next six months then I was glad it was her.

"Well congratulations, Jess," Daniel shouted over the melee of noise. "But before I let your prince get his hands on you, there is a little question I need to ask you."

Jess and I both looked startled. This wasn't anything that we'd rehearsed or been told was going to happen. Jess looked at me nervously and I shrugged as Daniel slowly walked towards her.

"Jess, you know that Kade here is a very rich man," he said in a serious tone. "And we know you've spent a lot of quality time with him over the last six weeks." He winked at the camera with a stupid grin, hinting at what had gone on in my room, and I really wanted to push the stupid jackass in the pool. Daisy may have been watching, and he wasn't helping my prospects of winning her back.

"Yes," Jess whispered, dipping her head to speak into his microphone, obviously forgetting that we were each wearing a radio mic.

"So, if I were to ask you to choose his love or his money, what would you pick?"

"I'm sorry?" she asked, confused.

I, however, wasn't. They were going to let her pick between dating me or taking some money, and somehow they were going to fuck with her. That was why Meredith told me I had to pick Jess. But if she took the money, that worked out for both of us. We wouldn't have to date. I'd be totally free to go after Daisy, and Jess would have a nice lump sum to help her go to acting school, her dream. So what the fuck was the catch?

"You can stick to the plan," Daniel said sweetly, "and date Kade for the next six months, which may or may not work out, or he will personally give you half a million dollars."

The gasps from the girls echoed in the stillness of the evening.

"Pick Kade," Natalie shouted.

"Take the darn money, sugar." That was Poppy.

Then all the other girls joined in, shouting out their preferred choice. I looked at Jess and something told me that while it wasn't great for me, she should pick me. Something was really off about this deal. Looking at her, though, I instinctively knew she was going to pick the money. Her lips were turned into a sad smile, and her eyes told me that this was a brilliant offer for both of us.

On that first night, nothing had happened between Jess and me other than a little kissing. We'd realized pretty much straightaway that there was just no chemistry there. I'd picked her because she reminded me of Daisy, but she wasn't her, and I just couldn't bring myself to try to pretend otherwise. So, I'd taken Jess into the bathroom, turned on the shower to drown out any microphones outside my room, and told her everything—well almost everything. I didn't tell her that I wasn't rich. I couldn't risk Meredith finding out that Jess knew and kicking her off the show. I did tell her that I really liked Daisy and just couldn't think of anyone else. Jess sighed with relief because she'd realized, too, that my kisses just didn't do it for her. So we agreed that whenever I could, if I couldn't pick Daisy, I'd pick her. I also told her that if she got to the final, she would be my pick. That way, I would be able to see Daisy, and that I'd give her some money. I just hoped that I made some from the show, not being the millionaire that she thought I was. Jess had laughed and said the viewers would realize that Daisy and I were meant to be together and Daisy would be in that final. I hadn't risked telling her that Daisy would *never* be allowed to be in the final. Jess didn't need to know what Meredith was up to, and the more I could keep from her the better. On every night I picked Jess, we played cards and talked until I made a bed on the floor and we fell asleep. I just wished the nights with the other girls had been so easy.

As Jess took a deep breath, my thoughts were suddenly back on the game.

"I'm sorry, Kade," she said in a timid voice. "But I'm going to take the money."

My heart sank as I heard Meredith's distinctive voice cry 'yes', realizing that she'd come down from the makeshift gallery in one of the bedrooms to witness this. That 'yes' confirmed to me that Jess was indeed about to be stitched up.

With groans and cheers from the ex-contestants, I flopped back onto my throne and waited for the sucker punch. It wasn't long in coming.

"You definitely choose the money?" Daniel asked.

Jess nodded and glanced over at me before turning her attention back to Daniel.

"Okay, so Jess chooses the money, folks, but you the viewers have seen Kade here," he turned and pointed at me, "living in this luxurious house with all its beauty and splendor. You've witnessed his household staff waiting on him, and you've seen his expensive clothes and the way he lives his life."

Fuck, I suddenly knew what they were going to do.

I stood up and took a step towards Daniel and Jess, only to feel Carson's hand on my arm.

"Don't!" he snapped. "It's her choice, and if you stop this, Meredith will do what she threatened."

I swung around to see him sneering at me. Gone was the suck up, pouty face he usually pulled when he wanted me to do something. I was no longer of any use. I was back to being Kade Sutton, homeless person.

"What you, and all the viewers don't know," Daniel continued, "is that Kade Sutton is *not* a millionaire playboy…"

He paused as everyone gasped.

"He is, in fact, Kade Sutton, homeless person."

It was a drop the mic moment. Daniel stepped back, crossed his arms over his chest, and watched as everyone dropped into silence and turned their stares to me.

"Kade?" Jess whispered.

I dropped my head, unable to meet her gaze. I wasn't ashamed of who I was, but I was ashamed that my friend had been made to look a fool on network television.

The girls all went crazy, crying out words like 'cheat', 'bastard' and 'fake', while I heard Natalie shout, "Way to go, Kade." I always did like her.

Finally, Jess pulled her shoulders back and walked to Daniel. "That's okay," she said. "He's a really nice guy and I'll always think of him as a friend."

My gut twisted for her. She was a sweet kid, but it didn't matter what she thought of me. There was no way she was going to be getting anything out of this, and I doubted she'd even want my friendship at the end of it. Daniel then confirmed what I suspected.

"The problem is, Jess, you chose Kade's personal gift, the money, and that means that, unfortunately, you go away from here tonight with nothing."

"N-nothing?" she stammered.

"Nope, nothing, nada, zilch, zero." Daniel tried to sound apologetic, but the smug bastard couldn't contain the little grin on his stupid Botox-filled lips. "Kade, has nothing to give you but that friendship you said you'll always have. So, Jess, thank you for taking part but we now have to evict you, too."

The hysteria that broke out was of epic proportions. A couple of girls tried to get to me. The nails were out and ready to do damage, and they had to be held back by two burly security men. Natalie was comforting Jess. Honey and Vanessa were holding court with a couple of other blondes. Everyone else was either shouting and pointing at me, or openly laughing at Jess for being so greedy.

"Let's go, Kade," Clint said, suddenly appearing at my side. "We need to get you into the house."

"Clint, I had no idea they were going to do this," I cried as he and a security guy led me away.

"You say so, Kade," he growled.

"I swear. I wouldn't have agreed to this."

"Just get into the house. Brody, come on guy," he said, urging Brody to follow us.

"Please, Clint, there are things you don't know." I hated that this man had no respect for me. I had so much for him, and loved that he'd looked after my girl when she was upset. Fuck, my girl! I just hoped that was still possible. She would know that this was Meredith's doing, and I just hoped that she realized her eviction had been, too.

As Clint silently led me back to the house, I looked over to take a final look at the crap going on around me, when movement in the shadows of the gazebo caught my eye.

"Just a second," I hissed to Clint, and moved away towards the figures.

Standing behind a trellis that had some plant growing

up it, I could see that it was Meredith and Honey.

"Here you go," Meredith said, passing Honey what looked like a check. "Three hundred thousand dollars that will go down as household expenses for this place." She gave a throaty laugh and hugged Honey to her.

"Thanks, Mom," Honey said, reading the check over Meredith's shoulder. "I'm just glad it's over. It's been an awful nightmare."

"I know, sweetheart. Now, go before someone notices you're missing. I've lined up an interview for you tomorrow, so lay it on thick about your nights of passion with the homeless guy."

Honey giggled. "I will, Mom. Don't you worry. You still have the footage of them?"

"Oh yeah," Meredith replied. "And I'll use it if I have to."

Everything stopped—my heart, the blood running through my veins, time, everything. She'd fucked us all, over and over again, and was going to continue to do so. This nightmare would not end tonight.

Chapter 39

NICHOLAS KING

"Oh my God," my daughter Claudia cried. "I can't believe it."

"What's that, honey?" Elizabeth, my wife, asked, coming into the room and sitting next to me on the sofa.

"That guy on the show I've been watching, he's a homeless guy. He's not rich at all."

"He's sooo hot." Brittany, Claudia's friend sighed.

I shook my head, not looking up from my newspaper. "I have no idea why you watch such rubbish," I grumbled.

"It's not rubbish, Daddy. It's really good."

"What the hell is it called anyway?"

I looked up at the screen to see some poor girl crying into the arms of another.

"I Wanna Get Laid By Kade," Elizabeth said on a sigh. "And before you say anything, you don't see any sex."

"So you've watched every episode with them?" I asked wryly, letting out a laugh when I saw a guilty blush on my beautiful wife's face. "You damn well like it, don't you?"

She gave me a coy smile and turned back to the TV.

"Kade doesn't look happy, does he?" Claudia cried.

I looked up to see what had her so excited, and almost choked as the face of Kade appeared on the screen.

"My God," I muttered. "He looks like Noah."

The face in front of me could have been my son. This Kade boy was a little darker and had longer hair, but they could have almost been twins.

"I know," Elizabeth agreed. "I think that's why Brittany likes the show so much, hey, Brit?"

"Mrs. King!" she gasped, but there was no disguising the blush in her cheeks.

"Ooh listen, Daniel's going to say something." Claudia shushed us all and leaned closer to the TV.

"So, I think that the byline of this show, not to judge a book by its cover, has been well and truly proven to be true. All these women flirted, plotted and tricked just to be the one who was picked to date Kade Sutton, playboy millionaire, when all along he was actually a homeless man we took from the streets. Kade Sutton, the only son of the late Shelby Sutton."

Elizabeth's head shot around and she stared at me wide-eyed.

"Nick? Do you think..?"

I didn't hear anything after that because I knew she was right. That was my son.

KADE SUTTON

Clint smuggled Brody and me out of the mansion that night.

The press were already there, braying for their first sighting of the new millionaire couple. Never did they expect to get the information Daniel Dickhead delivered during the final show. Those who had secured a slot close to the live outside TV feeds were being well rewarded for turning up early.

The temptation to expose Meredith and Honey was extreme, but I let sense kick in and decided to save that little nugget of information for another time. That witch Hennessey had shown the lengths to which she was prepared to go on numerous occasions, and I needed something to fight back with. I'd had enough of laying myself wide open. It was time I did what these fuckers did. I had to fight fire with fire.

After all, I still had to get my money out of her.

And I would. She could go fuck herself if she thought she was screwing me out of a second chance at living a respectable life. How respectable that could be after the deception I'd just been a part of was anyone's guess.

When I left the house of horror, Brody and I were hustled into the back of a minivan surrounded by kit and equipment. The girls were the unlucky ones. They went in the limos, and it was them who got all the media attention.

Clint was huffing and puffing about how the reaction to the news of me being a poor street dweller had been worse than they'd expected. I knew how he felt. I was still getting over it all, too. When I agreed to do this, I never really thought about the innocent girls who were being duped in front of millions for the entertainment of others. It was cruel. It was a small, simple word but it carried so much depth of feeling and gravity. I knew that what I'd just done was cruel. I'd intentionally hurt a lot of people.

After a couple of hours, Clint pulled up at a house in the 'burbs somewhere and swung the rear doors open, bathing Brody and me in moonlight. My pal wasn't one for being cooped up in a moving metal box, so he leapt out with wild abandon and began to search our new surroundings.

"You can crash here with me for a few nights until you get yourself sorted."

Though he'd offered, I could tell he wasn't happy about it.

"I… I… I don't know what to say. Thanks, man."

Clint dragged a suitcase out from under one of the boxes. "I can't believe I was part of that disgraceful shit storm back there. Consider this my good deed. Just because you came in with   nothing doesn't mean you have to leave with nothing. I packed your clothes," he finished, putting the case at my feet and inserting a key into the lock on the door.

"Oh, I'll get something. I plan on getting everything that fucking bitch owes me."

Grabbing my case, I followed him into the house.

"Bathroom is at the end of the hall, and your room is that door on the left." He pointed. "Mine is this end.

Kitchen and living room will be obvious."

Brody had decided to come and investigate inside now. "Bet you never thought you'd be giving me two house tours."

Clint ignored my remark and wandered off. He looked exhausted. "I'm gonna grab a beer. There's some soda in the chiller, too, if you want one?" As he ambled in the direction of the kitchen, his cell phone started to ring. "Yeah?" he said on answering.

Immediately, he put his finger to his lips, indicating I needed to be quiet.

"No, I didn't take him anywhere. I got out of that nuthouse."

At the worst possible time, Brody barked, causing us all to freeze.

"Yes, I have the dog. I wasn't going to leave him there to fend for himself."

The screeching from the other end of the phone confirmed my suspicions. Meredith was on the warpath.

"He'll turn up." I watched as Clint tried to placate the raging evil on the end of the line before hanging up.

"Guess she's thought of something else I can do for her," I mumbled, shaking my head."

Clint popped the lid of his beer and threw a *Sprite* at me.

"I fucking hated what you did to that poor girl, but when you've come from the streets, I can understand the lure of having more than nothing for a change."

I dumped the soda can on the counter top. This guy had offered me somewhere to crash yet still thought the worst of me. People with even the smallest amount of money and security always assumed that those with absolutely none also had no morals or standards. My lack of possessions didn't automatically mean I had no compassion or human nature.

"You know what, Clint, thanks for the offer of a roof, but I'll take my chances outside. Brody, let's go."

As we made it to the door we'd only just been welcomed through, he stopped me.

"You see that, that right there is what doesn't make sense. You screw her over and carry on, yet right now, you're prepared to walk away. What's your deal?"

It knew it was time to let someone in. I had a lot swirling around in my head. It felt like I was trying to boil the ocean when in reality, all I wanted was what was owed me and a chance to make it up to Daisy.

"I know what that night did to her. I had to take her home and she was in pieces, man. Her dad had to carry her inside her place. She was so upset she didn't even have the strength to walk."

Visualizing that scene was too much. If she never forgave me, I'd understand. I deserved to live in my own version of hell after Cory, but adding to it with Daisy was just another version of the purgatory I would go through while I was still on this earth.

"Tell me what's going on," Clint urged.

"Fuck. Having that one night with Daisy meant so much to me. It was perfect. Seriously, that girl had seen me at my worst. Hell, she fucking fed me and Brody for months. The last person I came across with her level of compassion was my foster mom. They could have been made from the same mould. Daisy was already freaked out because I'd spent the night with Jess."

Clint was mid-swig of his beer when he coughed and spluttered. "Freaked out? I picked up the pieces after that night, too. She was already in deep by then, my friend."

The information to condemn my soul to the fiery pits of hell just kept racing at me.

"Nothing happened with Jess. We kissed and it felt more like kissing a sister, so we struck a deal. She was going to be my get-out clause. I couldn't tell Daisy that, though. I sorta promised Jess. Shit, I only picked her because she looked like Daisy. The next morning, I couldn't get Daisy to speak to me so I threatened Carson.

That's how I ended up spending the night with her."

Clint's frame became alert then. "You mean you threatened Meredith?"

When I nodded at him, he looked incensed. "Fuck, Kade, why not put a rattlesnake in a box, shake it up and open the lid?"

"Cutting a long story short, Meredith showed me some footage of me and Daisy. Intimate footage. I couldn't risk that getting out in public. Then you became the icing on the ca-"

"Me?" he interrupted.

"Yeah, she'd doctored the camera feed from when you dropped my luggage off, made it look like you'd installed a secret camera. She was gonna hang you out to dry, too. I couldn't have her taking everyone down, so I did what was necessary, evicted Daisy and continued."

When I began my confession, Brody came inside and planted himself on top of my feet. He knew that if I didn't have some form of barrier, I would have quit and walked away sooner. I was looking down at him, contemplating his prowess and human intuition when Clint slammed his bottle in the sink, making both my dog and me jump.

"Like I said—viper. And she always needs to have the last laugh."

"She does," I agreed. "But I'm tired and I just want to get my money and make amends with Daisy."

Clint shrugged and accepted my plan for the immediate future. I retrieved the unopened soda can and turned for my bedroom. "One other thing," I said, stopping, remembering what else I'd seen. "Besides me, Daisy and the production crew, did you know anyone else in the house?"

He looked at me, unsure where I was going, but replied anyway, "No, the house team were all recruited on the understanding that you were a genuine rich guy. Less chance of an exposé being released to the paps. Why?"

"Did you know Meredith had a kid?" I watched very

closely for his reaction. This was the moment when my street smarts would tell me whether I could really trust him.

"That dried up old bitch? I've seen more juice in a shriveled up raisin. Meredith Hennessey was hatched in a lab. God should have made it a rule to never allow it to procreate in order to stop the evil at source."

It shouldn't have made me laugh, but it did. It was fucking hilarious.

"Well she does and I intend to use it to my advantage. That shriveled up raisin will not have the last word on this."

The next morning, Clint left for work early. A small note scrawled on the back of an old electricity bill told me he'd be back later and I was free to just hang out.

Hang out?

This wasn't a fucking holiday. I had my life to sort out. I had Daisy to win back, and let's face it, any hours, minutes or even seconds where I wasn't doing everything possible to make that right were just wasted time.

First things first, I wanted Meredith to understand that I wasn't going to cower away just because she'd blown up my apparent none-existence and poor Jess' life just because she was chasing some meaningless award.

I showered and put on some of the clothes Clint had had the forethought to pack for me, and after helping myself to a little dry toast, I wandered outside to see where the hell I was. We'd arrived like stowaways, and I was praying that we weren't too far to walk. A quick assessment of the surroundings and the bus stop at the end of his road told me there were a few miles between me and the network's office building, so we got moving.

I had lots of time during that walk to think about everything that had gone down, to think about how I was going to turn this around and live with the experience. I could easily rebel against the system and go back to the streets but it felt like such a waste all of a sudden. Living rough was once a necessity and then it became a choice, a clear way to force me into suffering for the bad choices I'd made and the life I'd taken as a result. I could still feel all that remorse and suffering with four walls and a roof over my head.

Brody and I easily ate up the miles, and it felt almost calming to be at one with the fresh air and to feel the concrete beneath my feet. With nothing but the clothes on my back, I carried on because if I didn't get what I wanted from Meredith, I was going to create holy hell and then simply go back to fending for myself with my best friend.

My plan was simple—get my money, get a little place, sort things out with Daisy and then enrich my life somehow.

When the office block loomed, I saw the huge billboard on the side of the building come into view with my face on it. It was like looking in a mirror in a funhouse, huge and out of proportion with the real me. My small glimmer of hope that no one had watched the show was dashed as I saw a man on a set of stepladders pasting a big sign across the bottom. He was brushing at it with a huge yard brush he kept dipping in and out of a bucket. Leaning across the street, I waited until he was finished and knew my hopes of it being a failure were wasted.

'Nominated for Best Show, People's Reality TV Awards 2016.'

I hated that I had been a part of something that would bring Meredith Hennessey fame, fortune and industry praise. So often in life, the light at the end of the tunnel was either freedom or a speeding train. Choosing the former told me this was my break. With an award up for grabs, the threat of what I knew was even greater to her.

Finally, I had the upper hand.

"Brody, come on, buddy. Let's do this." I smiled and he barked in return.

The building's entrance was under siege. Everyone seemed desperate to get the first glimpse of last night's aftermath. There was even a woman sitting on the floor doing a newsfeed from my usual begging spot. It was tasteless and vile.

"Kade, do you regret duping the public and those poor girls?" one shouted.

"Kade, just a few quick words about what it was like to go from rags to riches," another piped in.

"Kade, have you heard *Playgirl* magazine are offering you a million dollars to do a centerfold?"

The cameras kept rolling as I pushed them aside so Brody wouldn't get trampled on, and the light bulbs were flashing so much I was starting to see blurry spots by the time I battled into the building's reception area. Fortunately, security were on the ball and no one was able to follow me in.

"Mr. Sutton for Meredith Hennessy," I said, standing in front of a wide-eyed slip of a girl who seemed in awe of my presence.

"Uh… ah… um… one moment," she blustered before picking up the phone and hissing that Kade Sutton was in the building like some fan girl on speed.

"Her assistant will be down to collect you."

Those words were like rainbows and sunshine to my ears. I was finally going to see Daisy after all these weeks. I watched the elevator doors, not even daring to blink in case I missed her. People went up and down and Daisy never appeared. Brody sat facing the main entrance, seemingly bothered by the activity outside, until a pinch nosed blonde appeared in front of me.

"Kade, Meredith will see you now."

This wasn't Daisy.

Disappointment was growing inside me as we rode the

elevator together and the nameless face stared at me, putting me in a really bad mood.

"Is there something wrong?" I finally asked, not hiding the irritation from my voice.

"Not at all, just wondering what all the fuss is about." She shrugged nonchalantly.

"Yeah, you think? That makes two of us," I grumbled, following her through a maze of cubicles littered with people working on PCs.

She guided me to a seat outside the office door with the bitch's name on, indicating I should wait for Meredith. Brody got waylaid somewhere en route and caught up with me eventually. When I sat down in the chair, I saw Daisy's name plate on a desk in front of me. It was like a punch to the gut, finally realizing that she wasn't here. The desk didn't look occupied by anyone apart from piles of paper, junk mail and old coffee cups. It was clear that Daisy hadn't been here since the left to do the show.

What the fuck had I done to that girl? She hadn't even come back to work.

The longer I sat outside that office, faced with that empty, desolate desk, the angrier I became.

"Fuck this!" I shouted and stormed into Meredith's office.

The manipulative bitch was sat on the phone with her feet on the desk, laughing about something, which didn't improve my disposition.

"I've come for my money."

"One moment," she said in my direction, attempting to go back to her inane conversation. My life was literally up in the air and she wanted me to give her a moment? No chance. I strode across her office and disconnected the call for her.

"I've come for my money."

The smile that graced her face was one of satisfaction. "It's been nice doing business with you, Kade. You see these flowers?" She gestured to the window ledges, which were filled with vases. "All from industry peers, congratulating me on a job well done. I'm a shoe-in for that TV award."

"I don't give a fuck about that. Check. Now."

I stood wide legged with intent, crossing my arms across my chest, letting her know I meant business. She needed to know that I was going nowhere until I got what I was due. Sensing my seriousness, she opened a desk drawer and threw an envelope across the desk at me.

"Unfortunately, there were some business expenses, so I've deducted them from your fee."

The skin on this dragon was impenetrable. Even though she'd got what she wanted, she was still trying to screw me over. Ripping the envelope open, I saw that she wasn't lying. It was short by three hundred grand.

"Interesting," I began, heading towards the flowered vases, picking up the cards and reading them. Keeping hold of the first one I recognized, I walked over to the conference table in her office and picked up the handset, pressing zero for the switchboard.

"Yes, Ms. Hennessey?" said a voice.

"It's Kade Sutton here. Could you get Ms. Hennessey Kurt Sander's assistant on the phone? We're going to do a live radio interview."

"One moment," the helpful girl replied cheerily, and Meredith's face took on a panic stricken edge.

"What the fuck are you doing, Kade?" she growled, standing up behind her desk.

"Just letting your industry peers in to a few specifics," I replied, covering the mouthpiece. "You know, the scoop stuff—manipulating me, a poor homeless guy, putting one of your own assistants in the mansion under false pretenses, and vote rigging." Her demeanor changed as I carried on. "Oh, breach of contracts, and here's the best one. Wait, hang on." I paused for effect, listening to the switchboard operator. "They're hooking me into the live broadcast after the next commercial. Oh yeah, where was

I? Fraud. Ripping off the network to pay your own daughter three hundred grand of my money. Such heinous acts, some would say criminal."

Meredith Hennessey's skin palette went from flushed upper hand to pale and panicky in a nanosecond. She was so desperate to get to me that she stumbled and struck her shin on a coffee table.

"Fuck!" she roared. "Hang up the call. I'll pay!" I looked at her, trying not to laugh because no matter how hard she rubbed at her shinbone, the bruise was inevitable. "Didn't you hear me? I'll get accounts to write you a new check now."

"You do that because if I have to threaten this shit again, it will be a live TV interview, followed by your own interview at the Sheriff's office."

"Alright! Alright!"

I dumped the phone call and sat my ass on the edge of the conference table, keeping my eye on her as she walked to her door and bellowed at Lydia to call accounts and get an additional check. In an act of sheer bloody mindedness, she proceeded to tell her off for not getting the correct amount in the first place.

Fifteen minutes later, I had a new check in my hand and was ready to leave. "Did you fire Daisy?"

"No. She hasn't returned since the eviction night."

"Where is she?" I had to try to find out.

"Fuck you, Kade Sutton. You don't come in here, hold me to ransom and then expect me to give you information. I don't know or care where she is. Her shit is still in her desk and she hasn't picked up her final pay packet."

I wasn't going to get anything out of her. I'd just bested her. "Brody, let's roll."

Daisy's absence at the final show was expected but not seeing her here was really concerning me. She'd fallen off the face of the earth since I'd broken her heart. Fucking around with Meredith was a great distraction, and honestly, made me feel a tiny bit better, but I got one of the things I came for and being persona non-grata with a check and no checking account presented me with another challenge.

I ignored everyone as I wandered back through the office, building up the courage to face the press outside. They knew I was in the building so there was no way they would have left. The only thing I could do right now was head back to Clint's place and plan my next move as well as figuring out how to track Daisy down.

As I pushed and shoved my way through the cameras and radio mics that had doubled in number since my arrival, I decided to give them something to keep them occupied.

"Ladies and gentleman, thank you for your support during the filming of the show. I am under instruction not to conduct any interviews, but Meredith Hennessy has advised she will be down in the building foyer shortly and is happy to take questions."

Like the inconsequential homeless person I was, they were tempted by something more sparkly and took the bait. They all pretty much spun around on the spot and continued their information vigil, deciding she was the better scoop.

I was laughing at my own ingenuity as Brody and I wandered down the sidewalk, when a black town car pulled up alongside me. "Mr. Sutton, could I have a moment of your time?"

Okay, so maybe I hadn't managed to ditch them all. "No."

The officious looking thin guy climbed out of the back wearing the sharpest pinstriped business suit I'd ever seen. The crease pressed down the middle of the pants looked measured and exact. The shine on his shoes could have blinded me had they been reflecting the sun, and his tie was the perfect width and length. "I must insist," he tried again.

"I bet you do." In a moment of madness, the guy paced up beside me and stepped in front of me to get my attention. "You have three seconds to say your piece or get the fuck out of my way."

The guy looked wide-eyed and flustered. "Shelby Sutton!"

The name fell from his lips in a flash, like a throat punch.

"I beg your pardon." I leaned in to him, unimpressed.

"I represent King Enterprises and I've been instructed to contact you about Shelby Sutton, your late mother, I believe." When I didn't answer him, he looked at me puzzled. "Are you not Kade Nicholas Sutton?"

"Keep. Talking," I growled and watched as he swallowed, clearly afraid of me.

"I've been asked to bring you to our head office. I am not at liberty to discuss this on the street. Would you be so kind as to follow me?"

That was the big question. Would I?

Chapter 41

KADE SUTTON

As the guy waved for the town car to move forward, his expectant eyes remained on me.

"Mr. Sutton?"

The car idled next to us and I let out a long sigh. "Okay, as long as my dog is invited."

"I was told specifically to bring Brody with us, Sir."

The fact that he knew Brody's name caused me to pause, but then I remembered that every part of me had been laid bare to millions of viewers over the last few weeks, and my buddy was a big part of me.

"Do I get any hint as to what this is about?" I asked, walking towards the car.

"As I said, Sir, I'm not at liberty to say. I can tell you that my name is Maxwell, Maxwell Charter."

He held out his hand to me, so I took it and gave it a firm shake.

"Nice to meet you, Maxwell." Then, with a little trepidation, I got inside the car with Brody jumping in after me.

We drove for around twenty minutes, going deeper into the city towards the business district where the skyline was taller, sleeker and shinier. People were rushing along the sidewalks, each and every one of them either talking into a cell phone or tapping away at some sort of electronic device. I may have had a shit few years living on the streets, but believe me I would not have swapped it with these people for anything. Well I might if it meant I could have Daisy.

Finally, we pulled to a stop and Maxwell laid a hand on my shoulder to indicate that we'd arrived. I looked out through the car window, up towards the sky. I had no idea what King Enterprises did, but from the look of the building, I gathered it was pretty lucrative because it was one of the most sleek and shiny buildings of the lot.

"Just out of interest," I said to Maxwell, "what do King Enterprises do?"

"They do lots of things, Mr. Sutton, but Mr. King's main business is acquisitions."

I nodded. "Hence why they do lots of things."

"That would be correct. Now, if you'd like to follow me."

Brody and I trailed behind Maxwell as he smiled and nodded at the burly security man who held the door open for him. Maxwell's smart leather shoes and Brody's claws clipping across the marble floor were the only sounds in the vast foyer. A reception desk sat to the left of a bank of three glass elevators, and behind it was a pretty, dark-haired girl wearing spectacles. At first glance, I thought she was Daisy, and my heart lurched.

"Morning, Tiff," Maxwell said with a wave of his hand.

I gave her a quick smile and sighed when I realized she was nowhere near as beautiful as my Daisy.

"Morning, Mr. Charter," she replied cheerfully. "Mr. King has just arrived."

"Thank you," he replied, pressing the button for the elevator.

As we waited, Brody sniffed and licked at my hand by my side, trying to reassure me in his own way, and boy did I need it. A few seconds later, the elevator pinged and the door slid open. Maxwell ushered us in, following behind and pressing the button for the twenty-first floor.

We had to be in the quickest damn elevator on the planet because it appeared to take just a few seconds to reach our destination. Maxwell led the way, and as I looked at my surroundings, I was impressed. For an office building, this was real nice. The carpet under my feet was so thick that I almost lost sight of my feet in it, and there were two huge, expensive looking, brown leather couches either side of a mahogany coffee table. On one wall was a line of paintings, not prints but actual paintings, and each was individually lit. Opposite them, under the wall of brilliantly clean windows, was a mahogany side table with a coffee jug bubbling away and various plates of cakes and pastries that looked even better than those we'd been served in the mansion. Facing the elevator was a huge mahogany desk with another petite brunette sitting behind it. She wasn't wearing spectacles, but I still couldn't help thinking of Daisy. Shit, was this going to be my life if I didn't find her, my heart being rattled at the sight of every damn small, dark-haired woman I came across? I hoped not, mainly because I was determined that I wouldn't be without her for much longer.

"Hi, Mr. Charter," the girl said as we approached. "He's waiting for you."

"Thanks, Sherilynn."

As we wandered past, Sherilynn leaned forward and gave Brody a stroke.

"Cute dog," she said, smiling up at me.

"Thanks," I replied. "He's a good boy."

She gave him one last scratch behind the ears, and we continued on down a corridor of glass fronted offices until we stopped right at the end, in front of a pair of mahogany and glass doors. Maxwell gave two sharp knocks and then opened the door, walking directly in.

"Morning, Nicholas."

Behind *another* huge ass desk was a man wearing a charcoal grey suit. His greying head was down and he was writing something. As Maxwell spoke, the man I presumed was Mr. King looked up, dropped his pen and pulled off his grey steel framed spectacles. He pushed his chair back, stared at me, and blowing out a breath, raked a hand over his head.

"Thank you, Maxwell," he said quietly, his gaze firmly on me. "I'll let you know if I need you."

Maxwell left silently, clicking the door shut behind him.

"Please sit." He nodded at the black, leather chair. "I see you have Brody with you." His face broke into a huge grin as he held a hand out to my dog.

Brody went over, gave him a lick and then came back to my side. Mr. King stood and reached out his hand to shake mine.

"Nicholas King," he said with a warm smile.

"What's this about?" I asked, lowering myself into the chair.

"Your mother was Shelby Sutton, is that right?"

I bristled at the mention of my mom's name and squirmed in my seat.

"She was, but what does that have to do with you?"

Mr. King leaned forward, putting his elbows on the desk, and looked at the ceiling for a few seconds. He then looked back to me and I was sure there were tears in his eyes.

"Look, what's going on?"

"I guess I may as well just say it," he breathed out. "I think you're my son. Damn it, I know that you're my son."

Chapter 42

KADE SUTTON

The air rushed from my lungs at warp speed as his words registered with my brain. Did he just say I was his son?

"Excuse me?"

He pushed his chair back, and with his arms outstretched, rested his palms on his desk.

"I believe that I am your father, Kade," he replied, his voice quiet and controlled.

"W-what?"

"I know it's a huge shock for you, but I had a relationship with your mother twenty-six years ago."

Shock was putting it mildly.

This wasn't possible.

My mom hated rich people. She'd never have hooked up with a guy who wore suits that cost more than a damn family car.

What the ever loving fuck?

I dragged a hand over my face and left it covering my mouth as I stared at him.

"That's your only reasoning?" I asked. "That you had a relationship with my mom twenty-six years ago. She may have had another guy, one you don't know about."

Tenderness flashed in Mr. King's eyes as he shook his head.

"I don't think so," he replied softly. "Your mom and I, well, what can I say? It was a pretty intense couple of months."

A huge slab of anger pushed at my breastbone. "So damn intense that you left her when she was pregnant?" I snapped. "That much I do know. She said she was pregnant and you left. Other than that, she never spoke of you."

Mr. King blanched. "I never knew, Kade. She didn't tell me, I swear."

To be fair to him, Mom never did say that he knew, just that he left.

"You still split, though. Why?"

Mr. King took a deep breath and reached for a framed photograph on his desk. He picked it up and passed it to me.

"He's the reason why, Kade."

I looked down at the picture of a guy who looked a few years younger than me. I stared at it and drew in a breath. He was a little lighter in coloring than me, but other than that it could have been me. We were identical. The same blue eyes—Mr. King's blue eyes.

"That, Kade, is your brother, Noah," Mr. King said quietly.

I looked up at him and shook my head.

"I don't get it. Why leave Mom because of him? He looks a lot younger than me."

"That picture was taken four years ago," he explained, emotion quaking in his voice. "Noah is twenty-five, just like you. His birthday is January 10th. Yours, I believe, is April 5th. He's just three months older than you."

His words slowly registered as I looked back down at the picture of…my brother!

"Fuck, I have a brother." I drew in a shuddering

breath as I gripped the silver frame tightly. Then my anger rose again. "So, you were fucking around on my mom?"

"No, no I wasn't," Mr. King, *my dad*, cried vehemently. "I was married."

"Oh, and that makes it so much better," I bellowed, throwing the photograph onto his desk. "You were fucking married and had an affair with my mother?"

I pushed my chair back and stood up. Immediately, Brody was at my side, pushing his body against my leg.

Mr. King also stood, reaching a hand towards me.

"Please, Kade. Sit down and let me explain."

"What, let you tell me a load of lies about how your wife didn't understand you and that Mom was a shoulder to cry on? No, I don't think so."

"I swear it wasn't like that," he pleaded. "Just hear me out and then if you're still not happy, you can leave. But, I warn you, now that I know about you and I've found you, I will not be letting you disappear on me."

"Like you have a choice," I snapped. "I have lived on the streets for three years. I know how to be anonymous to everyone around me, so don't think I can't get myself lost in this city, because I can."

Mr. King's shoulders sagged and his face broke into a grimace. "And I am so damn sorry about that, Kade. That you ended up on the streets will be the biggest regret and sadness of my life."

I watched him as he picked up the photograph, lifting it back into place and then lowering himself back into his chair.

"Please, Kade."

With a sigh, I slammed back into the chair and nodded for him to speak.

"My wife and I were having some problems," he started, glancing at another photograph that I could only see the back of. "Things were really bad between us. She was angry all the time, throwing things and lashing out at me. Maybe we should have tried harder, but we were young and idealistic about how our marriage should be, and things were so bad we felt the best thing was to separate. We loved each other, but I just couldn't seem to make her happy, no matter what I did."

"That's when you met Mom?"

"Yes," he said with a reverent smile. "She served me my morning coffee every day for almost a month before we actually spoke. She said something that made me laugh, and I hadn't laughed in a long time. That was your mom, though." He sighed. "She made me laugh every single day that we were together."

He paused and seemed to be taking a moment, pinching the bridge of his nose. He was evidently feeling emotional and I was right there with him. The thought of my mom laughing and making everyone around her laugh was my happiest memory. Even when she was ill and in pain, she tried real hard to be cheerful.

"So what happened?" I asked when he finally let out a long breath.

"We were really happy, your mom and I, really happy. She knew about Elizabeth and that we were separated, and I told her from the beginning that I still loved my wife. Your mom, though, she said we should just take each day as it came and we would end up on whatever path we were meant to be on."

I smiled and shook my head. "She used to say that to me, too."

"Well, she was right about most things so I guess that must be one of them."

"If you were happy with Mom, how come you left?"

Why did you leave my mom and me? Why was your other son more important? They were the questions I wanted to ask, but as soon the thoughts came into my head, they just as quickly disappeared. He'd already said he didn't know about me, and I believed that.

"My wife, called me one day to tell me that she was pregnant. She was crying and said she'd heard that I was happy with Shelby, but she thought that I should know. She also told me that the doctor had said a hormone imbalance caused by the pregnancy had created her mood swings. When I left, she was already three months pregnant but had no idea. You see, she'd suffered from gynecological problems all her adult life; we weren't even sure she could have kids. That was why she had no idea she was pregnant. It was only at four months when she started to show and get other symptoms that she went to the doctor. When she called me, she was already five months gone. I told Shelby straight away, and we carried on seeing each other a little while longer, but we both knew that Elizabeth was who I should be with."

"So you just left?" I snapped.

"No, Kade, it wasn't that easy. I loved your mom, I really did, but I loved my wife more. We had a history. She was my High School sweetheart, and it was tearing me apart. Then I went to pick your mom up one night. We were going to the movies, but she wasn't ready. She just handed me a bag of my stuff I kept at her place and told me to go be with Elizabeth. We both cried and held each other, and…" His voice trailed off and tears pricked at his eyes.

"And what?" I demanded.

"And," he breathed out, "I told her that I would always love her and I asked her to call me if she needed anything. She must have known that she was pregnant that night. I think it was from one of our first nights together when we had unprotected sex. Shelby told me that she'd get the morning after pill, but I guess she never did. She must have been a couple of months gone when I went home to Elizabeth."

"Thank God she didn't tell you, hey, because it wouldn't do to have two little kids to support, would it?" My hands were gripping the arms of the chair so tightly that it hurt. It killed me to think about the pain and despair my mom must have felt.

"It wasn't that, Kade. I wasn't as wealthy then, I admit, but I would have supported you and would have wanted you in my life. Yes, it would have been hard, but I would have done it gladly. For Shelby, I would have done anything."

"Oh yeah, sure you would, after all you did love *both* of them," I scoffed.

Mr. King nodded. "I did, and I know that sounds cliché but I truly did."

"You just loved Elizabeth more. Yeah, you said."

Obviously stressed, his eyes closed as he rubbed his temple, a habit I knew I had, too.

"Mom never called you, so why didn't you call and check on her if you cared about her so much?" I asked, causing him to look up at me.

"I don't know, Kade, but I swear if I'd known, I would have helped you both out." His voice started to break as he pushed closer to the desk. "If I'd known about you and the sort of life you were living, I would have come and found you. I wish to God that I'd taken the time to call her or drop around."

A tear rolled down his tanned skin, and as he wiped it away, I noticed that we had the same hands—big with long fingers. Studying him carefully, I could see now the similarities between us. I had my mom's coloring and mouth, but I had his eyes and nose. Even our eyebrows were the same. Shit, maybe he went to the same salon as I did!

"What happens now?" I asked, reaching down for Brody, who was sleeping, evidently totally un-fazed by the revelations.

Mr. King looked up at me and smiled.

"I'd like you to meet Elizabeth and your brother and sister. That's if you'd be willing."

"They know about me?" I asked incredulously, expecting to be his dirty little secret.

"Oh course. In fact, Claudia, my youngest, she's

sixteen. She's been watching the show avidly and is beyond excited that you're her brother. Noah simply said, 'That's sick, he can help take some of the ladies off my hands'."

I sniggered at that. Noah sounded pretty cool.

"Yes," Mr. King said with a grin. "Noah is kind of laid back."

"What about your wife? What does she think about all of this?"

He smiled warmly and looked at the other photograph for a little longer this time. "She's excited to meet you and is pretty desperate to mother you. If you don't mind, of course."

My heart faltered a little at the thought of someone other than my mom mothering me, but I had to admit it would be nice.

"No, I don't mind, but I guess you'll want to do some sort of DNA test?" I asked.

Mr. King tilted his head and frowned. "No, I know that you're my son. You look like me, you're the image of Noah, and Shelby was your mom, so no DNA will be needed."

Wow, that was pretty trusting of him, but I supposed there was no denying that the three of us looked alike.

"About your mom…" he started tentatively. "Did she suffer much? I found out that she died of cancer when you were only six."

"She was ill for a long time, but we didn't know it was cancer until she died. We didn't have money for doctors, so she just tried to carry on through the pain. It was ovarian cancer and according to what my mom's friend told me, when I was older, the doctors said she'd had it for a while, but the symptoms didn't show themselves until it was too late."

Mr. King let out a long, shuddering breath and swiped at his cheek.

"I am so sorry, Kade. It must have been so hard for

261

you to lose your mom and then end up in the system. I wish…" As he leaned forward and gripped hold of the desk, a huge sob escaped from his broad chest as his shoulders shook.

I pushed up from my chair and went to his side, placing a hand on his back. As soon as I touched him, my heart slammed around and I had to swallow past a huge ball in my throat. This was my father, and I was touching him. My flesh and blood and he actually seemed like a good guy.

"Hey," I said. "It's okay. I was fine. Nothing bad happened to me."

His head snapped up and he stared at me with red-rimmed eyes, glistening with tears. "You should not have had to live in those places, Kade, and you should not have ended up on the streets."

"What's done is done. We can't change that. Maybe that's the path I was meant to be on."

With that, he pushed up from his chair and pulled me into his large frame, crushing me into a hug.

"I'm so sorry, son," he whispered. "So damn sorry."

It was then that I let my own tears fall. I was no longer alone. I had a brother, a sister, a woman who wanted to mother me, and a father who wanted me. People who would care about me, people who would want me to be safe. I had a family.

Now all I had to do was get Daisy, too.

KADE SUTTON

"How did it go with the wicked witch of the west?" Clint asked when we were eating take out later on that evening. Like a lot of other people who worked for them, like Daisy, he knew Meredith Hennessey was evil personified but needed the regular income.

"I got my money. I played a good hand. I don't think she'll fuck me over again, but who knows? I didn't see Daisy," I told him, unable to hide the sadness I felt.

"No one has," he confirmed, dipping an egg roll in some sickly sweet sauce. "Dropped off the face of the planet it would seem."

Brody was sat on the floor. He'd chomped his way through a few tins of dog food that Clint had picked up along with fresh bread and milk.

"So what's your next move, Kade?"

That was the million-dollar question.

Before, I was just a guy without a permanent place of residence and a big check in my pants pocket. My original plan was to cash the money, lay low until the furor of the show had died down, and then hunt Daisy out and spend my days begging for forgiveness.

Now, I was a son with a dad, a stepmom and two half siblings. I had a family who were excited about letting me be part of their world and I didn't know what to do with that.

So, along with a big ass check in one pants pocket, I had a business card with my dad's cell number and a twenty-four hour driver service in the other. And believe me, that weighed just as heavily as a bucket load of green.

"Hey, earth to Kade." He laughed snapping his fingers in front of my face, trying to gain my attention. "What's going on in that pretty head?"

"I can trust you, right?"

His eyes darkened at my insult. "Of course you can. I'm here, aren't I?"

I mumbled an apology and Clint raised his eyes to the heavens, pleading with someone to remove my stupid self from in front of him.

I dropped my fork, half spun and laden with noodles, back in the take out container. "I met my dad today," I told him nervously, watching as his brow furrowed with confusion, followed by his mouth dropping open to reveal half eaten kung po chicken.

Chewing quickly at super speed, he swallowed.

"I thought you were little orphan Annie, or rather Andrew?"

"Me too, but because my life isn't crazy enough right now, it seems the guy who released sperm inside my mom still exists and found me."

"Eww… less man meat references. I intend to finish this food. I have a figure to maintain. Back up. You sure he's your father?" he said in a Darth Vadar impression.

"He seems to think so, and I believe him. I just don't know what to do about it."

Clint picked his fork back up and loaded it up with so much food it was a wonder it all made it the short distance to his mouth, and that was before he had the challenge of wrestling it all in through his lips. I picked up another egg roll and thought about it, too.

All the time I spent in the system, I was desperate for a long lost aunt or family member to turn up. It was only when I moved in with Bernadette that longing dulled just a little. It never truly went away but the older I got, the less important that fantasy seemed. When my maturity kicked in, my belief in fairytales died and I placed that dream on the back burner for good. By the time I lost Bernadette, I'd just accepted the realization that I was never going to be rescued and loved. I had to do that myself. I allowed Cory and his mom to temporarily soak up some of the longing, but when I played such a pivotal part in Cory's death, I believed I didn't deserve to be saved.

I'd been shoveling food into my mouth while thinking all this through and it finally hit me. I no longer thought of myself as totally to blame for Cory's death. I just happened to be a part of the circumstances that led up to it. People make bad decisions all the time; it's how you learn from them that defines the path your life takes. Forgiveness can happen, even if you give it yourself. It doesn't mean you forget and make the same mistakes again.

"What's working in your head?"

"Just had a big fucking light bulb moment, that's what."

It would be stupid of me to walk away from the prospect of a family without getting to know them. I didn't want this to be another bad decision I was part of and more than that, I didn't want to make it through fear and without all the facts. There were thousands of kids, just like my younger self, who were praying for a second chance at family life, and I owed it to all of them and little Kade to give it a chance.

"Can I borrow your cell?" I asked him, and watched as he wiped his hands clean and fished it out his pants before handing it over.

I pulled the business card from my pocket, running my

finger across his name, Nicholas King, before smiling in understanding. This guy had meant something to my mom, enough that she'd given me his name. I shouldn't be mad that he'd left her high and dry with a bun in the oven. She was just as capable of reaching out to him and telling him about me. My mom made the brave decision to go it alone and let him go back and give his marriage a chance. The very least I could do was give him the same courtesy. All of a sudden, it seemed like a wonderful way to honor the memory of my mom, the woman I hoped had helped to arrange this twist of fate from her place in heaven.

The town car collected me and Brody from Clint's place the next evening. I'd agreed to go to dinner at the King's house, and as I sat in the back, I felt just as nervous as I had when I was travelling to the mansion. My only hope was that this was going to be a better, more enjoyable experience that had a more fulfilling outcome than just being palmed off with a check.

When we arrived at his house, my nerves peaked higher. Whatever was on the other side of that front door could be a real life changer for me, and although I told myself not to get my hopes up, the orphan in me pushed through and was secretly praying this was going to work out.

The driver pulled up, and as soon as Brody and I were out, he left, mumbling that he'd see me later when I was ready to be driven home. As I stood in the driveway, I looked up and was reminded of the big family house in the *Home Alone* movie. I wanted there to be chaos and normality inside, not pomp and circumstance. There were a lot of windows, a huge garage and a big tree on the lawn at the side with an old swing and tree house built in it.

Was this what I'd missed out on?

I don't know how long I'd been stood in the same spot, just looking up at the life that I didn't get. Even Brody was still, like he knew that what lay on the other side of the double wide fronted door could be a big game changer in our lives.

The security light blinked off, and all of a sudden, we were in complete darkness. The only illumination was coming from table lamps inside the windows and street lamps behind us.

"I tried to wait it out, but I'm nervous. I wanted you to do this on your own time, but the longer you stand here, the more worried I'm getting that you're not going to go through with it," I heard the old man's voice say, coming from the side of the house.

I looked in his direction as he nervously walked towards me, his hands in his pockets. My go to position when I was trying to hide the fact they were shaking.

"I understand if you can't come in, but please, don't give up before we've given it a chance."

"Sorry, I didn't realize I looked indecisive. I was just taking it all in and clearly more time passed than I realized."

I watched as the man desperate to be my father exhaled in relief. This wasn't going to work if we both kept thinking about the past, about everything we'd missed out on. We both needed to be present in the here and now as much as possible. "I was just thinking about how the last time I entered a big ass house, my life kinda got bent out of shape. It was more life changing than I could ever have imagined," I mumbled.

"I can't argue with that. I want this to be life changing, too, but for the better. For all of us."

Nicholas King tentatively reached out and touched my shoulder, prompting me to get moving. When I went to walk towards the front door, he stopped me.

"Round the back, son. Family don't knock on doors, we just walk in through the kitchen and make ourselves at home."

When he finished saying the word kitchen, Brody

barked and shot off as if he'd been given permission, and I knew what he was hunting for.

"I hope there isn't an unattended pot roast back there."

I didn't get the chance to take in much of the surroundings. It was dark but there were a few garden lights and a pool house by the side of a big manicured lawn. As we walked closer to the back of the house, I could hear laughter and smell home cooked food. My dad twisted and turned the handle on a replica stable door that lead into a large family kitchen.

"I see someone has made himself at home." He laughed, ushering me in before him.

I was greeted by Brody, perched upright, looking like a show dog about to do tricks, being fed by a pretty young girl.

"Claudia," My father said, exasperated.

"What? He likes pot roast. He stole one like every other day in the mansion. This way, we're sharing."

I smiled at her. "It wasn't every other day... was it?" I asked. I hadn't seen any of the footage that had been screened to the public.

"Near enough... There was this one day when he stole Mellings' lunch. This clever pup took that instead of the BBQ's meat that had just been pulled from the grill." She laughed, scruffing the fur under his jaw.

"Brodes... no wonder that guy hated me," I told him, squatting down to talk to my best pal. "Hi, I'm Kade."

"Claudia. Great to meet you. Dad was right. You do look like Noah. Poor you!"

When I stood up, my father was leaning on his elbows on the kitchen counter next to us, watching our interaction with a wistful look on his face.

"Clau-" a female voice started to shout from outside. "Oh, hello. I didn't know you were here. I'm running late." The gorgeous middle-aged woman who came crashing through a door into the kitchen was flustered. She was holding a shoe in one hand and a button down sweater in the other.

"Kade." My father stepped forward, his nerves right on the edge for all to see. "This is my wife, Elizabeth."

I stood up and walked over to her with my hand extended. Her nerves appeared then, too, as she first tried to shake my hand using the one with the sweater and then swapped it for the other, forgetting she was still holding a shoe and balancing on one heeled foot. "Damn it, this is what happens when Noah gets home late from the rink. I'm the one who ends up not ready."

"Rink?"

"Yeah, I play in defense for a local hockey team," came another voice.

My mirror image was stood peering round his mom. Our similarities were unbelievable and only made more prominent by the fact that we were so close in age. The fact that he was interested in hockey was just too bizarre for words. I thought for one quick moment that we could have played against each other or together, but if I'd been faced with my doppelganger, I would have remembered.

After Elizabeth finally found a hand to shake mine with, I extended it over to Noah straight away. I was keen to get the formal introductions out of the way.

"I played center in college. The center was cool and always got the girls."

He returned my handshake, laughing. "From what Claudia has been banging on about these last few weeks, it seems you're still an attraction for girls. So much you figured you'd move into a mansion with a whole boatload of them. Just how many pucks to the head did you take?"

"A lot." I chuckled, agreeing with him.

By this time, Brody had had enough of what was probably only a starter dish in his eyes, and he padded over to sit in front of me, twisting and turning his head with confusion between my half brother and me. The dog's mannerisms were comical. "I guess one of us needs to get a haircut, otherwise you'll find yourself with a new sidekick," I joked.

The ice was well and truly broken. My father seemed more at ease, Claudia was happy to immerse herself into all the crap that went on in the mansion, and even though I'd hated it and what I'd become while I was Kade the Millionaire, it was endearing to hear how she and her friends were addicted to the show. Noah was more like me than I thought possible, or was I more like him? It was hard to tell, and given time, I believed we could become great friends. My dad attempted to fill me in on extended family members, but he'd quickly pull himself back, worrying that he was going too fast. None of us stood on ceremony and I can honestly say I felt welcomed.

The dinner we ate was lovely and Brody was made to feel just as welcome as me, but no one really asked or spoke about anything that was too deep. Everyone was on their best behavior without being guarded, and even though I made a few jokes about things, I got the impression that everyone wanted this to work out.

When my father, Claudia and Noah got up to help clear the plates from the table, I stood up and joined in, only to be told to sit back down by Nicholas. I knew that none of us could rush this, but being made to feel like a guest wasn't how I wanted this to end. The little orphan in me expected the fairytale of open arms and getting stuck in. With Brody and I left in the family dining room, surrounded by pictures of my siblings growing up, I felt a stab of pain in my chest over what I'd missed out on.

I was taking a closer look at those pictures when Elizabeth came back into the room carrying a tray of coffees.

"The rest of them are loading the dishwasher. I have my team well trained. You either cook or clean up in this platoon."

"Is..?" I began "No, forget it." I was feeling unsure now that I was finally alone with the woman my mother and father betrayed.

"Please talk to me, Kade. I have a feeling this is as weird for you as it is for me."

Elizabeth wasn't posh or formal, even though they were well off and clearly not hurting for money. Her genuine approach was well received, and she'd appeared in the room at the time when I was beginning to wonder whether I'd ever fit after such a long time. Together, they had learned the art of family support and surviving as a strong unit. Right now, the only person I had like that was Brody and he didn't speak the same language as me.

"How can you welcome me in your home, knowing I come from a time when your marriage was suffering?" I asked honestly, deciding to just throw it out there. If we weren't straight with each other, this wouldn't work.

Elizabeth placed the tray down, grabbing a mug of coffee, and came to stand by me. We were both looking at a picture of Noah and Claudia hanging upside down from a supporting plank on tree house that was still outside. Claudia's hair was long, nearly brushing the grass, and Noah was wide armed, showing off how brave he was.

"My marriage wasn't just suffering. It was dying and all but over. Saying I was unbearable to be around is an understatement. I think that was what hurt Nicholas the most, especially after we'd been together so long. I fell pregnant with Noah and it knocked me sideways. I look back at that period of time with regret over so much, but I choose to focus on the good. Noah. I truly believe he saved me and he definitely saved my marriage. I now learn that my savior came at the expense of your loss. Yin and Yang—for every action there's a consequence."

I leaned over to the table and reached for a coffee.

"Nicholas was upfront about his time with your mom, and I have to take some responsibility for making him feel so unhappy that he sought out friendship and clearly more with another woman. I reached out to him when I learned I was expecting and we decided to give things another go. We had a lot of counseling and it was all put on the table, but it was important to leave that behind us so we could move forward together. I hate it when a child suffers for the sins of their parents. Besides, had the tables been turned, I'd want a good woman looking out for my two, no matter how long it took for them to find each other."

Should I have hated this woman? She could have been the thing that stood between my mom and dad being together and me having a happy and stable life. Had I been found by my dad when I was younger, I probably wouldn't have been able to deal with this situation maturely. I would have always seen myself as the outsider. I had to be realistic. The only thing that made sense was what I knew—my mom would still have died from that horrible disease and I would have missed her every day. It was time to move forward with my life and start believing I wasn't alone.

"I hope we can be friends," I told her.

"Friends," she said dismissively. "I'm not settling for friends. I want more than that and anyway, you're years behind the other two in the parental embarrassment stakes."

Elizabeth hadn't said she wanted to take the vacant slot left in my life by my mom, but it was heartwarming to know that someone wanted to care for me in that way. It didn't matter how old you were; everyone loved knowing that someone had their back.

"I reckon after what I've just done on TV in front of millions, I'm the one embarrassing you."

"Nonsense, it looked like spring break fun. Although, don't tell Noah I said that. I gave him no peace during his first spring break. Your father and I did our level best to time our phone calls for the most inconvenient time. I think we had just as much fun as he did." She winked.

My father joined us then, rolling down his shirtsleeves. "My chores are done, oh slave driver," he called, coming up behind us. "Oh, that picture... I used to tell those two all the time about acrobatics on the tree house. I think

Claudia fractured her arm about a week after we took it. Then Noah told us his dream of playing pro ice hockey. I went straight into the office and invested in the city's ER department. I figured we were about to get some good use out of it."

It was lovely to hear the normality in his voice. His nervousness about inviting me was getting less and less.

"What's your plan, Kade?" he asked me suddenly. The question came out of the blue. For years, I'd lived my life according to how I was going to survive the next mealtime without food or the next night without a bed, knowing the rain was coming.

"I have to make amends with someone I didn't treat very well, if I can find her. Then I need to find a place to live and consider some employment."

"Let me help?" my father urged.

His offer felt awkward and I didn't know how to refuse, but I knew I needed to. My second chance at life was mine and I wanted to do it on my own. I would rather have his emotional support than his financial backing and that wasn't how I wanted this relationship to begin. "Thank you, but I need to do this alone."

"I understand you won't take money, but there must be something I can do for you?"

"Find the love of my life so I can apologize?" I joked.

Only Nicholas King didn't laugh in response to my humor. "Of course I can. Who is it?"

Chapter 44

KADE SUTTON

Spending time with my dad and my new family for the last couple of weeks had been pretty awesome. Claudia and Noah gave me general sibling shit, joking around and punking me at any opportunity, while Elizabeth mothered me without the suffocation or sickly-sweetness of someone trying to get me onside. Dad—whoa, it was strange calling him that for the first time I can tell you—well Dad was great. He didn't pressure me into making any decisions about my future, but listened when I told him what I'd like to do with the money I'd earned from the show. He advised me but didn't preach, and was generally a great dad.

He did insist that I move into the house with them, just until I got myself a place, and he also suggested that I get an agent/advisor just to help me with the press furor that was still going on. Lots of people wanted a piece of me, with interviews in magazines and on TV and radio being offered. Plus, a couple of men's designers had approached me to be their next 'face of'. I didn't want to do any of it, but Rick, the guy I had temporarily hired to help me, suggested I do a couple of interviews to put my point of view across, and then retire gracefully from public life. Dad and Elizabeth wanted me to put a positive spin on the show: I'd found my family. After everything that they'd brought into my life, I was happy to oblige and said that in every interview. Dad had drawn the line at a family photoshoot, though, muttering something about us not being 'the Partridge Family', whoever the hell they were. Claudia sulked a little about that decision as she was desperate to be in a magazine, but I abided by Dad and Elizabeth's wishes and declined on their behalf.

Clint told me, on the day that I moved out, that he'd got a new job working as a voiceover artist for a kid's station. He was going to become the voice behind Mr. Dizzy Pants, a guy who travelled to different places just by shaking the legs of his pants. He insisted it was going to be the next big thing in kid's shows. He also told me that there was still no sign of Daisy at the station offices. Her desk still had a box of her stuff on it, getting dustier by the day, and Meredith had threatened to throw it into the dumpster on more than one occasion. What I didn't tell Clint, for fear of jinxing it, was that I knew where she was. My dad had employed a PI, John Carrington, who found out within two days where she lived and exactly where she had gone missing to. She was currently in London on the last leg of a European holiday with her parents. It had been real easy for him. He barely had to work for the money my dad had insisted on paying for him. When doing Daisy's background check, he realized that he knew her brother, Heath, from his time as a State Trooper. John gave Heath a call and told him that he was working on behalf of the station. He said that Daisy hadn't picked up her belongings and they were concerned about her whereabouts. Heath apparently gave him a real roasting, calling Meredith words that John wouldn't repeat, and adding in a threat to my balls for good measure. However, during his rant, he thankfully gave up the vital information.

So here I was, trying to compose a letter for her. I figured that was the best way to approach her to start with. I also figured it was the best way to keep my balls intact. Not that I didn't think I deserved to lose them—I did, and I would've been happy to give her a shot at them if it meant she forgave me. But if I knew Daisy, and I thought I did, she would be embarrassed and heartbroken, and she would need time to digest everything before making a decision. At least she might read a letter. Yeah, she might well burn it or rip it up as soon as she realized it was from me, but it was worth a try. And, if a letter didn't work then I'd have to risk my balls.

On what seemed like my millionth attempt, I was satisfied.

Hi Daisy,
I LOVE YOU.
Pretty out there, hey, and not really how I wanted to tell you, but needs must! I also wanted you to see those words before you destroy this letter because I'm pretty sure that you will.

I have so much to tell you about what's happened since I left the show, but all that can wait until I see you, and God I can't wait to see you. Thinking about seeing you again was all that kept me going for those last few weeks, so please agree to that.

I know I appeared to treat you badly. Shit, I did treat you badly, but there was a reason. Apart from I love you, there's something else that I wanted to tell you face to face, but I don't think I'd get the words out while rolling around clutching my junk – I just know that you're gonna kick my balls as soon as you see me. That means I'm going have to tell you now. I did what I did because of Meredith –
SURPRISE!

She filmed us making love, baby, and was threatening to leak it to the media if I didn't kick you out and stay until the end. If it was just me, well, I wouldn't have given a shit, but I couldn't let her do that to you. You are too special, too sweet and too pure to be touted to the highest bidder. I only saw a snippet of what she'd filmed, but there was no doubt it was us – you and me – making love on that bed. That was the best night of my life, and I would not have it tainted by that hideous bitch. So, I did as she asked, in the manner in which she asked me to do it. Truth? If I'd looked at you, I would have crumbled, come running after you and dragged you into my arms, but I couldn't risk that tape getting out. She also pinned it on Clint, doctoring up some footage of him delivering my backpack to my room to make it look as though he'd planted the camera. So you see, if I had walked, not only would you have been crucified but him, too. Clint told me what happened by the way, when he dropped you home, and I am so sorry, baby. Please apologize to your dad for me that he had to go through the pain of seeing his daughter so broken. I swear that I will never make you feel that sad ever again. I will do everything in my power to make you feel happy, secure and loved. Oh, and tell your brother that I would like to keep my balls if I'm ever to provide him with a niece or nephew – or maybe even both. Because that's my intention, Dais. I want to make a life with you, love you, have a family with you, because I know that you are my 'it', my forever, if you'll just forgive me and understand why I did what I did.

You also need to know that nothing happened between me and any of the other girls. I believe Honey has an interview coming out in National Enquirer about our 'nights of passion'. I swear down on Brody's life and my mother's grave, there were no nights of passion. The first night that I picked her, the night you left, I locked myself in the bathroom and wouldn't come out until morning. She wasn't happy, particularly as she had to pee in a vase that was on my dresser. Whenever I picked her after that, because Meredith insisted and I'll tell you why when I see you (yep I'm being optimistic here), the tub was my bed. Jess was different. I admit we did kiss that first time, but it was like kissing my sister – that's another story by the way – and we agreed we just weren't compatible, plus I couldn't get my mind off you. I told her how I felt about you and she was happy just to have the publicity for her acting career. Any other girl I picked while you were gone, well, they also knew straight from the off nothing was happening. Thank God none of them were as horny as Honey. Shit, if this wasn't so sad, I'd suggest that to Meredith as a title for her next show – As Horny As Honey!

Clint and Jess have given me their numbers (I've written them on the back of the first page), and have said if you want to call them to confirm any of this, you can. Me, I'm just hoping that you believe my word, but I understand if you want to be sure.

Everything that I said to you that night, everything I did was real, baby, I swear. I love you so very much because, not only are you beautiful, sexy, and sweet and have more smarts than anyone I know, you're also the kindest and most loyal person I've ever met. My mom would have loved you, just as much as I do – I just know it.

Someone has told me that I should look on the show as a positive, and at first, I found that hard to do. But now, I realize what they mean. That fucking show gave me you, and even if you don't forgive me and never want to set eyes on me again, at least I met you.

I was on the path I was meant to be on, and on that path, I had you for one perfect night in time.

Love always,

Kade (oh, and Brody sends his love, too) Xxxxx

Chapter 45

DAISY INGLES

The plane journey home from London wasn't the best. There I go again, trying to kid myself. It was awful. I watched that little plane graphic on the in-seat TV screen eat up the miles on the map and felt sicker the closer we got. I'd been able to hide in Europe. All of my troubles seemed so far away and unreal, like it had all been someone else's life, but now that avoidance tactic was coming to an end and it was all rearing its ugly head again.

I never expected to go on my parent's trip of a lifetime, but they insisted. After arriving home in such a mess, it was clear I needed to be honest with them. I started with how I still volunteered at the shelter and only started working at the network to save up money for mom's medication and their trip. When I finished with all the gory details of how Kade had betrayed me less than twenty-four hours after giving him my body, heart and soul, they were as distraught as I was.

If I think back to that conversation, we were all in tears but I'd never seen my dad so angry. I could lie and say the blame lay at Meredith's door, or even Kade's, but he was angry with me. I'd kept all of this from them. I'd put myself through the whole thing to buy them a life-enriching trip because he no longer could. Watching my pop walk out of our tiny apartment for his own sanity was as hard as watching Kade deceive me. My mom and I are essentially the same—selfless and would do anything to put others first—so while my pop calmed down, I let her console me and soothe some of heartache I'd been feeling.

Pop was in a much better mindset when he returned, but his one stipulation for spending the money from my time at the mansion was that I go with them. If I'd gone through so much pain to get them something they'd always dreamed of, the least I could do was share it with them. I didn't feel like going. I felt like crawling under a rock and never talking to another human again, but after thinking it over, I knew time and distance were the only things that were going to help me.

The following morning, with a vow to never switch the TV on again, I bought three plane tickets and three Euro-Hopper tickets, staying focused on the positives. I'd been through hell, but not as much hell as my mom and pop. I'd been let down, humiliated and had my heart shredded, but I'd done what I'd set out to do—make my mom and pop smile and be thankful for the second chance at life that they had together.

It was easy to avoid the aftermath of the show as we were boarding a plane when the episodes were being aired on a delayed schedule. I tried to be insignificant on the show and I sincerely hoped I was just as insignificant when I got home. Everyone would be focusing on Kade and his final pick. They'd be following them around and hounding them for the next six months, trying to see if it was working out and Kade the millionaire had really found his true love.

As I floated round the Louvre in Paris, St. Peter's Basilica in Rome and the Acropolis in Athens, I was completely enchanted with the history and experience.

When we moved onto Venice and the three of us took a gondola ride on the Grand Canal, the realization of how deep my feelings were for Kade started to fight through. I was in one of the most romantic places in the world, and I was sat in a traditional Venetian boat with my mom and pop. We passed couples in love, who were being serenaded and were so bewitched with each other that the scenery and architecture didn't even register with them.

My parents did their best to distract me, and it was when we were in Spain that it all hit me like a freight train. Pop and I had walked up the thousands of steps to the top of the Sagrada Familia in Barcelona. Mom was too tired and stayed at the bottom to people watch and have a cool drink, and because the queues were so big, our progress was slow. We'd been inside for hours, trudging up and down the stone steps, and we were tired so I designated the rest of the day a beach day. Sitting on a towel on the sandy city beach of Port Vell, I realized I was wearing one of the bathing suits that Lydia had chosen for me. It was red and sexy, but reminded me of the day when Honey had written on Kade in lipstick. As I was trying to push the memory to the back of my mind, a guy ran past me with a dog at his heels and he looked like Kade. The fluttering of my heart worried me. It confirmed I wasn't over him and that no matter how much time and distance I put between us, I would probably always be in love with him.

I just had to figure out how to move on and live with that. Kade was with someone else now, and I couldn't afford for that experience to jade my love life forever. Kade may have hurt me but I wasn't prepared for it to turn me into a lonely spinster. I knew I was always gun shy when it came to matters of the heart, and if nothing else, my heart's mangling in the mansion had taught me to be more cautious in the future. I needed to move on and accept life didn't always turn out the way you wanted it to.

We finished our tour of Europe in the UK—a few nights in Scotland, a hilly trip to Wales before spending the last days of our adventure in London. It was in London where I came across my first real information on I Wanna Get Laid By Kade. I caught the tail end of E! News Weekly and saw a report confirming that Meredith had indeed got the award she had been coveting. Her success in the mansion with Kade and the twist in the tale of him being homeless had captured a level of praise that even she wasn't expecting. That vicious creature was being hailed as some reality TV queen. I saw the moment she strutted down the aisle, accepting false praise from the industry vultures, barely remembering there was a team of people also responsible. Carson and Lydia were stood behind her during her acceptance speech, as she swung an award round, just so everyone could see it again and again, and thanked everyone apart from Kade and the girls who had been duped into her manic plan.

What a fudging cow.

As I dragged my frustrated butt off the bed in my hotel room to poke in rage at the TV's power button, I saw the footage switch to their roving reporter outside the theatre. She was all glammed up but pouting in disappointment that the two main stars, Jess and Kade, weren't in attendance. She finished her live broadcast by saying that there were unconfirmed rumors that Kade and his selected female finalist were exploring the possibility of how to get to know each other better under the media spotlight. She then surmised, with a wink and heavy look of insinuation, that they were probably enjoying each other's company somewhere right then.

Ugh! I needed to sort myself out sooner rather than later.

When we landed back in the U.S.A., I did everything possible to see it as a new beginning, forcing a positive mental attitude, forcing my brain to focus on overriding any thoughts of anything remotely Kade-like. My parents had had the most wonderful time, and seeing them appreciate life, each other and fall in love all over again against the back drop of a fountain in Rome made my suffering worth it.

The taxi dropped us off at my apartment in the early hours of the morning. Doris, my elderly neighbor, had been in to open a few windows and leave fresh bread and milk, so the only thing we needed to do was fall through the door and collapse into bed. As I shoved through the door with a smile, I was welcomed by a mountain of mail. There was so much that it was impossible to fully open the door and fit through with my luggage.

"Would you look at all that?" my mom said, surprised.

I had to agree with her. I'd never had that much mail. It looked like two years' worth had been dumped at once.

We put the jug on for fresh coffee and I slumped in a chair, taking in the familiar homely surroundings and scent. Mom and Pop had gone to freshen up, so I opened one of the many letters. It was from a TV network, asking me to appear on their daily talk show. Um… not a chance in hell! That piece of paper was quickly dumped on the floor. The next letter was from a magazine asking for an exclusive; that joined the other one heading for the trash. I opened another two in a similar vein, and the next one was almost like fan mail, which felt uncomfortable.

When I reached the next envelope, I opened it expecting to scan read it and trash it, but the words 'Hi Daisy, I love You,' hit me. In an effort to try to decide whether it was a crank letter or not, I flipped the pages over, seeing Kade and Brody's names at the end. They stopped my heart the same way it had when I first realized I was in love with him.

I couldn't read that now.

My hands were shaking so much I wasn't sure I could read it ever.

Chucking the letter on pile with the others like it had burned my hands, I ran for my bedroom and shut the door. As if the barrier of a door could make it all go away, I decided to stay there and hide, possibly forever.

283

Forever lasted for about three hours. Blame sleeplessness, blame the long plane journey or even jet lag, but the fact of the matter was, I wanted to know what the fudge was in that letter. I wanted to dissect every word and grasp the underlying meaning so I could torture myself some more.

In the darkness of the night, I pulled my big girl panties up and tiptoed to the piece of paper that was going to send me spiraling back into heartbreak. Without flipping on a light to alert the world to my apparent obsession with dismal emotions, I reached my lounge. Sitting in the chair, I braced myself to confront it only to peer over the side and find the pile gone. Leaning my hand over the arm of the chair and flapping it around like a duck's webbed foot trying to gain traction in the water, I felt nothing. In despair, I knelt on the floor and crawled around and around looking for the pile of mail. On my fourth circuit of the room on my hands and knees, the room was suddenly flooded with light.

"Mom, what the heck?" I complained, shielding my sensitive eyes.

"Oh Lord above. Robert! Go back to bed. It's just Daisy."

My pop appeared then. "I told you to wait for me. What if it had been someone breaking in?"

"Nonsense," she shushed him. "What's going on Daisy? Why are you crawling round the floor at this ungodly hour?"

"I was, uh… um… looking for my mail. I think there was a work letter in there I needed."

"Oh dear, I'm sorry, love. I dumped that lot in the trash chute before I went to bed. Now, who's for a cup of cocoa?"

Cocoa… Cocoa? I couldn't drink fudging cocoa. I felt sick. She may as well have dumped my heart in the chute with that letter. Now I'd never know what he meant to say to me.

Chapter 46

DAISY INGLES

"You okay, love?" my mom asked me.

The three of us were sat at the little table in my kitchen enjoying a multi-cultural breakfast. Mom had gone all out. Pop was quite happily enjoy eggs sunny side up with some almost burned and crispy bacon like the British, mom was enjoying a croque monsieur, a lovely French toasted cheese and ham sandwich she'd tripped across in France, and I was wrestling with a coffee. Just a solitary, uneventful and much needed coffee, like a typical American.

"I didn't sleep great is all, and I need to head into the office to collect my stuff."

"No, I refuse to believe my girl, who was brave enough to go on a national TV show, is worried about facing that vulture. Tell me what's got you in a pickle?" she asked all spritely.

I shrugged my shoulders and took another mouth incinerating swig of coffee, to which my pop immediately closed his newspaper and grimaced across the table. "No more secrets."

Fudge! He'd made me promise that in a moment of emotional weakness.

"I know I promised that I wouldn't let Kade and the show get me down, but, I... well... He wrote me a letter and I'm wondering what it said."

"Then just read the damn thing," my dad told me like I was stupid before picking his paper back up.

"I would but I don't have it any longer." The last thing I wanted was for my mom to feel bad that she'd thrown it away by accident.

"I don't get why you're so concerned, Dais. You said he was the last person on Earth you wanted to hear from."

"I know, but-"

"You said," she pointed, "that 'Kade Sutton can go to fudging hell,' when we were on the banks of the Seine."

God, she was right. I did say that. "Yeah, well-"

"You said," she began again.

"Alright! Jesus, Mom, I know what I said, but I can't help how I feel about him. I know he hurt me, but he started his letter with the words 'I Love You.' What if he means it? What if he explained everything in that letter and I go on with the rest of my life thinking he's a butthole and I'm wrong? What if-"

"Oh lord above, enough with the melodramatics," my dad burst in, shutting me up. "Give her the bloody letter, Heather. I'm trying to read the paper."

I didn't know what I was hearing, but my eyes did that funny comedy thing, like following a tennis ball across a court as they flitted between my parents.

"I was going to get more out of her than that, Robert!"

"I know, but she's was getting all... screechy and I want to read the paper."

The conversation continued between them like I wasn't there and they hadn't just confused the poop out of me.

"Stop talking," I said calmly. My mom, sensing she'd lost the advantage she was gaining with my dad, reached into the pocket of her apron and handed me the letter she'd claimed to have thrown away. "Why did you say you'd trashed it?"

"We needed to see how you really felt about him. I'd say there's unfinished business on both sides according to his love letter, so I'm expecting you to be the Daisy I raised, one with manners and good grace, and hear what he has to say before you completely condemn him."

As I took the letter off her, it felt like it weighed a thousand tons in my hand. I stood up and left the kitchen, retreating to the privacy of my own room to read it. When I put my hand on the door to close it, I heard my dad shout, "And your brother ripping his balls off will be the least of his worries if he upsets you again."

Two hours later, I was still in my room and my mom had clearly had enough. The anticipation over what I was going to do was killing her as much as me, and by the time she'd knocked on the door to ask, I'd read the letter so many times I could have rewritten it backwards.

"Well?" she asked, throwing her hands up in frustration.

"I don't know. I just don't know if I'm ready to see him."

"But what about the things he alluded to in his letter, his reasons? You know that wretched woman. It's not a stretch to believe what she was up to."

"I don't know. I don't know!" I screamed back at her, grabbing my coat and purse.

"Where are you going?" she wailed, following me out of the door like some deranged person. Although, let's face it, I was the deranged one.

"To the office. I'm going to get my stuff, and maybe I can take some of this frustration out on the snake who deserves it."

Leaving her standing, completely flustered and looking like she was about ready to strangle me with her apron strings, I pushed past her and headed for the office, in the perfect mood to deal with Meredith and Lydia.

There were no paps holding the building under siege. It was like a regular day. I drove past three times, wondering whether I could be bothered to go in and get my belongings. I didn't really have anything of value in my drawers apart from a few pictures of my family and friends at the shelter that didn't deserve to be trashed.

What I really needed to do was put this building in my past, face up to the women who had caused me so much upset and close it down with no regrets. I would not let that women chase me away like I'd done something wrong. I had friends who worked here and I did not want the last thing they saw of me to be that disastrous eviction from the mansion.

Decision made.

I would go in there and close the door on that part of my life.

It should have been that simple, but when I walked up to the building and took a cursory, sentimental glance at Kade's begging post, I felt the air whoosh from my lungs.

There, larger than life and more handsome than my brain could ever visualize, was Kade and Brody was waiting patiently beside him. Kade had his hands in his pockets, leaning against the wall, looking so panty meltingly gorgeous that I knew I needed to hear him out or I'd never be able to erase him from my heart.

KADE SUTTON -KING

"Please, Kade," Claudia whined. "It will take you ten minutes, that's all."

"Nope," I grumbled, cutting into my Christmas turkey. "It's been over two years and there is no way they even care anymore. And for the love of God, stop feeding Brody. A doggie weight loss class is not in the business plan."

"God, you're so grumpy." My sister leaned into Brody's snout and started talking to him in a silly voice. "Your daddy is a grumpster, a meanie grumpster. Yes he is, yes he is, yes he-"

"Claudia," Dad snapped. "You heard your brother. He said no. He does not want to meet all your college friends and have photographs taken with them, and Brody is starting to waddle. Lay off feeding him snacks. Your mom is just as bad, and between you, you're spoiling him."

Claudia was in her first year of college, and while I loved her dearly, she was a demanding little princess.

"Yeah," Noah added around a mouthful of food. "He's finished being a celebrity. Although, he was pretty crap at it anyway. The Brodester was the real star of the show."

With a grin, I threw a carrot at my brother and started to laugh, despite myself. Noah shook his head and continued to stuff his face. We'd become really close over the last couple of years since the show, and spent a lot of time together. At least we had until a couple of months ago when he'd moved to New York to work as a sports journalist. Journalism had been his major at college, but hockey had been his priority, working to get drafted from the farm team he played for. Unfortunately, just three months after I left the show, he suffered a career ending injury to his ACL, so he'd taken a cadetship at a sport magazine and then worked damn hard to get his job as one of the sports writers for the *New York Times*.

"Boys, please," Elizabeth chided. "Stop behaving like children. You're both grown men for goodness sake, and Nicholas, I do not spoil that little cutie pie."

Christ, even she was at the baby-dog talk now.

Noah and I giggled like little children, and I knew that if we'd grown up together, we'd have got into some real shit.

"You know Kade's problem, Mom," Noah said, taking a sip of his wine. "He needs to get laid. How long is it now?"

"Euw," Claudia groaned. "Purlease, I do not want to think about my brother having sex."

"That's the problem, Claude. He isn't."

Noah roared laughing, and while I couldn't help but smile, he was right. I was feeling real frustrated and was totally pissed, hence why I'd said no to Claudia's request to meet her college friends. I never said no to Claudia, ever!

"Leave him alone, Noah," Dad said with a smirk. "It's bad enough he has to cope with blue balls, without you giving him shit for it."

"Nicholas!"

"Dad!"

We all started to laugh as Dad shrugged his shoulders and gave us a 'wtf is wrong with that' look. God, I loved that man, and my Christmas gift to him last year had been to take his name. I was now officially Kade Nicholas Sutton-King. Yep, it was a mouthful, but I loved seeing my dad's eyes light up whenever he heard it.

"What's going on?" a sweet, sexy voice said at the doorway.

I turned to see my beautiful wife entering the room, and yep, my dick stirred. It had been six long weeks since I'd been inside her and I was sure my balls were actually a nice shade of deep purple, not blue.

"Oh God, Daisy," Claudia cried. "They're being disgusting and talking about you and Kade having sex."

Daisy's eyes widened as she looked at me, and then slapped my arm. "Kade!"

I pulled her into my side and kissed the top of her head. "I can't help it, baby. I miss you."

"Well, Kade," Elizabeth said with a sigh. "If you'd pushed a six pound baby through your meemaw, you'd want at least six weeks of abstinence."

"Mother, what the fuck is a meemaw?" Noah roared.

"Well if you don't know, Noah, then I think we failed when we told you about the birds and the bees when you were seven."

As everyone started to laugh and chatter, I turned to Daisy and stroked a finger down her cheek.

"Is he okay?" I asked quietly.

"Yeah," she said with a contented sigh. "He's perfect and I'm still not the only one who thinks so. I can't get Queenie to leave his side."

Queenie was our crazy little pug. I'd adopted her shortly after the show, and when I heard her name, I had to have her. It was fate. Both Queenie and Brody had played key roles in my marriage proposal. I was sure my plan was foolproof but I was extra determined to get the right answer, and using furry friends to make that happen was merely a back-up idea. Brody and Queenie got on like a dream, but as the pug was attached to my other little boy, Brody had the run of the kitchen both here and at our place. So yeah, he was getting a fat old boy.

Our son, Joshua Cory Sutton King, had come screaming into the world just six weeks and one day ago, and as Daisy said, he was perfect. He was a King through and through, although he did have Daisy's freckles and her good nature; he was a real placid, smiley baby and we barely knew that we had him, but shit we were so glad we did.

As Daisy helped herself to some more turkey, I couldn't help but stare at her. She was so beautiful, and I thanked God every day for bringing her to me. I'd thought at one point that I'd lost her, but thankfully she believed me when I said I loved her.

I'd been waiting in my old spot on the sidewalk every day for almost a week before she finally arrived at the office to get her stuff. I was pretty sure she wasn't back from Europe, but the day after I posted her letter, I made it my daily routine to wait for her. I couldn't risk her coming back early and missing her. I found out later that the first three days that I sat there, she was still in London, but hey, it wasn't like I wasn't used to sitting on the street all day. It just happened that this time, I had clean clothes on every day and a real home to go to every night.

At first, when she spotted me, she just looked at me, and I thought that she was going to turn and run, but she didn't. She cried out my name and ran to me, almost knocking me off my feet. The kiss we shared was amazing, and it took a lot of strength not to bury myself in her right there on the sidewalk. She had her legs wrapped around me, her hands were clutching at my hair, and she was pushing that hot little body of hers as close to me as possible. All while I cupped that perfect ass of hers in my hands and tried hard not to bust my zipper with my hard on.

I can remember every touch, every breath and every emotion in that kiss. It felt like years of misery and sorrow just slipped away, and were replaced with light, love and happiness, all wrapped in the beautiful package of Daisy.

We had an awful lot to talk about that night. I told Daisy everything that had happened, and I had to stop her from going over to Meredith's house and punching her. It was the first and last time I'd heard Daisy curse.

"That fucking cunt!" she screamed. "I'll fucking kill her."

Yep, my baby had a filthy mouth when she wanted to, and I don't just mean cursing. Sometimes, I wish I'd let her have at it with Meredith, but the bitch wasn't worth the criminal record. Dad managed to get the video of Daisy and me from her, though. It appeared she was scared of someone. I had no idea what he said to her when he visited her at the network, but according to Maxwell who went with him, Meredith looked as though she was going to shit her pants. As for Honey, she never did do her interview about our 'nights of passion', but she did star in Meredith's flop reality show, A Honey for Honey. Who knew Honey was actually a lesbian? Not me, that's for sure.

"What are you smiling at?" Daisy asked, nudging me with her shoulder.

"Nothing, baby. Just thinking how blessed I am."

She gave me the sweetest of smiles and snuggled into my side.

"I wonder how my mom and pop are getting on?" she asked. "It's the first time we've spent Christmas apart."

Daisy looked out to the vast, snow covered lawn and sighed. Her parents had gone on a cruise that Daisy, me, Heath and his wife Caitlin had all paid for as their Christmas gift. Heather was much healthier nowadays, so she and Robert had been doing a lot more travelling but had always wanted to go on a cruise, so we'd obliged. They still lived in Daisy's old apartment and had a good life now that they could finally enjoy it.

Heath never did rip my balls off, hence the arrival of Joshua, but he did bruise my jaw. I took the punch, though, because I figured I deserved it, but we were good now and he was one of my closest friends.

As for me and Daisy—after our quiet family wedding six months after the show, we set up a second animal shelter using some of my money from the network. Dad helped me to invest the rest, and that paid for the upkeep of the shelter and for the salary of two other people, Sarah and Drake, to work there alongside us. We also provided respite for owners who were ill and needed help with their pets, as well as providing free or dramatically reduced cost veterinary services for those who didn't have much money.

Our lives together consisted of each other and our families. We were careful who we let into our world. Some of that was down to our time in the mansion, but a lot of it was down to only wanting to share our world with the people we loved. There was a lot we could hate about the mansion, but we chose to see the positives of it bringing us together. We also met our very dear friend, Jess. She was still in our lives, even though she was a mega movie star, and she helped out with PR for the animal shelter. Daisy and Jess got on like BFFs should, and we were thinking of asking her to be Joshua's godmother.

When we weren't at the shelter, our time was spent at the center that Dad had set up in my mom's name. It was a center for kids who were either from one-parent families, or were in the system and needed a place to have some fun. Daisy and I organized a lot of fundraising events for it, but seeing as Dad and Elizabeth donated a huge fucking great chunk every year, The Shelby Sutton Center did okay. In fact, it did more than okay and had been highly commended by Social Welfare, with them sending kids to us all the time. Daisy and I didn't run it. We had a real good team of professionals to do that, but we loved being there and seeing the kids having fun.

Taking a sip of my wine, I watched as Daisy chewed on her food, looking contemplatively into the distance.

"You okay?" I asked, taking her hand in mine.

"Hmm," she said with nod. "Just thinking about what you said, and you're right, we truly are blessed."

I looked around at my family, all laughing and joking at Dad trying to take a selfie with Claudia's cell.

"Yeah, baby, we are." I lifted her hand and kissed it. "Very blessed."

"You know what else?" she said with a little grin.

I recognized that glint in her eye. It was bright and dazzling, especially as she wasn't wearing her glasses.

"What's that?"

"Well," she said, squirming in her seat. "You do know it was actually six weeks yesterday since Joshua was born?"

"Yeah, I do," I said slowly, hoping I wasn't wrong in what she was getting at.

She put her mouth against my ear and whispered seductively, "So, that means I wanna get laid by Kade tonight."

Yep, there went my cock. Straight up like a flagpole.

"You okay with that?" she asked, dropping a kiss to my bicep.

"Oh yeah, I am definitely okay with that."

"Good, 'cause I love you, Kade," she whispered, swallowing hard. "So much, and I am so lucky that I found you."

"And I love you, too. But, baby, there was nothing lucky about that. That was because we were both on the path that we were meant to take."

THE END

Printed by Amazon Italia Logistica S.r.l.
Torrazza Piemonte (TO), Italy

11906782R00172